CW00496931

The Last Colony

Ron Culley

Edited by John McManus

Grosvenor House
Publishing Limited

This book is published by
Grosvenor House Publishing Ltd
Link House
140 The Broadway, Tolworth, Surrey, KT6 7HT.
www.grosvenorhousepublishing.co.uk

This book is a work of fiction. Any resemblance to
people or events, past or present, is purely coincidental.

A CIP record for this book
is available from the British Library

ISBN 978-1-78623-501-5

Previous books by Ron Culley

The Kaibab Resolution. Kennedy & Boyd 2010.
I Belong To Glasgow (foreword by Sir Alex Ferguson)
The Grimsay Press, 2011
A Confusion of Mandarins. Grosvenor House. 2011.
Glasgow Belongs To Me. Grosvenor House
(electronic media only) 2012
The Patriot Game. Grosvenor House 2013
Shoeshine Man. A one-act play. SCDA. 2014.
One Year. Grosvenor House 2015
Alba: Who Shot Willie McRae? Grosvenor House 2016
The Never Ending Story (Editor) Downie Allison
Downie 2018
Odyssey: Travels On A Bucket List.
Grosvenor House 2018

Web address
www.ronculley.com

Preface

Let me start by explaining why many people should not read this book.

British Unionists will loathe this book. They should not read it unless they seek enlightenment. Scottish Nationalists will also hate the book if they seek a dry and dusty account of British Imperialism and its implications for the future of Scotland although, I confess, that is rather what the book is about.

This book is a *novel;* in some ways, a *roman à clef,* a light read. It nevertheless addresses many of the features that trouble those within the Independence movement but does so within the context of a dramatic fiction. Great efforts have been made to avoid the suggestion that attitudes or behaviours of living personalities are true reflections - indeed I happen to know for example that the present Head of Regions and Nations for the BBC at the time of writing is a fine, upstanding and highly intelligent native of the Scottish Western Isles and not is as represented between these covers. Equally, I'm unacquainted with the Brigadier who leads the 77th Brigade and I'm sure he's not as foul-mouthed as he's presented in these pages. However, strenuous efforts have been made to ensure that the true facts relating to those persons now deceased - especially in controversial circumstances - are accurate.

As ever I am grateful to my family for permitting me the time to write this book and am more indebted than mere words could convey to my editor John McManus whose wise and cautious advice guided my hand. His time and effort in making sure that I didn't make egregious mistakes have been essential to me and this book is much the better for his many interventions. However, where I've strayed from his counsel the responsibility is mine and mine alone.

I'm also grateful to those who attended public meetings where I discussed the contents of this book prior to publication and who encouraged me (as did my editor) to change the title *from 'The Butcher's Apron'* to *'The Last Colony'*; a much better title.

Ron Culley

Introduction

In the days before Scotland secured its independence from the rest of the United Kingdom, ever-more frantic attempts were made by the British Establishment to influence and suborn the democratic wishes of the Scottish electorate.

Internationally, the British Establishment had been well used to dealing with upstart nations. Having reached its peak in 1913, Britain was the most extensive empire in history and for over a century was the world's colonial superpower. At the commencement of the First World War in 1914, the British Empire held sway over four hundred and twelve million people; twenty-three per cent of the world population at the time, covering a quarter of the total land area of the globe. Roly-poly gangster capitalist Winston Churchill boasted that he controlled the largest Muslim population in the world given that the Empire presided over half the Muslim believers in existence at that time.

There are 195 countries in the world today and Britain has invaded or otherwise thrown rocks at all but twenty-two of them. So the British Empire didn't develop following cheese and wine parties and a subsequent measured analysis by nation-states of the benefits of the protection of the British Crown. Rather, Britain has a history of creating colonies by employing cruelty, pillage, theft of natural resources, slavery, war-crimes, ethnic cleansing, murder, manipulation…and blood.

Not without reason was the Union flag of the United Kingdom referred to as *'The Butcher's Apron'*.

The *Butcher's Apron* also flew over the mainland of the United Kingdom and the British Establishment was just as energetic in the protection of its interests closer to home. Domestically, the UK Security and Intelligence Services had form. Files released under the Freedom of Information Act show that as early as April 1951, a government agent attended an SNP gathering in Hyde Park in London to keep a close eye on party leader Robert McIntyre who had made history by becoming the first SNP Member of Parliament after winning a by-election in Motherwell six years earlier. In those early days, the agent had confined himself to keeping with the usual requirement of passing on transcripts of meetings, listing those who attended and offering a commentary on the mood of the assembly.

That rather benign approach to domestic security and intelligence matters changed however. In 1969, violence erupted in Northern Ireland and the British government became involved in a bloody campaign that was to last for a quarter of a century. Over three thousand lives were lost and the British Establishment went to great lengths to use all the powers at its disposal to meet their objectives including the black arts of the security services.

And heaven help anyone if it was decided that they required to be interrogated as the British military had extensive practice in utilising techniques of hooding, sleeplessness, beatings, sensory deprivation, starvation, isolation, choking, blinding, freezing and deafening. These instruments of torture had most recently been used under the *Butcher's Apron* in Malaya, Borneo, Palestine, Cyprus, Brunei, Kenya, Aden, Malaysia and the Persian Gulf. It was only when they were deployed on British shores that a measure of unease became evident within the body politic of the United Kingdom.

The American Journal of International Law cited the British powers which it had conferred on its security forces thus; '*The following are prohibited; Violence to life and person, in particular, mutilation, cruel treatment and torture, outrages upon personal dignity, in particular humiliating and degrading treatment.*'

Very civilised! Unfortunately for the poor souls who were subjected to interrogation, a further qualifying clause also governed the behaviour of the men and women silhouetted by the bright lights.

'*The precise application of these general rules in particular circumstances is inevitably to some extent a matter of judgement on the part of those immediately responsible for the operations in question.*'

This clause effectively gave *carte blanche* to British interrogators and subsequently resulted in the British Government being found guilty of torture by the European Court of Human Rights in 1976.

And in more recent years the security services had gone beyond their mere note-taking role and had infiltrated all of the major opposition parties in the UK, had placed MI5 operatives at the heart of a number of Trades Unions (Stella Rimington, the former head of MI5, admitting that the agency targeted union leaders during the Mineworkers' strike, arguing that they were using the dispute to bring down the elected government) and had inserted undercover officers within the anti-nuclear movement, in some cases developing intimate relationships to deepen their cover.

Infiltration was no means constrained to those organisations mentioned or within Northern Ireland. According to a report obtained by the Guardian Newspaper and the *Undercover Research Group,* a network of activists that research police infiltration, the Socialist Workers' Party alone had twenty-four undercover officers deployed over a thirty-seven years period. Four of them deceived women into sexual relationships while using their fake identities. One spy met one of his wives during his deployment and had a child with her. The scale of the infiltration of the SWP – far larger than any other political organisation – is revealed in a database compiled following investigations by the Guardian which lists one hundred and twenty-four legal groups that have been spied on by undercover police officers since 1968. Anti-nuclear, anti-Fascist, anti-apartheid, feminist, anti-poll tax, animal rights groups, the Aldermaston Women's Peace Camp, CND, National Union of Students and the National Union of Teachers were all infiltrated by Government spies. They even infiltrated that renowned organisation dedicated to general mayhem, anarchy and the overthrow of Western civilisation; the Young Liberals! The governments and their agents over the past several decades were taking no chances!

Essentially, citizens who joined entirely legitimate organisations dealing with animal rights, the environment, anti-nuclear, anti-apartheid, anti-imperialist, anti-capitalist, anti-racist, anti-war, Trades Unions, Irish issues or civil rights matters could easily have been dealing with an undercover Government agent, not the friendly supporter to whom they believed they were talking.

In 2012, Prime Minister David Cameron was forced to the Dispatch Box to inform Parliament that an official enquiry into the 1989 murder of Northern Ireland lawyer Pat Finucane had discovered 'shocking levels of State collusion between Loyalist paramilitary killers and MI5, Police and Military Intelligence'. In 2019, *thirty years after the murder*, the UK Supreme Court ruled that all previous investigations into Finucane's murder had not satisfied the European Convention on Human Rights' procedural obligations to carry out a coherent and vigorous investigation. In a unanimous judgement, the five UK Supreme Court judges made clear that the previous reviews were ineffective and failed to meet human rights standards.

British Intelligence also paid Freddie Scappaticci during the thirty years of the 'Troubles' in Northern Ireland to infiltrate the IRA and kidnap, torture and kill on their behalf without being brought to justice.

And in order to ensure that criminality of these and other offences went unnoticed - or if it was, that the reporting of that criminality was presented in soft focus

- a unit within the BBC vetted all applicants to ensure that no one was employed who might offend their mission of serving the interests of the state. 'The Observer' revealed that MI5 has long been vetting BBC appointments, basing its operations in Room 105 in Broadcasting House. MI5 was concerned not only that subversives might influence televised debate but also that the trades unions representing engineers might be infiltrated by Communists and the like and that in consequence, important coverage might be sabotaged. The political vetting process was also designed to ensure that any staff that became 'contaminated' with Socialist or Communist ideology *following* appointment could subsequently be denied promotion or refused attachment to duties deemed unwise.

In addition to secretive infiltration of legal entities, the UK Government's Investigatory Powers Act 2016 specifically permits 'the use of agents in criminality' and permits a secret oversight mechanism (known as 'The Third Direction' in Intelligence circles) whereby 'Covert Human Intelligence Sources' may commit *authorised* criminality. These illegal acts have been available to agents for some considerable time and certainly since the early 1990s but were only brought under judicial review by retired senior judge, Sir Mark Waller in 2012 at which point he was instructed by Prime Minister David Cameron to examine only the operation of the policy, not to offer any opinion on whether any actions so undertaken were lawful or not.

British Prime Minister Theresa May has refused to publish any official guidance to MI5 in this regard as 'it would undermine national security'. Nonetheless, the Investigatory Powers Tribunal approved a finding that GCHQ, MI5, MI6 and Special Branch officers within the Intelligence Community routinely over a period of fifteen years operated outside of Section 94 of the UK's Telecommunications Act. In addition, the Investigatory Powers Tribunal President, Sir Michael Burton acknowledged that the Foreign Secretary had 'rubber-stamped a general direction that included a very broad form of words that permitted spy agencies to do whatever they pleased' and subsequently criticised the behaviour of the UK's spy agencies in a document (IPT/15/110/CH) which will never be seen by the public.

A heavily redacted, three-page MI5 document *entitled 'Guidelines On The Use Of Agents Participating In Crime (Official Guidance)'* states that 'the service has established its *own* procedures for authorising the use of agents participating in crime'. So, that's all right then!

In summary, the British security services believed themselves permitted by governments of all stripes to be able to infiltrate any legal organisation, to interrogate suspects without regard to constraints on torture or humiliating behaviour and to authorise criminal behaviour by their agents.

All of the foregoing are matters of fact and are capable of simple verification. What follows is the fruit of my imagination...or is it? The British Empire over the last century has gradually fallen away to the point that excluding the prospect of the re-unification of Ireland, the only colony left available to them to plunder is...Scotland.

Scotland is Britain's last colony. It covers thirty-two per cent of the area of the UK, but has only eight per cent of its population and has but fifty-nine of six hundred and fifty Members of Parliament at Westminster thereby finding itself locked into a political system that offers no democratic way of triggering its claim of right by its own volition.

Scotland is the largest producer of oil and the second largest producer of gas in Europe. It has an eighty per cent share of UK's North Sea assets ... more if it gave itself permission to explore its west coast and recovered the English/Scottish maritime boundary under international law which Tony Blair appropriated in 1999 to annex 6,000 square miles of Scottish waters to England, including the Argyll field and six other major oilfields.

It has a coastline of some 10,250 miles compared with that of France which has a coastline of only 2,130 miles. While Scotland dominates green energy within the United Kingdom in terms of wind power and hydro-electric power, in terms of tidal power it is possessed of 25% of the estimated total capacity for the European Union and up to 14 gigawatts of wave power potential; 10% of EU capacity.

In addition, Scotland lands over 60% of the total fisheries catch in the UK at its ports. There are over two hundred and fifty thousand lochs in Scotland, each capable of producing top quality freshwater. Loch Ness holds the most water with 7.4 million cubic meters (a cubic meter is one thousand litres); which single loch holds more water than all the English and Welsh lakes combined. England is parched so the UK Government propose to expend fourteen million pounds building a super-canal to take Scotland's water south to England. They've already taken the oil.

The UK berths its nuclear submarines at Faslane on the Gareloch, where the submarines are based and Coulport on Loch Long, eight miles away, where the warheads are stored. An independent Scotland would return them to England which would face an enormous cost in constructing a customised dock in Milford Haven in Wales or in Plymouth.

The Times' Higher Education World Rankings has placed five Scottish universities among the top two hundred; more per head of population than any other country in the world. In addition, tourism, whisky, other food and drink, professional, scientific and technical activities all see money pour into Westminster's coffers.

And when Scotland is compared with other smaller nations within the European community such as Sweden, Denmark, Norway, Ireland, Iceland, Rumania, Finland, Austria or Portugal, other than Norway, it has more natural resources within its boundaries but often has poorer economic performance, tied as it is to its larger, colonialist neighbour to the south.

Scotland is Britain's last colony but as the world entered the twenty-first century, Scottish Independence was on the rise. It threatened the status quo of the Establishment, the economy and the resources available to the United Kingdom. It had to be put down...hard.

MI5 were instructed to act to save the Union and retain Scotland as a servile British colony shackled to Westminster...the last British colony.

Chapters

Chapter One

The Third Direction

"Bloody Jocks!'

The right forefinger of Brigadier Sir Jonathon Pennington stabbed urgently at the intercom button on his desk connecting him to his secretary.

"Miss Evans, I'll see Commander Cavendish shortly. I have Jeremy Ogilvie with me just now. Ask him to wait and can you cancel my tickets to centre court this afternoon? Phone my wife, explain that I've been caught up in something and order some flowers from Blooms. I'll collect them on my way home."

Lifting his finger from the device he repeated his invective. "Bloody Jocks!"

He lifted a file from his desk and without opening it waved it at his deputy, Ogilvie who sat at the other side of his large, nineteenth century, inlaid mahogany desk.

"Henry Cavendish! He's a fucking incompetent! The second son of the ninth Earl of Thornwood who's first cousin once removed to the Queen just slightly behind his half-wit cousin, Oliver, another of his breed who in between snorting coke with the coxless rowing team or enjoying the benefits of daddy's investments, inherited wealth and the ancestral home, has been given public responsibilities far beyond his abilities over in Paris."

1

"I read the file, boss. If seventy-eight particular people die, he becomes king of England."

Pennington nodded his agreement. "Fucking minor royals! These inbreds pop up all over the place and are indulged by people of intelligence whom I respect but who buckle at the very notion that we might operate on merit rather than because some individual, born of royal blood is presumed fit by divine right to rule over the rest of us mere mortals who are their subjects."

"And Cavendish is a case in point?"

Pennington shook his head sadly. "Cavendish is a very minor and very irritating case in point but I'd better indulge him." He lifted the folder and placed it in a desk drawer. "Perhaps if you leave by the side door, I'll see what on earth Henry Cavendish has to do with the good people of Scotland."

Ogilvie left as Pennington rose, straightening his Charles Tyrwhitt tie, his scowl transforming to a practised, welcoming smile as his guest entered the large office ushered in by Emily Evans, an elderly spinster who had worked in MI5 since leaving university. He strode towards his guest, his outreached right hand offered in greeting, his footsteps silenced by the deep-piled Axminster carpet.

"Henry! It's so nice to see you again. Glad you've recovered from our little mishap in Manchester last year."

"I'm just pleased it's been concluded, Brigadier. It may have taken us eleven months of patient investigation but many people could have been killed had we not taken the actions we did."

Pennington remembered his impatience.

"Indeed! Well, to business. Thanks to your request for an urgent meeting, I've been denied an afternoon with my wife at Wimbledon. I gather you want to speak with me regarding the northern hordes."

Cavendish accepted Pennington's gestured invitation to take a seat in a comfortable armchair set aside from his desk area. He smiled.

"If by that you refer to our cousin Scottish countrymen, then yes…"

Pennington interrupted. "I forget myself, Henry. If I'm being denied lunch, I won't be denied a lunchtime Glenmorangie…especially if we're discussing its country of provenance. Might you join me?"

"A small one. No water."

Cavendish continued as two large whiskies were poured. "Brigadier, our chat today is off the record. "I'm requested to invite your participation in a highly confidential…and when I say 'highly confidential' I mean almost certainly wildly *illegal* exercise to help maintain the integrity of the United Kingdom." He accepted a glass and grimaced his mock disapproval at the generous measure. "It's been made clear to us in the Home Office from the very top that all efforts are to be made to thwart the democratic rights of the Scots in securing independence. It's also been made clear that the gloves are off. If and when there are transgressions, the preference is that they be covert but if they come to light there must be deniability…which is why I would very much like the assistance of your people in the Counter-terrorism Unit."

"To do what, exactly? Most of the boys in the dirty tricks department have long retired with serious damage having been caused their liver or are currently advising some of our largest conglomerates on how best to take advantage of their staff, customers and competition."

Cavendish sat forward in his seat. "Let me explain further, Brigadier. We've an operational unit covertly dealing with this Scottish matter. Over the past years we've managed to position the nation's broadcaster against independence; ignoring positive stories, exaggerating negative ones. We've a coordinated digital media presence that does the same thing as well as infiltrating the pro-nationalist cause and displaying them in a bad light. The print media takes care of itself given their foreign ownership and right-wing agendas and the two major parties are as one in opposing the dissolution of the kingdom. We've beefed up the Scottish civil service in Scotland and tasked them with putting a Union Jack on everything that's positive. However, polls show an irritating reluctance of Scots to side with our point of view and we now face the prospect of a real fight to maintain the status quo."

"And this matters why?"

"Well, apart from three hundred years of a shared history, it's now regrettably a matter of record that if Scotland had sole access to the oil and gas that lie beneath its waves, it would have a huge and embarrassing balance of payments surplus. We, in turn would be denied that revenue. They would have us at material disadvantage when the inevitable English requirement for fresh water becomes a national emergency; immigration policies would certainly differ and would provide easy access to England by illegals unless we rebuild Hadrian's Wall. They might choose to introduce policies that would run counter to our strategic national interests such as their avowed determination to see the removal of our nuclear deterrent from Faslane. Our friends in industry are most concerned about the Scots' disinclination to assist their ambitions for fracking and a recent direct approach by the Director of the Central Intelligence Agency not to mention our American colleagues in their State Department are currently apoplectic at the prospect of new political hands controlling the key shipping lanes used by the Russian fleet around Cape Wrath."

Pennington sipped thoughtfully at his whisky.

"I'm not much taken with the place myself. I had occasion to visit a place called Paisley recently and to be honest it offered this visitor no inducement to loiter long." He grimaced at his recollection. "I'm very aware of our past activity in Scottish affairs but we must remember that these initiatives were undertaken in the context of a sympathetic House of Commons, low polling by the Nationalists and a Labour Government in Scotland. It made things much easier. As you yourself say, there is a much greater appetite for independence up north these days and a wary administration in Holyrood." He paused in thought. "Much as I empathise with your problem Henry, our charter limits us to investigating and engaging with actions of persons and organisations which may be judged to be subversive of the state." He rubbed the rim of his glass on his lower lip. "More recently in MI5 we have been rather more careful and on several occasions have had to resist the natural tendencies of ministers and their senior officials to equate subversion with any activity that threatens their policies or even challenges the existence of their government."

"Of course, Brigadier. We're all well aware of the charter but there's no denying that in this instance the Scots place a dagger at the throat of the United Kingdom. Without becoming over-dramatic, Scottish Independence would have a calamitous effect on our economy, our

security, our border control and our international status."
He struggled for a clincher to his argument. "And, finally,
heaven forfend, they'd probably get rid of the monarchy."

Pennington dismissed the remainder of his glass of
whisky in one movement and placed the empty glass on
a nearby table.

"Ah, yes…the monarchy. Heaven forfend!" replied
Pennington with more sarcasm than he'd intended. He
paused and gathered his thoughts. "Her Majesty's
Security Services cannot and will not be caught up in
adventurism such as you describe, Commander. It may
easily not end well and if it were ever shown that we'd
participated in an anti-democratic act against the
northern half of the Kingdom there'd be hell to pay."

"But you see our dilemma, Brigadier," responded
Cavendish acknowledging the new formalities in their
conversation. "Left to its own volition, '*this sceptered
isle…this earth of majesty*'…"

"Yes… '*this earth, this realm, this England*'…"
interrupted Pennington. "I'm disinterested in your
romantic Shakespearean arguments for our intervention,
Commander. My organisation has to be rather more
hard-headed…more in line with the philosophy that in
international affairs, '*the strong do what they can and
the weak suffer what they must*'." He permitted himself
a smile. "You prefer Shakespeare. I studied classical
Greek antiquity and its approach to political realism."
He looked wistfully at his empty whisky glass. "Have
we learned nothing from Northern Ireland?"

A silence was allowed by both parties, broken by
Cavendish.

"And I should reiterate that my request for your cooperation comes right from the top. The question was raised

inviting reflection on your use of 'The Third Direction'."
He raised the inflection at the end of his sentence as if it
were a question inviting further contemplation and continued. "Might you consider inviting your specialists in
counter-terrorism to look into this quietly so as to cause
confusion and division in the ranks up north...or should I
ask the assistance of the Director General?" he enquired
with the merest hint of menace.

Pennington permitted himself a wry smile at
Cavendish's attempt at insouciance, ignoring the implied
threat.

"The Counter Terrorism boys are in the bad books
right now. While the great British public can rightfully
feel safer as a consequence of our monitoring and
engagement with honest-to-goodness terrorism, when it
comes to dirty tricks perpetrated upon citizens of the
realm, we've not covered ourselves in glory. The CIA
seem very much better suited to this kind of work. We
don't appear to have the in-built guile! We've had to
ensure no Fatal Accident Enquiry into the shooting of
SNP Vice President, Willie McRae, manage the Enquiry
into anti-nuclear campaigner Hilda Murrell, we've had
to arrange for all files on the death of Dr. David Kelly,
the scientist behind the denunciation of the weapons of
mass destruction in Iraq, to be classified for seventy
years and we've kept a lid on everything to do with the
sad demise of Robin Cook once he resigned from the
Cabinet and started speaking out against the Iraq war
and supporting Scottish Independence. I could instance
many others. Our expertise seems to lie in legal and
political cover up, not in executing clean strikes against
subversives. However..." he grimaced and nodded his
head in resigned acquiescence. "You say this comes

from the very top and that 'The Third Direction' was encouraged?"

Cavendish nodded.

Pennington allowed a silence. "Very well." He paused and leaned forward, leaning his elbows on his knees. "We are both aware that Mohammad Hudaibi is still at large following our action against his terrorist cell in Manchester last year. I have to inform you that there is no further news of his whereabouts. *That* is what you came to ask me about today. I will diary our meeting as such." He rose to his feet and extended his arm, offering a farewell handshake. "As you leave, write your home telephone number on a piece of paper and leave it with Miss Evans. You will be contacted by telephone by someone who may be of assistance. You may advise your superiors quietly that your request for the deployment of 'Third Direction' resources has been successful...but formally, for the record and with deep regret, MI5 cannot assist due to our requirement to remain faithful to our charter. I will not involve our Counter-terrorism people." He indicated the door, signalling the end of the meeting. "Someone will contact you by telephone. Arrangements to pursue matters further may then ensue but I'm afraid the Home office will be required to lead on this. You personally will meet with the operative who will contact you. You, personally will be responsible for providing any resources he requires although we can make certain items available to you once removed so there is no overt connection between MI5 and the actions you propose. I wish you luck in your endeavours."

Cavendish shook his hand and left. As the door closed, Pennington sighed deeply.

"Fucking minor royals!"

Chapter Two

The March

The breeze had stiffened slightly causing the sea of Saltire flags to flap more briskly in the wind as the long march of supporters of Scottish Independence made their way noisily down the city's Saltmarket towards Glasgow's famous sward of grassed parkland abutting the River Clyde. At the head of the marchers, somewhat incongruously, a cadre of Sikh *Dhol* drummers thumped out a Punjabi *Bhangra* rhythm supported by three men in full Highland dress each playing the war-pipe. Occasional *Esteladas*, the unofficial flag of Catalonian independence, bobbed in the midst of Saltires and at intervals, marchers pushed prams within which had been placed battery-powered amplifiers belting out Scottish songs favoured by the marchers who sang along noisily. Whistles, air-horns and shouted slogans intensified the cacophony.

In an attempt better to communicate with his friend Charan Singh, Lachlan Macdonald cupped his hand at the side of his mouth the better to defeat the blare of the be-kilted piper on his right.

"Charlie…once this march reaches Glasgow Green, I'm for heading to the nearest pub. I've heard all the speeches before."

"We need to show willing, Lachie. People'll notice if we head off without sticking around for the inspirational bit! Questions will be asked!"

"There's maybe fifty thousand here, Charlie. Who's going to notice?"

Singh smiled and relented. "Okay. Mine's a pint of Cooncil Lager if you're buying."

"Ah'm buyin'.

"Then I'm drinking."

In unison, they linked arms and marched extravagantly in step to the martial piping of the retired Black Watch piper next to them who, as if he were urging them forward in the *Battle of Falaise Pocket,* was playing with gusto the quick march of his old regiment; *'Hielan' Laddie'.*

The Whistlin' Kirk pub first sold alcoholic refreshment to the denizens of Glasgow in the year 1750 and had done so continuously since then. Situated on the old Jail Square abutting Glasgow Green on a route that leads from the city centre to Celtic Park, the pub had become associated with those who have a soft spot for the football team which plays there; the Irish tricolour being displayed prominently on its walls. It is situated immediately across the Saltmarket from Glasgow's High Court of the Judiciary which itself opened for business in 1813. In consequence, it transforms the Whistlin' Kirk which hosts thirsty clients who are required to buy a bacon roll with their vodka or lager from eight o'clock in the morning, to a watering hole later in the day for lawyers, QCs and their clients following their departure from court. Few of the accused enjoy a glass prior to their appearance in court, usually because they'd been transported there in the rear of a prison van. A fortunate minority having been discharged visited the now somewhat tired and tawdry small bar which was nevertheless possessed of a decent gantry and pleasant bar staff.

Busy due to its popularity and further crowded due to the number of marchers who'd abandoned the cause in search of refreshment, the crush impeded Macdonald and Singh as they made their way slowly and apologetically through the throng to the bar muttering "'Scuse me' and 'Sorry, pal' as they eased their way.

They sought eye contact with a sturdy, fierce-looking barman and a pretty barmaid whose shoulder tattoos suggested a partiality for Glasgow Celtic FC. Each was busily serving those who waved paper currency signalling their drouth. A pin-striped suit at the bar behind Singh pronounced loudly to two others, criticising those who marched outside in clipped tones. Macdonald took stock; greasy hair, a tie so stained with dribbled food that had it been put in a pot of water and boiled it'd have made a nourishing bowl of soup, an unlit small cigar bouncing on his lips and a large glass of red wine threatening to spill its contents as his outrage rose.

He shook his head and remarked to Singh, "Lawyers are fuckin' arseholes!"

A customer next back from the bar heard his comment and responded.

"Hey, that offends me!"

Macdonald understood Glasgow bar culture. Immediate steps required to be taken to lower the temperature and avoid escalation. He held a hand up in apology.

"Sorry, pal. You a lawyer?"

"Naw," he guffawed. "Ah'm an arsehole!"

Realising the absence of threat and appreciating the joke, Macdonald returned the smile.

"Aye, very good. That deserves a pint. Can ah get ye one while I'm at the bar?"

A facial expression that attempted to convey *'that's not necessary'* with *'that would be very welcome'* was interpreted accurately by Macdonald. "What'll ye have?"

"A Guinness would be good."

Having completed the transaction, the three moved over closer to the front door of the pub where reduced noise levels and fewer topers permitted conversation.

Macdonald offered his free hand in friendship.

"Lachlan Macdonald." He gestured to his friend. This is Charan Singh. Everyone calls him Charlie. People call me Lachie."

"Thanks for the pint, boys. I'm Tam Sim"

"Bet that's the shortest name in the pub today," smiled Singh. He continued cheekily, "Sounds Chinese."

"Well, I used to stay in Garnethill. Big Chinese community there." He took a long draught of his Guinness. "On the march then?"

"Aye," responded Macdonald. "You?"

"In a manner of speaking," grinned Sim. "I'm Special Branch. Here to make sure you don't blow up the High Court or something."

Both marchers exchanged glances. Macdonald recovered first. "Fuck's sake, Tam. Should you no' be out there photographin' everyone and their granny frae behind a bush?"

Sim retained his broad smile. "Och, we've got that well covered. I've been on more march surveillance duties than you've had hot breakfasts but that crowd out there are happy, peaceful and the tunes are great. Anyway, I'm a quiet supporter of Scottish Independence myself. I'd rather have a pint with two fellow supporters than look for bomb-throwers that aren't there."

Singh's glass was held motionless on his lips. "Hope no one sees us talking to you then. It wouldn't do our reputations any good. Missed all the speeches and blethered away to the fascist secret police in a dark corner of a pub?" he asked rhetorically but with a smile of his face.

"Ach, I'm harmless. We're not interested in people like you who are just expressing a political preference. To be honest, we're trying to protect you."

"Aye, how's that?"

"Well, the one thing that might torpedo your ambitions is the wilder wing of the movement. Some of these boys are more interested in causing violence than in achieving political goals."

"The Scottish National Liberation Army?" Macdonald became animated. "They're no longer a force and anyway there's loads of evidence that they're a false flag operation set up by you boys to give the independence movement a bad name."

Sim pursed his lips in mild disagreement.

Macdonald continued. "So how come Westminster have sealed all security documents relating to the SNLA in the seventies when they were active?"

Singh developed the argument. "And by exception, why have these files been sealed for fifty years? Not the usual thirty."

Macdonald returned on descant. "And if you're a gamblin' man ah'll take a hundred of your English pounds that that ban is extended when the fifty years is reached if we're no' independent by then."

Sim's smile remained unperturbed. "Wow! You guys know your stuff. This *matters* to you!"

Macdonald bristled. "Everyone in the movement knows how sleekit you guys are. This matters to *everyone*. Perfidious Albion right enough!" He sipped at his pint and decided to ease back. "Ah mean, *you* seem okay but honest to God, see the Government down south an' its battalions of secret polis? They're a' bastards!"

"Well, I've only been south of Carlisle to catch a plane at Manchester Airport the odd time. Not a big fan of the Metropolitan boys myself." He glanced at the several Irish flags adorning the walls and asked ironically, "So do you boys prefer the sporting talents of Rangers or Celtic?"

Macdonald had practiced his punchline on many occasions before. "Manchester United are ma local team."

"That's a broad Glasgow accent you have. Local team?"

"Ah'm a citizen of the world!"

All three laughed and continued their conversation. Sim bought a further round of drinks.

"So you guys students or what? You look like students."

"Charlie here is studying criminology at Glasgow. Wants to be a polis like you!"

"Do I hell! I want to be in traffic. I fancy the motorbikes. Not sneaking around trying to frustrate the cause of independence like Big Tam here."

The smile didn't leave Sim's face as he nodded at Macdonald. "And you?"

"Ah'm studyin' nuclear physics at Glasgow."

"Really?"

"Naw. History. Ah'm no' *that* clever."

"More clever than me, Lachie. Two 'O' Grades and a six foot frame with attitude got me into the polis. When I grew up in Glasgow, university wasn't on the cards for the likes of me."

A third and fourth pint was consumed courtesy of Sim before he indicated he'd better get back to his duties.

Singh drained his glass. "Mr. Sim, I'm reviewing my future job options. Fast motorcycles like I fancied or being permitted to drink four pints on duty like you?"

"Trust me Charlie. I've known boys in Traffic who've done both!"

"We'll walk you out," smiled Macdonald.

Outside they shook hands and made small talk about how each had enjoyed the banter.

Sim deepened his pockets with his hands. "I'll maybe look you guys up some time. I'm not interested in the SNLA. Maybe sometime you could talk to me about what you know about *Sìol nan Gàidheal*."

"*Seed of the Gaels*? They're banned?"

"Proscribed," corrected Singh.

"Anyway we know fuck all about them."

"Nevertheless, I'll maybe look you up for a chat. They're a group within the Nationalist movement that are making increasing threats of violence."

"And just how are you going to 'look us up', Tam. You don't know where we live or anything."

Sim's tone became weary. He nodded at Singh. "Your name is Charan Singh. You study criminology at Glasgow University. You're a member of the SNP, I'd guess. Maybe the Greens. That accent suggests Giffnock or Milngavie, but probably Pollokshields. Middle-class anyway. The surname Singh marks you out as a Sikh." He turned to Macdonald. "A history man, Lachlan, eh? Except your accent suggests maybe a scheme upbringing. First of your family to go university, maybe? Pollok, Drumchapel, Easterhouse or Castlemilk? And you're a Manchester United fan so you'll drink in sports bars because you don't have enough cash to buy satellite broadcasts...unless you watch illegally at home using one of these pub-bought gadgets." His smile grew broader. "I could get you the jail for that, eh?" He held both men in a steady gaze. "Trust me boys. It would take me all of two minutes to find out whether you preferred Stork to butter."

Macdonald and Singh glanced at each other, unsettled by Sim's summary of their background.

Sim stepped back as a red Swiss-made pen-knife fell through a hole in his coat pocket and landed at his feet. Macdonald picked it up. "You dropped this."

Sim received the knife in the cleft between his thumb and forefinger.

"Thanks. Be in touch, boys."

As he disappeared into the crowds still milling around he took a plastic evidence bag from his coat pocket and dropped the pen-knife into it, sealing the adhesive top.

Chapter Three

Treasure

Mrs Sheila Maugham hugged *Methuselah*, her Belgian Warmblood which had just been put through her paces by her daughter, Mirren. Three extended rounds of show-jumping in the family field behind their farmhouse just outside Fenwick in Ayrshire had tested the horse which now stood, biddable but still sweating in the barn where she lived with a further three Warmbloods, all owned by the family.

"I'll take it from here, mummy. Daddy will be calling soon for dinner."

Agreeing the proposition, Mrs Maugham departed. Her daughter hosed the legs and belly of the large horse and washed off the saddle patch with warm water, all the time talking in a comforting sing-song voice to her mount. Satisfied, she washed the tail and brushed off dry sweat and mud before cleaning the feet and coronet bands, checking all the while for any knocks or cuts. Finishing, she put on a sweat rug with a jute blanket on top before leaving him with his feed.

Mirren Maugham was a privileged young lady; an only child who'd inherited her mother's beauty and her father's fierce intelligence. Blonde hair usually cascading beyond her shoulders was tied up in a tight bun and her slim figure was accentuated by the riding outfit she wore. Now in her mid-thirties, she'd been educated at not inconsiderable expense at prestigious Glasgow Academy for Girls before reading history in Cambridge. Her Ayrshire accent, never broad, had been cultivated, Anglicised and had passed muster for many years in many of the great houses of England where she had spent most of her adult life. On many occasions she'd witnessed eyebrows being raised when she'd confessed to her Scottish heritage. 'Really?' ventured one admirer only weeks previously. 'I was sure I could detect Wiltshire!'

A career in the family's farming business held no interest to a young woman who had developed an assertiveness and confidence that complimented her obvious intelligence. In her Honours year she'd been asked if she'd be interested in joining Britain's security services with promises of early seniority, an exciting lifestyle, a decent salary and a pension that would permit her to continue living a life of privilege in the autumn of her life. During a diet of interviews where she did most of the interrogating, she impressed her purported interlocutors and was brought into the fold, barely catching her breath as she spent time undertaking various tasks in grand cities such as Rio de Janiero, Mombasa, New York and closer to home in Reykjavik as well as roughing it in less salubrious stations in Belgrade, Belfast and Brindisi.

Following a period of a two years during which she understudied the Principal Private Secretary who looked after the office of the Secretary of State for Transport and subsequently the Secretary of State for Scotland, Mirren Maugham was provided with effusive testimonials, a sandpapered CV which was sufficiently honest to allow investigation and a hike in salary to match that on offer by the Civil Service in Scotland which sought a Director General for Constitution and External Affairs focusing upon leading the Scottish Government's work on intergovernmental relations, Europe, constitutional issues and supporting Cabinet decision-making. Importantly she was tasked with Ministerial support and personnel issues. Reporting directly to the Permanent Secretary, Scotland's most senior civil servant, her more important relationship, secretly, was to Brigadier Sir Jonathon Pennington in MI5.

To protect her identity, she was given a code-name; '*Treasure*'.

* * *

Sweating profusely, Arnel Pacquiao slashed and cut at the uppermost section of the tough *Abacá* banana cluster at the top of the plant grown on the *Villa Escudero* Plantation in his Philippine work base. The product of his labours was further processed and its fibre sent to Meycauayan where it was refined and used to make paper more expensive but tougher than that manufactured from wood pulp. After treatment, the *Meycauayan* mill produced *Abacá* pulp that had been steamed, pressurised and formed into a Manila Envelope used throughout the developed world. Despite the premium price being exacted for the product, Arnel Pacquiao received but a pittance for his labours.

The batch of envelopes manufactured as a result of Arnel's efforts were sized to take A4 documents and exported to the United Kingdom as Manila Envelopes and an element of the ship's contents found their way onto desks located within the Scottish Parliament in Holyrood, Edinburgh.

One of these envelopes was now filled with documents; a detailed and restricted copy of the advance itinerary for the following week (including personal time) of the First Minister of Scotland, a schedule detailing problems with Scotland's major hospitals, Ministerial dismay being expressed at the flawed unification of Scotland's police forces and the illness records of Cabinet Ministers. Two separate intimations of civil action being proposed against the Scottish Government and an early whisper of sexual impropriety by a member of the SNP parliamentary group in Westminster and one in Holyrood were also included. Finally, a page listed the detailed weekend activities proposed by individual Cabinet members.

Mirren Maugham took a sheet of blank paper from the printing machine located beside her desk and taking a pen wrote only the word '*civil*' in the centre of the page before sealing the envelope and placing it inside a briefcase where it remained for some minutes before being carried from the Parliament buildings at Holyrood.

Some thirty minutes later a man in a tan suit could be seen sitting on a bench in Edinburgh's National Galleries of Scotland admiring Landseer's painting '*The Monarch of the Glen*'.

After some moments had passed he turned to Mirren Maugham who had just seated herself beside him also apparently lost in admiration of the painting.

"Doesn't this painting capture the grandeur and majesty of Scotland's highlands and wildlife? A twelve point stag" He shook his head in wonderment. "It's magnificent."

After further contemplation of the painting he patted his knees with both hands as a signal that he intended to rise and did so, collecting in the process of leaving the brown leather briefcase Maugham had brought from the Scottish Parliament.

Treasure had successfully passed on the first batch of information of interest to Her Majesty's Government's domestic counter-intelligence and security agency.

Chapter Four

Contact

Commander Henry Cavendish lived in Chelsea, in London. Divorced these last seven years due to routine and prolonged absence on duty and bid farewell by a younger wife who enjoyed exercises offered by her gym instructor usually but not always denied his other clients, Cavendish's work was his life. An education commencing in Eton and ending in Cambridge where he studied English literature found him joining the Royal Navy Submarine Service as a Lieutenant and leaving it as a Commander; two promotions but seven ranks away from the top job. An opening in the civil service within the Home Office proved timeous and desk operations suited him; a man with little life experience but with royal connections and a wide and upper-class contacts list.

An early evening slumber watching television news was interrupted by his home telephone ringing. Scratching his thinning hair he reached for it, gathering himself.

He yawned his reply. "Cavendish!"

The voice in his ear was indicative of a Scottish accent...*Glaswegian*, he thought, just like his sonar operator when serving on HMS Vigilant, the third

Vanguard class Submarine to carry Trident nuclear missiles.

"I was told to phone you by Brigadier Pennington. He says you need my help."

His mind still swimming from his rude awakening, Cavendish spent a few seconds in confusion. Then he remembered. "Eh…ah, yes. The Scottish thing?"

"The Scottish thing!"

A short silence ensued broken by the caller.

"Tomorrow morning. Eleven fifteen. Cross Keys pub in Lawrence Street, Chelsea. Know it?

Cavendish faltered. "Eh, yes. It's near me." He attempted conversation. "They do a nice *Prosecco*."

"Not interested. Don't be late. I talk, you listen! It'll be quick."

Chapter Five

The Arlington Compact

As Commander Cavendish returned his phone to its receiver down in London, Lachie Macdonald raised his arm in welcome as Charlie Singh entered the portals of the Arlington Bar in Glasgow's Woodland Road.

"Over here, Charlie," he called as he rose to buy his friend a drink.

They both approached the bar. "Usual?" asked Macdonald.

Without waiting for affirmation, he asked the barman for a pint of Tennant's Lager and while it was being poured, turned to continue the conversation they'd both had following their engagement with Tam Sim three days earlier.

"What the hell was all *that* about, eh?"

"Bit scary, Lachie. What got me was how friendly he was. Then, before you knew it, he'd turned into a hard-nosed polis." He accepted the lager from the white-shirted barman and sipped at its froth while his friend paid. "We won't hear from him again. It's just second nature to these guys to mess around with people to see if they can learn anything of interest."

"Teach you that in your criminology class, eh?"

"Nah, watching cop shows on telly."

"Aye, well, ah bet you end up like that if you join the cops. Sleekit…two-faced!"

"Nah, I'm more the Sherlock Holmes type…on a motorbike!"

The two friends continued their banter and focussed upon the exams each had two weeks hence. Drinking alcohol in most Glasgow pubs could be expensive for students even in old traditional hostelries like the Arlington so each sipped their lager slowly. The booth they'd chosen had torn leather upholstery and had seen better days but the atmosphere in the bar was convivial and they'd both become used to its tawdry and down-at-heel appurtenances.

As the lager in each glass stood only an inch tall, the barman approached and placed two fresh glasses before them. Macdonald and Singh looked at him, eyebrows raised.

"From your pal ower therr," growled the elderly barman hoarsely.

Both craned their necks around the studded leather edge of the booth in a choreography that would have done justice to any of the contrived sit-coms on television that evening.

Tam Sim stood at a raised pedestal table a pint of Guinness in his left hand, his right waving only its fingers at the boys. Smiling in a cartoonish fashion, he mouthed the word, 'Hello'.

The students withdrew their necks and held each other's gaze. Macdonald broke the silence.

"Aye, well so much for Sherlock Holmes, 'Constable We'll-Never-Hear-From-Him-Again'!"

"Coincidence?" asked Singh.

His question remained unanswered as Sim approached the booth.

"Shove up boys. I've a fat arse. Budge up, Charlie!"

Singh responded with such alacrity he almost spilled the fresh pint of lager that had been set before him.

Macdonald was more measured. "Hi Tam. Fancy meeting you here in a dump like...well a dump like the Whistling Kirk. You obviously like sticky carpets."

Sim nodded his appreciation at Macdonald's wit and sipped his Guinness. He shrugged.

"Sticky *situations* more like, maybe."

Macdonald's eyes studied his shoes for a moment before raising his gaze to meet Sim's.

"Ah *knew* you'd be trouble."

Singh was perplexed. "Lachie. Don't be rude!"

Sim took his cue from Singh. "Aye, Lachie. I've just bought you both a pint. Didn't your mammy not tell you not to be cheeky to police officers."

"My mammy was brought up without much of an education in Pollok but she knew not to use a double negative in a sentence!"

Sim laughed a genuine laugh. "*Touché*, Lachie. *Touché*!"

"Thank you for the pint of lager, Mr Sim."

"*Sergeant* Sim, Charlie. Could you not tell from my bearing?"

Singh wasn't used to pub banter and unsure whether to compliment Sim on his bearing or to take his lead from his pal, Lachie, fell to mumbling a repeat of his gratitude for the pint of lager.

Sim gestured at the pint of lager before Macdonald. "Drink up, Lachie. I've a wee favour to ask and it'd be nice if the three of us could discuss it over a friendly glass."

Charlie Singh lifted the fresh glass to his lips as requested incurring the wrath of Macdonald.

"Charlie you're not goin' to be much of a polis if you do everything that strange men ask you to do in pubs!"

Singh slowly lowered the glass and wiped the froth from his lips.

Sim intervened. "Don't you worry, Charlie. If you're a cop you need to get used to the idea of obeying commands. You and me should have a wee chat sometime. I could help you if you're serious about assuming the office of constable. Genuinely. You seem a good type." He paused as if thinking. "You're not an axe-murderer are you?"

Singh spluttered his denial while Macdonald shook his head reproachfully.

"Look Sergeant Sim. We've got exams soon. We're only in here for a couple of beers and a blether. Let's cut to the chase. Why have you followed us half way across Glasgow to buy us a pint of lager?"

Sim set his Guinness squarely on a beer mat and pushed it a couple of inches away as if indicating that it was time to come down to business.

"Well, as it happens, Lachie. I do have a wee task I'd like you to conduct. A simple wee task. Essentially I want to give you each fifty quid to allow you to buy yourselves drink to your hearts' content."

"And where *exactly* would we drink to our hearts' content?"

"In the *Failté* Bar in St. Vincent Street."

"And why there, Sergeant?"

"Because that's where some of the top boys in '*Seed of the Gaels*' drink."

"Undercover work?" asked Singh excitedly.

"Aye...in a manner of speaking," responded Sim. "Nothing dangerous. I give you a few Nationalist badges to wear. You don't approach anyone. You do nothing but enjoy a few drinks. If people approach you, that's different. You allow yourselves to be spoken to and all you need to do is remember the names of anyone who talks to you and what you discussed. If everything goes well, I could keep you in beer money for quite a while and have a chat with you about joining the police force once you get your degree, Charlie."

"Aye, but supposin' we tell you to go and take a flyin' fuck to yersel'!"

Sim affected a more serious demeanour. "Then the beer stops and that knife you handed me outside the Whistling Kirk, now covered in your fingerprints, turns up covered in the blood of the victim at a serious assault scene!"

Chapter Six

Whisky and Water

The Cross Keys pub in Chelsea's Lawrence Street was still in the process of opening. A distinct aroma of disinfectant assailed Cavendish's nostrils as he shouldered the solid front door, gaining entrance and surprising a young man busily engaged in removing chairs from atop tables, placing them below.

"Sir! You're in early. Can I help you?"

Aware that coffee would be the sensible order, Cavendish found himself saying, "A glass of your delicious *Prosecco* would be the perfect way to start the day, eh?"

The bartender busied himself attending to the order while Cavendish found a booth he reckoned was sufficiently discrete. As his *Prosecco* arrived, so too did his interlocutor of the previous night.

"And whatever my friend here is having…" offered Cavendish.

A burly man, perhaps no more than five feet, six inches with an unshaven complexion and a heavy coat that concealed nether-wear that Cavendish calculated accurately had probably been purchased from one of those pre-loved shops he'd heard about.

The man hesitated, fixing his condemning gaze on Cavendish's *Prosecco*.

"Fuck's *sake!*

He was rebuked instantly by the young bartender, clearly unused to such malediction. "Sir!"

His reproach was met by a dark glower.

"Black coffee. Blacker than you've ever made it. Put more black in 'till you think I won't drink it then put extra black in it." He looked at Cavendish's Prosecco and considered the option. "And a large Macallan… Eighteen years' old if you have it. He's paying!"

The bartender scampered away as Cavendish continued in his well-schooled, polite demeanour whilst trying to come to terms with the suppressed aggression of his guest. He waved a hand at a seat opposite, attempting a confidence he didn't feel. "Please…make yourself comfortable."

John Kelso took his seat without removing his coat and studied Cavendish for a few moments before growling in a Glasgow accent, "I know a lot about you. You know nothing about me. That's the way it'll stay. I don't work for you. Other people direct my talents. I ask all the questions and you don't ask any." His impatient gaze was removed to the bar where his whisky was being poured. "Your job today is to tell me what keeps you awake at night and my job's to take away your nightmares."

John Kelso had been a Regimental Sergeant-Major with the Black Watch prior to a belated career stint in the Special Air Service for covert tasks in Iraq that required his unusual abilities and having retired had been offered some light-duty, completely above-board security tasks which had found favour with his superiors. Over some years these had edged into more felonious activity and he had discovered an appetite and a talent for responsibilities which would end his freedom if not his life were matters to go amiss. He could be relied upon to work alone and had a few trusted colleagues on whom he could call; equally skilled in the black arts as was he. He understood his value so was not inexpensive and could kill a man in several different ways. Two women had already been dispatched at his hand. His rise in the confidences of the security services was more as a consequence of his wily and guileful cunning and he possessed an accomplished history as a burglar due to a misspent youth in his home city before joining the army. Importantly, he was on no one's radar screen. His activities whilst illegal were completely deniable by the authorities. His one shortcoming was a simmering rage and a hostility towards other human beings that bordered on constant eruption. Cavendish had not expected to meet someone like John Kelso.

Somewhat discomfited, Cavendish attempted to bring the conversation round to something more to that which he'd anticipated.

"Are you acquainted with Brigadier Sir Jonathon Pennington?"

The lines on Kelso's forehead deepened. His eyes narrowed. "I thought you college boys were meant to be smart! Did you fucking study English at school?"

Cavendish's eyebrows were by now somewhere near his receding hairline.

"Err…"

"Because *I* did. And you just asked me a question. Did you realise that was a question? Did you maybe think that was a statement…a proclamation…an announcement? Didn't you hear me say that I'd ask questions. Not you?"

The young barman approached with Kelso's Macallan and placed it before him.

"Your coffee will be along in a moment sir."

"Where's the water?"

"Water, sir?"

Kelso sighed deeply while staring intently at the glass in front of him. "Look son...for future reference. You never serve whisky without placing a glass with a wee bit water on the side. You don't make your own assessment of how much water to put in. You don't drink whisky neat. You don't drink whisky with ice. You don't drink whisky with anything fizzy inside it." He raised his gaze to meet the eyes of the bartender. "So run along now and get your favourite customer here a wee glass of water so he can enjoy this..." A thought occurred. "Is this eighteen years old?"

"Indeed so, sir."

Kelso nodded his satisfaction and returned his gaze to the glass before engaging with Cavendish's look of stupefaction and confirming his requirements.

"Water!"

Left alone, Kelso took control of the conversation. "Now, Commander Who-Gives-A-Fuck, my understanding is that you clever types want to make sure that Scotland doesn't do a very sensible thing and separate itself from you wicked and incompetent bastards here in London. You've taken care of media matters, you've hired teams of people to stop your social media messages being absolutely dominated by an army of individuals in Scotland who now have the evil eye on you, you've bought the favours of foreign politicians to align with your agenda, got your banking and commercial pals on-side and threatened grandmothers that they'll lose their pensions if they cheer when Scotland scores a goal at Hampden. You accuse senior Scottish politicians of sex scandals without any substance to the claims and just let the stories run for months in the press. They just love that, the press, eh…they just *love* that."

A small ceramic gravy boat containing water was placed before him by the waiter who beat a hasty retreat.

"So far, so right on the money, Commander?"

"Pretty much," replied Cavendish feigning *sangfroid*.

"But here's the rub, Commander. The polls show that you're about to lose this battle of wits…that my fellow countrymen are up to all of your ploys." He poured a *soupçon* of water into his glass, hardly disturbing the surface of its contents and took a large draught, almost emptying it. "What you need is to put this political battle onto a playing field that better suits your abilities to control it, eh?"

"That is rather the essence of my discussions with…."

Kelso interrupted. "Fuckin' 'essence of my discussions'…? Is that a 'yes'?"

A coffee was placed beside his whisky, the bartender timidly asking if it was to Kelso's liking."

Kelso's gaze never left Cavendish's face. "Probably not black enough, son." He paused. "Leave us."

He turned again to Cavendish's concerns. "What you need according to the people who sent me here, is to militarise this thing. To allow you clowns to send in the troops to protect the people, eh? To make Scotland like Northern Ireland was back in the seventies and eighties?"

Cavendish protested mildly. "Well perhaps not entirely…"

"Frighten the lieges, eh? Get troops and cops on to the streets. Show the Nationalist movement as the thugs that they are, eh?"

"It wouldn't go amiss if doubts were to be raised in the mind of some that there was a violent undercurrent in the Nationalist movement."

Kelso smiled his first smile of the day. "A violent undercurrent…a nasty, violent undercurrent." He lifted his cup of coffee and drank it in one gulp. Placing it noisily atop its saucer, he lifted the whisky and finished it. "Then that's what you'll get." He stood, noisily pushing back his seat. "I'm informed that you're the…" He struggled to find the right word. "*Individual* I should be in touch with if I need assistance…but I fucking hope I don't."

Leaving, he hesitated. Glaring at Cavendish his voice lowered almost to a whisper. "I fucking *hate* cunts like you!"

Goaded into a riposte he regretted saying as the words left his mouth, Cavendish murmured just loud enough for Kelso to hear, "You might be a proud Scotsman, but you still take the King's shilling in order to do down your countrymen."

Kelso stiffened, bristled and walked towards the door.

Cavendish had made an enemy.

Starring straight ahead, he allowed a few moments to ensure that Kelso had left, sipped generously at his *Prosecco* and fumbled in his pocket for his phone, turning as he did so to ensure visually that the door remained closed with his adversary on its other side.

It took but a moment to find the office number for Brigadier Sir Jonathon Pennington; their relationship insufficiently close to require personal contact details.

As ever, the call was answered by the dutiful Miss Emily Evans.

"Good morning. The office of Brigadier Sir Jonathon Pennington. Who may I say is calling?"

"This is Commander Henry Cavendish. I met on Wednesday with Sir Jonathon. If it's possible, it's imperative that I speak with him immediately."

"Please hold."

Some moments later Pennington took the call, having first muttered quiet invectives to himself along the lines of having anticipated Cavendish's contact.

"Henry. Good to hear from you."

Cavendish disposed with his usual practised pleasantries.

"Brigadier Pennington, I've just met with the man you've allocated to deal with one of the most important, restricted and clandestine tasks Her Majesty's Government have on the books."

"Ah, so you've met Kelso?"

"Well, I'm sure I don't know *who* I've met. He was not particularly forthcoming on that front…on *any* front for that matter. He was rude, aggressive…"

"Yes, he can be a little assertive and straightforward in his communications, sometimes and I'll grant you that he's not overburdened with a sense of fun."

"Brigadier…if this man was under my command when I was in the services…"

"Indeed, Henry but he was not. Kelso has talents, perhaps *hidden* talents I'll grant you that might not be found to be crucial on board one of our submarines."

"Frankly, Brigadier, he was an abhorrent individual. I find it almost impossible to imagine that there is any way I can work with him on a matter as subtle as this one."

Pennington's patience, never in great supply, frayed.

"Cavendish, you're a decent enough chap and you may have spent time in the navy but you don't deal well with the ranks, do you? You really only feel comfortable in the company of people of your own social standing who are possessed of privilege and quality footwear."

Surprised at the rebarbative tone of his superior, Cavendish was reduced to hapless spluttering.

"But, Brigadier...."

"Look old chap. I never imagined he'd by now be inviting you to Club *Prive* at *L'Escargo* and suggesting French Martinis before getting down to discussing the establishment of a committee to further your agenda. Kelso is a warrior. Once in Iraq he was wounded in the thigh and declined anaesthesia in favour of biting on a leather belt. As I say, a warrior.

Now, you came to me asking for the assistance of MI5. That was denied for reasons of maintaining our charter. However, we have other arrows in our quiver and using Kelso provides deniability. I know he can come across as aggressive, largely, I gather because he was badly injured in Afghanistan which resulted in him being discharged following the insertion of a substantial steel plate in his head. Apparently the man could walk bollock naked through an airport security device and trigger every alarm in the place. He doesn't seem particularly to enjoy the company of those such as you and me but

I assure you, he has the ability to get the job done. It may surprise you to know that he was a soldier who worked himself up to the rank of Regimental Sergeant Major, in the process going to night-school and obtaining a law degree. He served with distinction in the SAS and in recent years he's carried out several covert responsibilities, sometimes alone, sometimes with people of whom I've no knowledge but whom he advises are his equals. He's never failed us. He's never left a trace of his involvement. I've no reason to doubt that he'll be just as successful as you wish him to be. My dear fellow, if I were you I'd work hard at finding him all of the resources he'll ask of you. You can trust him with money, arms and confidences. If he needs political favours, I'd find ways of having them granted. I've briefed him. *You've* briefed him…"

"Well, I wouldn't say that, Brigadier. He hardly let me speak, the scoundrel. He looked like a down-and-out ruffian."

"Trust me Henry. It wouldn't surprise me if the next time you met him, he was dressed in a Saville Row suit, wearing a monocle, smoking a cigar and speaking in a clipped German accent. Last time I met him he was wearing expensive golf wear in Muirfield Golf Club and speaking most entertainingly and amusingly. He's quite the character…if no stranger to the grape!"

Cavendish measured Pennington's comments for some moments and shook his head resignedly.

"Well, I'm sure I don't understand how your more covert establishment works, Brigadier but I accept your guidance as ever."

"Good chap. You should know that I've also provided him with details of an agent in Scotland lest he needs immediate support in an emergency."

"And am *I* to be provided with details of this agent?"

"Not necessary, Henry. Find a way of giving Kelso all the support he asks for. You won't be disappointed. Trust me, this will have been a performance designed to ensure that you understood him to be someone who expects to get his own way in all tactical matters." He permitted himself a smile. *Sounds like he was successful.*

Cavendish bid farewell and pushed the red button on his phone, ending the call. He looked to gain the attention of the young barman and waved him over.

"A large Macallan," he asked. "Eighteen years."

Receiving silent confirmation of his request, he decided to supplement it and to change the habit of a lifetime. "Eh...and with some water on the side."

At least Kelso wasn't a complete barbarian when it comes to the finer things in life, he reflected.

Chapter Seven

A Speech to the Faithful

As guests filed into the Algonquin Hotel on West 44th Street in New York a piper dressed in the blue and green colours of 'Hunting McLeod' played *'the Black Bear',* a hornpipe traditionally employed by army regiments as they return to their barracks. His shoulder plaid was held in place by a large badged crest of the McLeods bearing the clan's inscription, *'Hold Fast'*. To the Americans who passed he looked every inch their image of the Scottish warrior if the bone-handled Bowie knife atop his right sock in place of the traditional *sgian dubh* was overlooked - as indeed it was. To many of them it was merely a marketing ploy by the hotel; some smiled, others groaned at the sound of the bagpipes but for a select group of one hundred and seventy wealthy New Yorkers however, it was a perquisite of an evening spent celebrating their Scottish heritage - however distant. Many of the guests bound for the hotel's Oak Room had attempted to adorn their business suits and dresses with tartan regalia they believed showed the world their Scottish connections others wore highland dress, all were in good spirits.

Tartan Day was some six months away but preparations required to be made. Money had to be raised.

As guests assembled, *Friends of Scotland* President Andrew Buchanan stood just inside the room greeting everyone. Prior to being introduced to him, an assistant stood behind a table in the hallway; a nubile young lady dressed scantily in a short tartan skirt and a deep-cut top who beamed a supplementary welcome and handed out name tags so Buchanan could address everyone by their first name as they entered as if they were life-long friends. The bonhomie worked well.

Two guests were marked out for a special welcome; Cornelius (now Cornie) Donaghey and Struan McAllister. They arrived together and were enveloped in Buchanan' bear-like embrace where, after some affable salutations, he whispered an invitation that was more of an instruction to meet with him outside the Oak Room once Alan Bannerman had proceeded to deliver the financial report and explain the need for continued support for the cause of supporting Scotland's political and social renaissance.

Buchanan, a Scottish-born white goods magnate throughout the eastern seaboard of the United States and with a Boston accent now as broad as was once John Fitzgerald Kennedy's, was expert at building an audience into a fervour of excitement. He drew on his own journey as a young man from Garenin, a remote croft in the north-east of the Isle of Lewis whose centre of population, Stornoway was an hour's drive away. Every so often he'd lapse into the few words of the *Gaelic* tongue he could remember in order to impress those who hadn't a clue what he'd just said but, as a result, were convinced of his true Scottish heritage and of his right to be President of their gathering for a seventh year. Humorous, intelligent and passionate, he introduced Alan Bannerman and left the podium as the crowd roared their approval, smiling all the way round the periphery of the assembly to the huge oak doors that led to the corridor outside. He was joined by McAllister and Donaghey.

"Well done, Andrew. They loved you!" McAllister was his usual ingratiating self

"Well, I sincerely hope so. That speech must have taken me two minutes to write!"

Donaghey brought the conversation to the business in hand.

"I have all the items we sought."

Buchanan was anxious for detail. "Where'd you get them?"

"Gun fairs in Michigan, Santa Fe, Birmingham Alabama and Las Vegas. None of them are traceable."

Buchanan grabbed Donaghey by the lapels, in the process dislodging the sprig of heather he'd pinned there. He whispered aggressively in his ear. "We don't mention gun fairs, weapons of any description or anything that might alert the FBI. For all you know, you complete idiot, I might be an undercover agent who's just trapped you into serving who knows how long in a Maximum Facility Federal Super-max Prison in downtown Colorado."

As Donaghey attempted an apologetic explanation, Buchanan' face broke into a wide smile.

"C'mon, Cornie. If we can't trust each other, who the hell can we trust?"

He looked theatrically to the left and right of the hallway and hugged his conspirators even closer.

"What d'you get?"

* * *

Buchanan returned to the Oak Room and edged his way back to the podium where he took his seat beside other office-bearers. Some minutes passed before he was called upon by the speaker to address the gathering.

He opened his arms wide. *"Failté.* Welcome! *Alba gu bráth!"* He stood beaming at his audience as if attempting to gauge the tone of his message before proceeding.

"My friends, ladies and gentlemen, I have been privileged to hold the position of President of this wonderful organisation for several years now but this evening I intend to pass the baton to someone with more fuel in the tank than me. I know I could pass for a young man in his forties but the fact is that I reach the grand old age of seventy-six next year."

A murmur of polite objection met his short pause.

"I am a relatively healthy, touch wood and if I might say so, a relatively *wealthy* man and although I seek presently to stand back from the front line, I want to go out with a bang; to leave with a message of hope and to make two announcements that will cause a small measure of consternation in the ranks of the British Imperialistic Establishment."

He paused again and took a sip of his whisky.

"Although proud to have been born in Scotland, my formative years were spent here in America; in Boston to be precise. And as I made my way in life and built my fortune, I spent many an evening in the pubs, bars and clubs of my new city. Most of these were patronised by our fellow Celts, the fighting Irish - one or two of whom are here this evening..." He broadened his smile and waved at the rear of the assembly, "Sean and Declan, I see you." He returned to the scribbled notes before him.

"That pair spent too many hours attempting to persuade me from the straight and narrow. To have me forsake the Highland Malt of my forbearers and drink instead what *they* call whiskey...a spirit called 'Tullymore Dew', a bottle of which I now use to disinfect my floor mop."

Gales of laughter shook the room, enjoyed by Buchanan's two Irish friends as much as the Scottish contingent.

"But the stories they shared on many an evening had a profound effect on me for they told me of bombings and maimings and death and destruction on the island of Ireland. They told me of suspicion and fear, of enforced poverty and the ethos that's it's not the power you possess in any given struggle but the will to endure, to suffer any loss, any privation or impairment in order that ultimately you achieve your goal. Well, I have to say, that while there's an old saying that the most important lesson we must learn from history is that we always *fail* to learn from history; and while I suspect it's as true now as once it was, it's a lesson that's not lost on *me*. I built a commercial empire on logic, on rationality, sure, on taking risks but not on ignoring the lessons learned by those who'd gone before. And it's as true in commerce as it is in politics. Improving your lot by means of privation and impairment makes no sense to me. The only prospect of progress is by means of the ballot box. By persuasion, not by pugnacity; by friendship not fighting; by cooperation not coercion."

Some tepid applause allowed him another sip of his whisky.

"Today in Scotland we find ourselves subject to the English crown. While we have fifty-nine political voices, England has five hundred and thirty-three. They call it democracy but the union of parliaments was supposed to be one of two equals coming together in partnership but it's become the very opposite of that, of the subjugation of Scotland by England. When every single local authority in Scotland votes to remain in Europe, but England votes to leave *we* have to leave. We seek to have our powers returned to us from Europe but the five hundred and thirty-three English politicians - both Conservative and Labour - vote to have them retained in London. That's not democracy my friends. That's brutal colonialism!" Further applause.

"And when in 2015 Scotland sent fifty-six out of fifty-nine members of parliament to Westminster supporting independence for Scotland, the Conservative Government appointed the sole Unionist Conservative Member of Parliament as Secretary of State to ensure that their rule over Scotland was absolute. Scottish Labour had to nominate some joker from Newcastle in England as their shadow-overlord so depleted was their forces. That's not democracy my friends. Scotland is their last colony and they mean to keep it that way!"

Prolonged applause encouraged him to raise his arms in acclamation before continuing.

"They steal Scotland's oil over decades, commission a report on its economic implications but when it shows that an independent Scotland would have the strongest currency in Europe along with Switzerland and Norway, they lie about its quantities, tell Scots that they're too poor, too stupid and too small to handle a complex matter like North Sea Oil and slap a *'Top Secret'* classification on the information, deeming it to be sensitive information so restricted and secret that it must be protected by law. It worked for thirty years, buried in the vaults of Whitehall in London, ladies and gentlemen. Thirty years while they sucked the oil wells dry. That's not democracy, my friends. That's theft. That's colonialism."

By now, many were on their feet.

"The constitution of our organisation pledges allegiance to the Scottish flag, to the Scottish Parliament and to the Scottish people. Everyone here today supports the notion of independence for Scotland - and we are fortunate enough to have cheque-books that allow us to make a small difference."

A few in the front row waved wads of dollar bills.

"Well, I am better placed than most to make a small difference and this evening as I step down from my duties - but not away from my friendships nor the cause that we all espouse, I would like to announce two investments I am making which I hope shall advance the day when Scotland attains its rightful place in the United Nations between Saudi Arabia and Senegal. First, I am making a personal donation to deepen the coffers of the Scottish National Party in Edinburgh in the sum of one hundred thousand dollars."

A prolonged applause rang out as he continued.

"My second decision was based upon my life-long distaste for British Imperialism. There are almost two hundred countries in the world and the British state has, at some point in its history, invaded and established a military presence in over one hundred and seventy of them. Indeed, we live in one of them ourselves, do we not? And is not Scotland one of the last footholds of British Imperialism? Its last colony? It is not without good cause my friends that the flag of the United Kingdom is known the world over not for democracy, the mother of parliaments, justice for all...but for bloodshed and domination. It is not without good cause that almost all of the countries they once ruled have now achieved independence and cast off the occupier's yoke. And it is not without good cause that the flag of the United Kingdom that flew over their occupied capitals is called by those oppressed, 'The Butcher's Apron!'

But you all know me well and are aware that I enjoy a bit of mischief now and again so I bought a horse ladies and gentlemen, an Arab stallion with an established pedigree which I'm having trained in the rolling hills of the Curragh in Ireland where we are fortunate to have signed up with one of the world's top horse training facilities. I'm confident that we here tonight who are members of our horse-racing fraternity will soon be losing money on my horse once I enter her in some sprint races. And in order to inflict maximum embarrassment upon the commentators who will have to describe his progress in the race, I attempted to register this fine steed with a name that would bring shame and dishonour to the British Establishment as it enters the final furlong and its name..."*the Butcher's Apron...* is being shouted by commentators and punters alike. But the British Racehorse Authority disallowed the name!"

Some light-hearted booing was heard.

"And this at the same meeting where they allowed, '*Wear The Fox Hat*'!"

Much laughter and cheering ensued as Buchanan clasped his hands and raised them to shoulder level as he acknowledged the reaction of his membership.

"And so to my second announcement…as I won't be beaten by any aspect of the British Establishment!" He allowed a few seconds to heighten the drama. "As many of you also know, apart from losing my money on racehorses, I also lose my money attempting to keep rather a fine yacht afloat. Now it's a good boat I have, the *Scottish Thistle*…but not as fine a vessel as I've had built at a staggering cost of some four million dollars. The fastest transatlantic crossing was achieved by a wonderful craft, a trimaran called *Banque Populaire V,* an offshore-racing specialist. It made the journey in three days, fifteen hours, twenty-five minutes and forty-eight seconds. Well, I've bought its sister ship, converted it, made improvements and it's being sailed from Boston Yacht Haven in two days' time. It will travel first to Stranraer in Scotland…a slightly longer journey because I want it first to berth in God's Own Country and then to the Royal Yacht Squadron at Cowes in the Isle of Wight in the English Chanel where it will compete in the Round the Britain and Ireland Race; one thousand, eight hundred and five nautical miles round the British Isles. The race will be followed all the way by aerial photography, camera vessels and on-shore reports. Progress will be reported nightly on the national evening news. And although they stopped me naming my new stallion as I'd wish, they couldn't stop me naming my yacht so I very much hope you will join me in cheering on our new yacht, '*The Butcher's Apron*'."

Loud cheering ensued as Buchanan gestured to four figures seated in the front row to stand.

"And here are four of the twelve boys who will win that race and embarrass the British Unionists. Give 'em a wave boys….from left to right, our Skip, Sam Ferguson, son of the New York City Police Commissioner Thomas Ferguson, a good friend of ours whose antecedents come from the border village of Selkirk in Scotland. Next, Bill Cook, as American as they come but he has a Scottish terrier back home. Then, Alastair McLeod, whose parents, Bill and Mary hail from Edinburgh and finally Seamus O'Neil an Irishman who is just as passionate about Scottish Independence as his forbearers were about Irish freedom back in 1916." He raised his arms and gestured applause. "Let's give them some encouragement."

He sat down before being hauled back to his feet by Alan Bannerman who, to overcome the cheering, whispered a yell in his ear that he'd forgotten to raise the matter of fundraising.

Buchanan took more cheers before leaning into the microphone and silencing the audience. "Gee, I forgot, I forgot. Thanks, Alan."

He waited for the noise to subside.

"Now later on we have a band who will give us some good old Scottish fiddle music while we enjoy some hospitality but first, there are two receptacles at the end of each row. The larger of these, the black one, is set to hold cash dollars or cheques which will be needed to deal with some of the costs associated with Tartan Week, so give generously. You'll be going into your organising groups in a moment where you'll have to make progress against the programme we agreed at our last meeting. The second, the red bucket is to permit our four heroes in the front row and their eight fellow crewmen to take a tour of Scottish distilleries after they complete the Round Britain and Ireland yacht race. They'll want to stay in good hotels, perhaps play some golf at the best golf courses in the world and enjoy two weeks recovering before they bring *'The Butcher's Apron'* back home to Boston. Give till it hurts!"

As he sat for a second time, a be-kilted man in the furthest row from the front stood cheering with those around him before sitting and writing a final note on his cell phone. Its concluding word was, 'Harmless'. He pushed the send button transmitting his account of the meeting to Jefferson Carter the Third, Assistant Deputy Director of Operations (Western Hemisphere); his boss in the CIA.

Chapter Eight

Bryson's Farewell

The sun dipped perfectly behind the mountainous volcanic plug of Alisa Craig, darkening its profile and bathing its halo in a rich, red glow as it headed into the Irish Sea for the night. Sitting on a rotting wooden bench outside a small remote cottage in the Carrick Hills above the Ayrshire coast watching this phenomenon, Jack Bryson sucked on the remnant of a cigarette he'd rolled only minutes before. Satisfied that there was no more tar, nicotine or acetaldehyde to be inhaled, he coughed and wiped the tears from his bloodshot eyes. A further bout of quiet weeping developed into a coughing fit compounded by an aching, shoulder-wrenching, mute wail. In contrast to his dark and sombre mood, a nearby stream burbled, leapt and sparkled in the evening sunshine as a consequence of heavy rain earlier in the day.

Bryson was a large man. Six feet four inches in his stocking soles, a lifetime in the service of his country had seen his muscular frame develop in tandem with his fearsome combat skills. Recent years of functional alcoholism had reduced his outward athleticism only marginally although many of his internal organs were fast approaching their use-by date.

Jack Bryson was a sniper…had *been* a sniper. At his best he was the most accurate shot in the British Army and had been called on many times to demonstrate this. Even when gloriously drunk he could hold his own with most of his peers. Lauded by his commanders and comrades, forgiven his frailties by the same men, Bryson had become an important member of the Special Air Service and had served in most of the world's trouble spots during a decade of risky adventures before a drunken assault on a priggish officer had seen him reluctantly but dishonourably discharged. A small sum set aside to benefit a daughter he'd barely seen since her birth twenty-two years previously had been used instead to purchase a small Ayrshire cottage accessible only by a precipitous footpath down to the village of Ballantrae which in the seven months he'd owned the property had been walked mainly by him - and then mostly to replenish his dwindling drinks cabinet.

Bryson breathed deeply occasioning a further coughing fit. Still seated on his bench he spread his fingers and considered his outstretched hands. They each shook in consonance, one with another.

"Couldn'y hit a coo's arse with these if ah wis haudin' its tail", he murmured to himself.

Permitting himself an uneven if half-hearted smile, he shook his head regretfully. *Best shot in the British Army? Best sniper in the SAS? I wouldn'y win a teddy-bear at a shoot-em-up stall in a Barnum and Bailey funfair.*

He passed his hand across his unshaven chin then collected a tumbler half-full of Scotmid supermarket blended whisky - a marked comedown from the expensive malts he'd used to drink - and swallowed its contents in one gulp returning the empty glass shakily to the windowsill beside him. Levering himself from the bench by means of a nearby bin whose contents clinked as he disturbed it he rose and pushed at the front door of his cottage, the bottom edge of the long-swollen wooden frame dragging noisily across the flagstone floor.

A rope he'd prepared earlier had been knotted at one end and looped by means of a slip knot at the other. Clumsily he placed the knurl over the top of the door using his weight to close it, pinning the rope securely. Despite the relatively low ceiling and the corresponding height of the door, Bryson yet had to stand on a small stool so his head was positioned above the top of the door.

Weeping quietly again, he placed the rope around his neck. *So it's come to this, eh?*

Nodding to himself as if to confirm the finality of his decision, he rose to his full height.

Some seconds passed.

"Fuck it!" He pushed his right foot down on the edge of the stool which clattered sideways and dropped him the short distance to oblivion.

Chapter Nine

The Caledonian Committee

Brigadier Sir Jonathon Pennington called the meeting to order. Seven men sat around an antique oak Victorian table each thumbing through a new paper Pennington had distributed, dissipating the earlier light banter.

"Let's make this quick chaps. A brief summary from each of you if you don't mind and I'll speak to the paper I've just issued." He turned to the tanned and impeccably dressed colleague on his immediate left. "Jeremy, why don't you start?"

One by one, verbal reports were made on recent Scottish polling, conversations with newspaper owners, social media commentary and the latest shifting political views being exhibited by Members of Parliament of all affiliation with nuances discussed and assessed. Cavendish's recent activity was recorded with all present, perhaps taking their lead from the tone of Pennington's initial introduction, diminishing his fitness to fulfil any obligation beyond advising on the correct form of address when in the presence of an archbishop.

Pennington thanked Giles Wexford for his final comments before turning to his own paper which was a distillation of the information provided by *'Treasure'*.

"Nothing particularly of interest from our prime agent in Scotland. Some innuendo regarding the relationship between the Cabinet Secretary for Environment, Climate Change and Land Reform and his local Chairman as well as an interesting relationship that's developing between the Acting Deputy Leader of the Labour Party and one of the Conservative and Unionist List MSPs for Central Scotland who have enjoyed hill-walking with each other in recent months and who propose to conquer a mountain named Ben Macdui in the Cairngorms this weekend. I am to understand that when last these two fellows climbed three thousand feet they each joined the 'mile high club', so to speak." He laid his paper on the table. "Still, it makes a change from the buggering of small boys that seems still to occupy the spare time of many of their Westminster counterparts." He held his hand up, his palm facing Giles Wexford who appeared ready to comment, silencing his contribution. "Finally, as you've probably surmised, I should advise that MI5 have been approached formally by the aforementioned Commander Henry Cavendish under instruction from the Cabinet Office. They seek our formal participation in illegal escapades he proposes in Scottish affairs. I reminded him of our charter and denied our assistance. That is the end of the matter. However, very quietly and not for minuting I have allowed access to informal support under the terms of the Third Direction and we may or may not find that this yields results."

He warmed to his subject, recalling his days as an amateur Shakespearean thespian, raising his arms as if addressing an army. "We must all recall the wisdom of

Marcus Tullius Cicero who lived on this earth some one hundred and six years prior to Jesus of Nazareth. He said, if I remember the lines I delivered to an attentive audience during my Cambridge days, 'A nation can survive its fools, and even the ambitious. But it cannot survive treason from within. An enemy at the gates is less formidable, for he is known and carries his banner openly. But the traitor moves amongst those within the gate freely, his sly whispers rustling through all the alleys, heard in the very halls of government itself. For the traitor appears not a traitor; he speaks in accents familiar to his victims and he wears their face and their arguments, he appeals to the baseness that lies deep in the hearts of all men. He rots the soul of a nation, he works secretly and unknown in the night to undermine the pillars of the city, he infects the body politic so that it can no longer resist. A murderer is less to fear."

He lowered his arms and his tone. Jeremy Ogilvie mimed smiling applause at the soliloquy.

Now, I have another meeting so unless there are additional pressing matters, let us appeal to the baseness that lies deep in the hearts of all men and foment treason from within. Our business here today is concluded."

Chapter Ten

Only Six Armalites

A bowloader shell cut gracefully but muscularly through the waters of Boston's Charles River urged on by a cox whose metronomic voice shouting *'catch'* penetrated the mid-morning riverside quietness of the township of Cambridge on the outskirts of the city. Across the river, the older aspect of Harvard University stood in counterpoint to the modern edifices which occupied its west bank. Some short distance downriver, an ivy-covered mansion stood back from the waters in its own grounds. A sleek, powerful Bentley car slowed at its entry was admitted remotely and drove unhurriedly along its perfectly surfaced driveway cutting through its equally perfectly manicured lawns before parking.

Andrew Buchanan stood in his elegant four-columned *tetrastyla* portico and welcomed Hank Donaghey and Struan McAllister to his home before walking them through to his conservatory and out into his expansive rear lawn.

"Let's start with our usual ritual."

All three opened the top four buttons of their shirts and revealed chests void of electronic devices. They hugged as a threesome, in doing so feeling for any wires that may have been adhered to someone's back. Satisfied, McClellan took the lead

"We only discuss things outside boys. Today we'll talk at our barbecue pit. I checked it earlier. As they sat, he reached and turned on some music to disguise their conversation. The fiddle of Ali Bain and accordion accompaniment of Phil Cunningham filled the air.

"Can't be too careful!"

"Great speech the other night, Andrew," said McAllister quietly, just so they could hear him speak. "We raised one hundred and twenty-three thousand dollars...getting on for a thousand dollars a head...and the twelve boys will enjoy their Scottish tour if they can find a way to spend twenty-eight thousand."

Buchanan smiled. "I'm sure they'll try."

"Yeah, great speech, Andrew," agreed Donaghey. But I think your bit about '*The Butcher's Apron*' went down better with some than the passages about peace and harmony and conciliation."

Buchanan turned up the volume just as the Eagles began singing of standing on a corner in Winslow, Arizona. "You guys know as well as me that I lied through my teeth! When I spent those nights as a youth listening to Sean and Declan and their parents and friends talk to me in bars of the Irish struggles, we didn't talk the hand of friendship, we talked more of Pádraig Pearse the great Irish barrister, poet, political activist and revolutionary who understood that violence against the oppressor, which resulted in the Easter Rising in 1916, was the only way..."

"If memory recalls, he actually said, 'blood is a cleansing and sanctifying thing and the nation that regards it as the final horror has lost its manhood. There are many things more horrible than bloodshed and slavery is one of them!"

All three men started in alarm as a tall bearded man addressed them from the other side of the barbecue.

Buchanan spoke first. "Jesus, you near scared the livin' daylights out of me, Murdo." He beckoned Murdo Monteith to join them and addressed his two other guests. "I was going to introduce my house-guest in a moment once we'd settled." He beckoned the stranger to join them. "Boys, this is Murdo Monteith. He's one of the crew that's taking *The Butcher's Apron* over to Scotland and'...He slapped his thigh in appreciation. "He's also a main man in *Seed of the Gaels* back in Scotland...Sorry, Murdo I can't get my tongue round the Gaelic pronunciation."

Monteith took a seat at the marble table and held his hand out in friendship to McAllister and Donaghey. "Good to meet you boys. The work you do is invaluable to the cause."

Buchanan explained. "He's staying with me for a couple of days. Murdo's worked hard to ensure that the authorities, if they were watching, would not see him visit me...lots of manoeuvres he's explained to me - even though because of his prowess as a yachtsman, they know for sure that he's here in the States what with the race and all. So will the Brits."

Monteith beamed a smile at the group but addressed McAllister and Donaghey directly.

"Andrew here tells me you've managed to acquire an arsenal of quite some proportions!"

Both men looked at each other and then at Buchanan to invite approval to discuss the matter further.

"It's okay, boys. Murdo's the man who'll take possession of what you've procured when it arrives over in Scotland."

Buchanan nodded his assent again. "Tell him, Struan!"

McAllister was hesitant. "Have you checked him for wires, Andrew?"

"Yeah, yeah, yeah," confirmed Buchanan, quoting the Beatles who were now singing about a Lonely Hearts Club Band led by Sergeant Pepper.

"Well, from gun shows in several States we've got twenty Heckler and Koch HK 91 rifles, six Armalite AR 15 assault rifles and four AK 47 assault rifles. All legal but bought using assumed names and false ID."

"Tell him the prize, Struan."

McAllister continued. "We met a guy.... seemed straight enough. Ex-military. Brought back a Red Eye surface to air missile-launcher from Iraq. Cost us ten thousand dollars!"

Buchanan smiled at Monteith and awaited his acclaim. Instead, Monteith nodded solemnly and eyed the threesome.

"Are the weapons here?"

Donaghey answered. "No. A warehouse in Hartford, Connecticut. Halfway between New York and Boston." It's secure. We know the owner."

Monteith grimaced. "The guy *seemed* straight enough? You boys might just have bought yourselves a considerable amount of jail time."

Smiles vanished as they digested his comment.

"The Yanks are many things but they're not dumb! The FBI and CIA have countless agents trying to sell illegal arms to individuals whom they then either jail, blackmail or surveil in order to land a bigger fish. Now you guys might have been lucky and bought from a real nut-job who managed to bring a top secret weapon back from a war zone. It *could* happen. But I won't touch it. I know you're doing your best but I managed to sneak up on you without trying, there could be a bug underneath your chair, wiretaps are common and usually worn on the chest but there could be a surveillance van outside with telescope mikes trained on you, there could be a bug inside the Red Eye capturing your every word."

All three stiffened and looked nervously at their surroundings.

"Don't worry, they need line of sight and we're not overlooked here. I swept the area earlier with a counter-surveillance radio frequency device that would detect electronic signals and there's no sign of anything built into or hidden in the barbecue or the surrounding wall. No dust or debris where someone might have drilled a hole and secreted something. Now if we talk further about every single purchase of these rifles and I'm satisfied, I may be interested but we have to do something quickly about the missile launcher. So here's what you do. Before you leave here you phone a weapons dealer…a reputable one… and you tell him you want to have the device disabled; deactivated and made inoperable. You tell the guy you want either to loan it to a museum or you're thinking of starting a collection. You'd like his advice. You're an amateur who'd like to get started in collecting weapons. Either way you go on record quickly and make sure that the authorities can't accuse you easily of being a terrorist." He paused to check their understanding. "Follow?"

All three nodded.

"Let's hope when you leave here you're not met by a series of Jeeps carrying guys with guns. Who knows if they have Andrew here as a person of interest - although last night's speech was masterful." He grinned. "Peace and love, baby!"

"Were you there?" asked Donaghey.

Buchanan laughed. "Who d'you think was playing mandolin in the band during the social at the end?"

Buchanan' grin was infectious. Monteith was contaminated. "I came in with the folk group. They let me sit in at Andrew's request. Their repertoire is pretty standard stuff so my beard and I weren't out of place."

McAllister was impressed. "The band was great. You were pretty nifty on the old mandolin and tenor banjo."

"It was good fun but I was just hiding in plain sight. I listened to the speeches from the wings when Andrew was speaking." He half-stood and produced a grey pewter hip-flask from the rear pocket of his cargo trousers before seating himself once more and grinning at the group. "Glenfidich, twelve years old and I don't share." He unscrewed the small flask-top and took a swig. "Why don't you guys go inside, search the web for Boston's top antique or contemporary weapons' dealer and make the call that might get you off the hook if the Feds pounce. I'll sit here and contemplate life with the help of my Glenfidich until you return and explain in *very* precise detail how you came by every single weapon you have in your consignment…and we only shift six at a time. The IRA learned that back in the day. Losing six Armalites isn't too bad. Losing everything would be a blow. Plus it's easier to disguise and hide six rifles. Always small and regular consignments. Now make that phone call!"

Chapter Eleven

Failté

Macdonald and Singh stood outside the *Failté* Bar in St. Vincent Street and inspected the badges they'd each pinned on in Macdonald's flat an hour before.

"Right, we play the simple ba' here, Charlie. If that arsehole Sim wants to give us fifty quid each for drink, that's *his* lookout. We have a few beers, say no one spoke to us and return to our exams. Get him to hell out of our lives."

"*Aye*...but he maybe gets me into the police!"

Macdonald pointed to the sky and Singh followed his direction.

"Look! There's a pig flying over the roof of the pub!"

"Aye, very good. But he might help me. Anyway, it's quite exciting going undercover like this. A wee adventure!"

Macdonald wasn't to be moved. "Absolutely not, Charlie. That cop's evil. He's prepared to land me in trouble if we don't help him! That's bang out of order. So we go in. We have a few drinks. We cause no trouble. We leave. We report nothing to Sim and we get our lives back. We don't come back under any circumstances. Eh?"

Singh nodded. "Okay."

Holding each other's gaze for a second they pushed at the battered green swing door of *Failté* and entered. The pub was dark and only a few solo drinkers stood at the bar. At the far end a group of six people were gathered around a table which had not benefited from having had spent glasses removed. It was easy to deduce that quite a few rounds had been consumed. At the far end of the table, a long-haired, bearded man wearing a red tartan bonspiel tammy pulled over his left ear held court.

"Two pints of lager, please. Tennent's," said Macdonald.

"No way, Lachie. We've got a couple of bob. I'm having a foreign beer." Singh scanned the pumps. "Could I have a pint of Stella, please?"

Wordlessly, the barman poured as requested. Macdonald awaited the conclusion of the transaction as Singh hung his small backpack over the back of a chair at a table towards the far end of the bar. Macdonald returned with two pints.

"What the hell are you doin', Charlie? Let's move nearer the door. When someone from that crowd orders a round they'll pass us. The idea is to avoid contact not encourage it!"

"Just sit down and drink your beer, Lachie. We'll have a quiet night wherever we sit. And remember, we can't leave until the pub shuts. I'd bet anything that Sim is sitting outside watching everything.

Macdonald measured his friend's perspective and sat.

Two pints later both had loosened up and conversation focussed upon their studies. Over the hour they'd sat there, different members of the group had approached the bar and ordered more drinks but hadn't engaged them in conversation. As Macdonald finished his third pint he rose.

"Right, Charlie. What's it to be? Cooncil lager or more of that foreign muck you're drinking?"

"More of the same please my good man. And some plain crisps if they've any."

Macdonald stood at the bar awaiting attention and inspecting his twenty pound note while another customer was being served nearer the door.

"You guys having a night on the tiles?"

Macdonald turned his head to attend to his inquisitor. Beside him holding a clutch of banknotes in order to purchase more alcohol for the group at the rear of the pub was a young woman aged in her late-twenties. Her blonde shoulder-length hair framed an impossibly pretty face. Macdonald found himself unable to respond. She paraphrased her question as a statement.

"You two seem intent on drinking this pub dry."

He found his voice.

"Eh, no. We're students just talking about our exams and having a couple of pints to forget what we learned today."

"What are you studying?"

"Eh, me? History...at Glasgow Uni."

"I'm there too. Reading English with Latin. Haven't noticed you around."

"Well the Uni has over twenty-six thousand students so it's pretty easy to miss people."

She smiled and moving the notes from her right hand to her left, shook Macdonald's hand. "My name's Bonnie. Bonnie Gabriel." She stepped back slightly to provide a better perspective. "Love your long hair. Very Byronic. Makes you look sensitive. Poetic!"

Macdonald found himself discomfited, unsure if he was being teased. "I'm Lachie."

"Well it's nice to meet you, Lachie. Short for Lachlan?"

"Yeah. Is Bonnie short for anything?"

"Matilda. My parents were aspiring upper-middle class types and wanted to have me live my life with a daft English name so when I was sixteen I told them both that I would no longer answer to my given name and that if they wanted to capture my attention they'd better get used to calling me Bonnie. "

"Jesus, that'd have taken balls..." He stuttered. "Er, I mean..."

"Christ that doesn't worry me."

"Who's first?" The barman interrupted their conversation.

Macdonald attempted courtesy. "Eh, this young lady..."

Gabriel cut in. "It's okay, I'm buying." She nodded at the group. "Same again. And two pints of whatever this pair are drinking."

Macdonald protested. "Oh, no...no..."

The barman had by then turned away to begin to fulfil the order.

"Don't be daft. My parents had the good grace to die two years ago and leave me sufficient funds to buy strange men drink if I choose." She nodded at Macdonald's chest paraphernalia. I like your badges. 'Independence for Scotland'. You Scottish National Party?"

"Yeah". He gestured at Singh who was observing the conversation from afar with a perplexed look on his face. "We both are. We go on all the marches. Monthly meetings. Leaflet our streets. That kind of thing."

"Us too. We meet here on Tuesday and Thursday nights, often on a Sunday night and drink ourselves stupid while we plot the downfall of the English Establishment."

She continued speaking. Macdonald understood the main thrust of what she said but was attempting to do so while taking in the physical beauty of his benefactor.

Bonnie interrupted his reverie.

"Eh, Lachie?

Macdonald was brought round.

"I don't mind buying you a pint but would you mind terribly not staring at my boobs?"

"Jesus…I wasn't…I mean, they're…I mean…"

Bonnie ignored his protests and carried the first of two pints over to her friends, returning to find the balance of four drinks awaiting her attention.

She smiled her request. "You might be good enough to help me over with these?"

"Eh? Oh, sure." Macdonald lifted two of the glasses and accompanied Bonnie to the back table.

"This here's Lachie," said Bonnie. He's a supporter."

There was a general round of welcoming gestures. Macdonald was at a loss.

"Eh, hi…em…I was just going to get me and my pal some plain crisps. Would anyone like a packet?"

A chorus of 'Ayes' saw him return to the bar where he was joined by Singh.

"Lachie, what's going on?"

I'm getting that crowd a round of crisps."

"Crisps?" asked Singh incredulously. "A round of *crisps*?"

"Thought it was the least I could do. That lassie bought us both a pint."

"Aye. I saw you chatting her up. She certainly seems well-proportioned."

"She just gave me a row for looking at her boobs,"

"Jesus, Lachie. You shouldn't be looking at a woman's breasts."

"I wisn'y. Anyway, it was only a glance."

"A glance at her breasts is just a quick *look* at her breasts."

"A glance is a just a glance."

"Even a *glance* at a woman's breasts is unseemly."

"When did you start usin' big words like 'unseemly'."

"Unseemly isn't a *big* word."

"Need help with those crisps?" Bonnie appeared at Macdonald's shoulder.

"Jeez…eh, no. I'm fine. Eh, Bonnie, this is Charan. Everyone calls him Charlie."

"Hi, Charlie. So what's so unseemly?"

Singh froze. Never comfortable in the presence of women, he now had an extraordinarily pretty woman ask him a question he had no idea how to answer. He looked to Macdonald for assistance.

"Me buying crisps when you bought us drinks," lied his pal.

"Ach, away! C'mon and bring these crisps and your pints over and give us some of your chat."

"We should really be going. We've got exams soon," Singh finished lamely.

"Then why did you stand at the bar two minutes ago with the sole intention of ordering two more pints? Don't be shy. Everyone's nice. They're all fellow travellers politically. Come on. I'm fed up with these same old faces. It'll be good to have some new patter."

Surrendering to Bonnie's blandishments, they carried their drinks over to the rear table. Singh returned to collect his back-pack and found Macdonald ensconced next to Bonnie while he had to sit on the remaining seat next to the large bearded man who looked like he was an extra from Braveheart. He glowered at Singh.

"So you're SNP?"

Singh nodded, eyes front, focussing on drawing out the froth of his pint so as not to be drawn into conversation.

"Both Nationalists?"

Macdonald tried to rescue his pal. "Aye. Independence for Scotland!"

"I'm Angus MacDhuibh. The English call me MacDuff." He eyed both students. "You got names?"

I'm Lachie Macdonald and my pal's Charlie Singh. He's a Sikh from the Punjab in India but he's as Glasgow as I am now."

"As Glasgow as he is," repeated Singh quietly still with the pint at his lips in readiness lest asked another question. "Independence for Scotland..." he whispered in as convincing manner as possible.

MacDuff's face broke into a broad smile. "Then you're welcome here." He put his bear-like arm around Singh, spilling some of Singh's lager. "You're *both* welcome here!"

Macdonald opened his bag of crisps *pour encourager les autres*. "Wire in everyone."

As people delved into the depths of the crisps bags, conversation fractured as various discussions ensued between members of the group.

Macdonald found himself deep in conversation with Bonnie about their respective courses while Singh found himself paired with MacDuff who was explaining the group's ethos in a growl.

"We don't have much to do with the SNP, Charlie. They're not keen on us. We're an ultra-nationalist organisation that is fed up with the English people in Scotland who are fuckin' white settlers imposing their *lebensraum* of rapacious Anglo-Saxonry on us colonised Scots. It was the English moving north that lost us the referendum, son. Normal Scots want independence but the English state and its colonial arms; the police, security services, armed forces, Inland Revenue, the media...they have the whole deck stacked against us."

Singh nodded enthusiastically, the pint tumbler still poised beneath his lower lip. "Absolutely!"

"We are content to leave party political action to the Scottish National Party, the Greens, Scottish Socialists, Solidarity and the Scottish Parliament. We prefer more direct action and will not stand idly by and watch our country being used, abused or betrayed by enemies both internal and external," he rumbled.

"Absolutely!"

MacDuff paused. "You know, you two guys seem okay. You should come along to our wee sessions. You might learn something. And coming from the Punjab you'll know about the dastardly effects of British imperialism as much as we do. These boys robbed you blind, segregated your country and left you with a railway, the English language, the most complex administrative system in the world, poverty and deprivation!"

"You bet! Meeting up sounds great," said Singh trying to be conversational. "You here every night?"

"Mostly Tuesday, Thursday and on Sunday but that's mostly when some of the guys bring their guitars, fiddles and what not and we have a session."

He consumed two thirds of a pint of Guinness in one visit to the glass as Singh looked on in astonishment at his capacity for consumption.

Recognising his young friend's stupefaction at his appetite, MacDuff explained.

"Ye see, Guinness is just hops, barley, malt, water and yeast...it's basically a *salad*!"

He laughed uproariously as conversations continued round the table for further rounds.

Finishing their beers, Singh caught Macdonald's eye and signalling his discomfort non-verbally both stood intimating their imminent departure. Bonnie walked them to the door.

"Promise me you'll come back on Thursday night, eh? It was great chatting to you, Lachie. Maybe see you in the library anyway. Nice meeting you, Charlie." She kissed both on the cheek as she bid them farewell. "See you soon, boys."

A flurry of assurances saw both men back on the street.

"Let's get out of here," urged Singh. "We report to Sim and never darken the door of that pub again. That big MacDuff guy is scary!" He sensed Macdonald's unease at his suggestion.

"Well, maybe we could go back *one* more time."

"Aye, just so you can stare at Bonnie's *patakas* one more time!"

"That's out of order, Charlie. We happened to have had a long conversation about dialectic materialism and the insidious effects of bourgeois ideology on the proletariat."

"I *watched* you staring at her breasts…and you were pronouncing the 'g' every time you said 'fucking'! You were trying to talk posh and look intelligent just to impress her!"

Macdonald smiled. "Now *you're* being unseemly!"

Chapter Twelve

The Miscalculation

John Kelso approached the cottage slowly. He'd climbed the steep hill to the smallholding but was hardly out of breath. He stepped to the open door and listened. The rough '*caw*' vocalisation of a departing crow was the only sound to be heard. Still Kelso waited. After a minute's assessment, he stepped quietly into the doorway and peered into the darkness.

As his eyes accustomed themselves to the gloom he observed the small hallway illuminated minimally by light available through an open doorway from which the door appeared to have been torn from its hinges. Beneath the door a pair of feet was evident.

"Jesus!"

Quickly, Kelso moved towards the doorway and noticed a protuberant arm lying stilled towards the uppermost section of the door. He lifted the flimsy wooden structure and placed it to one side. Beneath where it had been was a prone body whose neck was constricted by a thick rope. He recognised the person immediately, his hands going immediately to the neck, loosening the rope. He placed his index and middle fingers to the side of the windpipe to check for any systolic blood pressure. The presence of a carotid pulse was strong. Kelso started when, having released the rope slightly, the body before him gave out an enormous snore before beginning to stir.

Relief and outrage fought for emotional supremacy. "Bryson…you were an arsehole when I first met you and you're an arsehole today. Were you trying to off yourself?"

Bryson eased himself on to his hip and looked at his interrogator with narrowed, quizzical eyes.

"Kelso? What the fuck are you doing in this neighbourhood?"

"Well, I *was* going to offer you a well-paid, short-term job that made good use of your military skills but there's no way I'm going to tie my horse to a wagon that's falling apart."

Bryson manoeuvred himself into a sitting position and dusted his arm.

"Well, you got *that* right." He looked at the buckled door frame. "Canny even top myself properly."

"Jack, you couldn't hang the weight of a picture on the back of that wee door. And you thought it'd hold *you*?"

"Miscalculation."

"Well thank Christ physics wasn't one of your strong points."

"Don't have many of *them*, Johnnie-boy."

Kelso leaned his back against the opposite wall to Bryson and slid down so he'd assumed the same eye-level.

"Jack…when we were together in the SAS…did anyone ever outwit us?"

Bryson shook his head. "Naw."

"Did anyone ever out-fight us?"

A smile crept across his face for the first time in months. "Naw…And no one ever out-drank us either,"

"Kelso grinned at some reminiscences. "That's for sure."

Bryson looked around at his small living room. "I'd offer you a cup of tea…the whisky's finished."

"Jack…Jackie-boy. We need to get you back up and running." He looked at his giant but emaciated frame. "When did you last eat a fish supper?"

"That would be a while back. I've been dining out on cheap whisky recently."

Both men fell in to an easy conversation during which they rose while Bryson showed Kelso his cottage. A living room, a bedroom, a small kitchen and a toilet with a stained bath.

"And you own all of this entire estate, Jack?"

"Everything you can see in all directions." He sat on one of two kitchen chairs. "I live here with spiders so big I can hear their footsteps." He suddenly became more morose. "I used the money I'd saved up for my daughter, Rachael. Missed her wedding. I've never even met the man she married. She won't know if I'm dead or alive. But I invested in this cottage and the wee patch of weeds outside." He sighed. "I just decided enough was enough. Didn't feel I'd a friend left in the world. I'd let down what remained of my family. Couldn't afford another bottle of duff whisky so I chose the coward's path, got drunk, threw a strong rope over a week door and said my goodbyes."

Kelso sat on the remaining chair. "Well, I'm back in your life now, Jack…and I'm back with a proposition that will pay you enough to fix all of your problems bar the bevy."

Bryson raised his eyebrows as if to invite further information.

"See, Jack. Over the past five years I've been acting as a well-paid gunslinger for Her Majesty's Government. Doing stuff they don't want called out for. The money's been excellent and the job I've got going now...well, money's no object. It helps that I've a boss who's a posh fucker who doesn't know what end's up. I bullied him from the off now he's scared to deny me the price of a pint. I can hire who I want and you remain invisible to the authorities. There's no audit trail precisely because they don't *want* any fucking audit trail. You'd be a number on a report *if* that. For maybe two or three week's work I can put fifty grand in cash in your pocket - tax free. You could drink it or get yourself back on your feet."

"Christ, that's a fortune! And what's in it for you?"

"Well, that needn't trouble you, pal. You just need to know that I can out my hands on any amount of cash, get pretty much any weaponry I want and can get access to privileged information."

In the absence of a response, Kelso's impatience surfaced.

"Look, I could probably do this job myself. It's pretty straightforward. Say the word and I'll walk back down that hill and out of your life. Just let me know and I'll strengthen the front door so you can have another go at lynching yourself."

Bryson demurred. "S'not that I don't want to do it, Kelso. I just don't want to let you down."

"That's my look-out." He held out his right hand across the kitchen table.

"You in?"

Chapter Thirteen

The File

The Scottish Cabinet meeting had just concluded and most of those attending had remained for some informal chat and some coffee or tea. The mood was light although the First Minister and the Cabinet Secretary for Justice were speaking with a quiet earnestness about the recent decisions taken by the Police Investigations and Review Commissioner which had found disfavour with the broadsheets. The Cabinet Secretaries for Health and Sport and that of Rural Economy had found humour in the re-telling of the after-match celebrations of a shinty team on the Isle of Barra and the Secretary for Transport, Infrastructure and Connectivity made detailed arrangements with the Deputy First Minister for some joint speaking engagements to which they'd just committed. Some senior civil servants chatted with their political master about the meeting that had just ended and three waiting staff urged more coffee on those assembled while helpfully removing used crockery.

Unnoticed, a file was left carelessly atop a confidential report on the Police Investigations and Review Commissioner while a coffee cup was refilled. When the cup was filled, the file was lifted and its owner moved on having innocently collected the report.

After a short while, those assembled left. *Treasure* had obtained the report as requested.

Chapter Fourteen

Unseemly

"I've spent my teenage and student years getting you out of trouble but this time it's serious. If you walk through that door. I'm walking in the other direction."

Macdonald clasped his hands to his chest and made pleading motions. "Charlie you're my best pal. Best pal *ever*. We've both…well *I've* known a few girls…and I've never met anyone like Bonnie." He placed his left hand on Singh's shoulders to emphasise his point. "She's beautiful, well-proportioned…as *you* pointed out," he reminded his friend, "…and she's bright, our political outlook is the same…"

"Aye," Singh rejoined, "And she's loaded and is clearly a young lady who's used by *Seed of the Gaels* to recruit horny and impressionable young men like you!"

Macdonald sought a compromise. "Look, Charlie. How about this? We have a pint…I mean there might be no one in the pub but we get to show willing for Sim… and after one pint…just *one* pint, if you in your wisdom think I'm being recruited to the *Seed of the Gaels* by Bonnie, you just say the word, eh…'*Unseemly*' and we both leave. Immediately. Instantly. Straight away! Eh?"

Singh relented but emphasised his reservations. "You know I don't like swearing but sometimes you are a complete…fucking…idiot!" He looked at the peeling green paint on *Failté's* door and repeated with some emphasis to Macdonald the essence of their deal.

"The code-word is '*Unseemly*'!"

Not feeling particularly nonchalant but valiantly attempting to fake it, Macdonald, with Singh in his wake, pushed at the door and headed for the bar, his heart leaping as he noticed the same group in the dark interior of the bar; Bonnie giggling at someone's remark.

Pretending to ignore them, Macdonald waited for attention. Barman Sean O'Leary had served the clientele of *Failté* for three years and had developed a certain insouciance when serving them. His gaze didn't leave the sports' pages of the Daily Record for a good ten seconds before disinterestedly asking Macdonald for his preference. During this time a member of the group had drawn the attention of Bonnie to the students' arrival and she arrived at the bar just as Macdonald had ordered.

"Bonnie!" exclaimed Macdonald as if she was the last person he'd expected to find there.

"Well if it isn't my two favourite new friends," she smiled.

Macdonald was nothing if not experienced in the world of courtship. "Can I get you a drink?"

"Thanks but I've two untouched at the table. Bring your beers over. It'll be great to continue our chat."

Singh rolled his eyes and told himself that he'd be as well saying '*Unseemly*' while the pints were being poured. As inwardly he condemned the stupidity of Macdonald, Bonnie looped her arm around his and tightened her grip in a friendly fashion. "You sit beside me, Charlie. I hardly said a word to you on Tuesday."

Macdonald's jaw dropped leaving his mouth resembling the opening to the Clyde Tunnel as Bonnie shouted over her shoulder that he should sit in the spare seat next to Angus.

* * *

Singh, at first nervous and inhibited in the presence of Bonnie's transcendent beauty, had been put at ease by her personal charm and interest, feigned or not, in his academic and professional ambitions. After the consumption of his first pint and with the entirety of Sim's fifty pounds still in his pocket, he ignored Macdonald's silent but repeated mouthing of the word '*Unseemly*', and offered to buy a round of drinks.

Bonnie put her hand on his as he put it inside his trouser pocket and shook it...the nearest Singh had come to an erotic experience. "Not at all, Charlie. I'm on the bell. Is it the same again for everyone?"

At the far end of the table, general conversation ensued for a while before MacDuff confided in Macdonald.

"She's some girl, Bonnie, eh? She's got a few bob now that she inherited some fucking estate in England but she isn't sticking it in some protected overseas account in Bermuda she's helping the cause."

"By buying everyone drinks?"

MacDuff grinned, showing a gap in his teeth where his upper incisor used to be positioned.

"An army marches on its liver!" He laughed uproariously at his wit.

Macdonald wasn't as taken with his repartee. "She told me you guys are the Glasgow section of S*eed of the Gaels*. So Bonnie's just the quartermaster in charge of bevy?"

This sent MacDuff into another paroxysm of laughter. "An important role…and one she's comfortable with. But she has other uses as well."

Sourly, Macdonald asked "Membership and recruitment?"

Aided doubtless by earlier consumptions, MacDuff threw his head back in a hooting laugh.

"The lassie's no' a minger and she's minted so that helps, ah suppose." Nah, she does wee odds and ends for the cause." His laughter subsided. "I like you, Lachie. Most other people here are feart of me and think I'm goin' to eat them but you're good. You've a wee bit aboot ye. You'd be a good man to have at ma side if you'd join the cause."

Macdonald was still in a churlish mood. "Aye, and what cause would that be, Angus?"

MacDuff took on a serious demeanour "Look around ye, son. Your nation is being raped and pillaged and all the politicians do is talk about bread tomorrow. In 1973, as soon as it was evident that Scotland sat on trillions of pounds worth of oil. What did the Westminster Board of Trade do? Eh? They closed the Scottish Stock Exchange in Nelson Mandela Place. They said it made more sense to *merge* the Exchanges and at a stroke there was no way to measure the quantities of oil that came ashore. And the Scottish politicians of the day - both Labour and Conservatives colluded with them. They did hee-haw! We're up against dark forces, Lachie, both in Scotland and in England. They'll stop at nothing to make sure they can still plunder our oil, tax our whisky, fish our seas and steal our water." He warmed to his task as Macdonald glowered at Singh who was now whispering in Bonnie's ear and she with a broad smile on her face.

Fuckin' unseemly, thought Macdonald.

"Christ, they'll use all of the organs of the state against us; MI5...the lot! Jesus, the determination of MI5 to protect the Establishment goes right back to 1924 when they forged the Zinoviev letter and sent it to every editor in the UK sayin' it had come from the head of the Communist International in Moscow and was urgin' British communists to give support to the plan of the first Labour government to recognise the Soviet Union and to set up cells in Britain's armed forces. A flat lie designed to scupper Labour. They sent it right at the start of the General Election that year and surprise, surprise, Ramsay MacDonald's Labour Party got gubbed...not by the Tories but by MI5! Look at what happened to Willie MacRae, a true Scottish patriot. He single-handedly stopped the English dumping their nuclear waste at Mulwhacher in the hills above Ayr. He helped our cause, rose to the rank of Vice-Chairman of the Scottish National Party and was about to reveal a list of paedophiles in Thatcher's government when he was shot in the back of the head. He'd been followed out of Glasgow by Special Branch officers in two cars. The gun was found at distance from the car. His briefcase was removed and returned minus his files and the Coroner pronounced the cause of death as suicide before they'd even found the gun! Suicide? My erse!" He took a large draught of his pint of Guinness which almost emptied it and continued. "Thon boy Doctor

David Kelly? He gave evidence that proved that Saddam Hussain had no weapons of mass destruction worth a tinker's cuss but Blair and Brown wanted to support the Yanks so he took a walk and despite everyone saying he was as chirpy as the chirpiest of fuckin' chirpy crickets he's found with his wrist slashed…but there's no blood. If he'd cut an artery it'd have skooshed over half the forest he lay in but…nothin'? They found a quarter of an inch of blood on his trousers and he'd needed to have been a contortionist to make the cut that killed him. Another suicide? No way!"

He nodded his gratitude as a further pint of Guinness was supplied him.

"Robin Cook? He resigns because of Bush and Blair's determination to kill wee Iraqi weans, *majestically* destroys the Government's argument to go to war in a historic speech in the Commons, denies the existence of *al Qaeda*, supports Scottish Independence and opposes Israel's war on the Palestinians…then he goes hill-walking up Ben Stack in Sutherland, in the far north of Scotland, with his new wife. Now listen, son. It's a matter of fuckin' record that MI5 agents were working as diary secretaries for senior Labour Party politicians and Cook was stupid enough to shag then marry *his* diary secretary the year he'd become shadow foreign secretary. So who knows, eh? Maybe she loved him… mibbes she worked for MI5 or Mossad!" Half the Guinness disappeared in another titanic swallow. He wiped his mouth with his free sleeve. "Then he apparently falls on the mountain but fortunately another hill-walker who just *happens* to be passing by - and has never been seen since - has a mobile phone that can get a satellite signal that's as likely as gettin' one on the dark side of the moon and a helicopter wheechs Cook to Inverness but his new wife is telt to walk down the mountain hersel' and while he's alone in the helicopter he's pronounced dead wi' a heart attack!" He readied the glass for another attack. "And *she* has said not word number one ever since. Not a fuckin' cheep! Convenient, huh?"

Taken aback by the ferocity of Macduff's onslaught, Macdonald could only respond, "Well, ah knew about Willie McRae!"

"Even today! *Today*!" he repeated, loudly. The Scottish Resistance, great servants of the cause...I spoke with their heid bummer...their top man, James Scott. He was tellin' me that he's had three people die in very suspicious circumstances in the last four months. All suicides! The Scottish suicide rate is zero point one percent. Ah looked it up! James tells me that three people out of about fifty of his troops have topped themselves. That's six percent! Unusual, eh? It's about sixty times the national average! Sixty times!"

MacDuff scratched vigorously at the tartan bonspiel that held tight his unkempt locks. "These people are vicious, Lachie. No morals! During the Brexit negotiations they fuckin' bugged the conversations of their European counterparts. Fuckin' allies! They bugged their own citizens; people who were relatives of the Lockerbie bombing and who became inconvenient when they started to organise and seek the truth. Look at what they did in Northern Ireland. To protect the loyalist base they sent in paratroopers to snuff out the early rebellion of the Catholic minority who were just demanding their civil rights. They assassinated thirteen of these poor fuckers in one go...just to make a wee point that the British Army wouldn't be messed with. They gave arms to civilians to do their dirty work for them and shot people willy-nilly; blew up non-aligned musicians....Do you think for one fuckin' second that London would hesitate to do the same up here when we've got a lot more in the way of assets that the fat cats in the Establishment count on? Trust me son, there'll be a bloody street war before Scotland's free and we need to be ready to meet the challenge. *Seed of the Gaels* is a necessary part of the movement to free Scotland. The movement doesn't like us but remember these noble words son, written on the sixth of April 1320, 'For as long as but a hundred of us remain alive, never will we on any conditions be brought under English rule. It is in truth not for glory, nor riches, nor honours that we are fighting, but for freedom – for that alone, which no honest man gives up but with life itself." As he concluded his angry monologue his voice had risen and had captured the attention of the other customers in the pub. He stood from his chair, rose to his full height and in a steady gaze, contemplated the roomful of people now transfixed by his spiel. "Ah need a pish!"

Macdonald's demeanour changed as Bonnie freed herself from her conversation with Singh and took Macduff's seat next to him.

"He's brilliant. Isn't he?"

Attempting something close to a non-committal response, Macdonald replied, "Aye. He's some guy!"

"He's willing to give his life for the cause. Just because he's in here most night drinking doesn't mean he isn't engaged in other ways. Lots of times he's away doing things he won't tell us about. Top secret!"

Maybe drinking in other pubs thought Macdonald uncharitably.

"I know he makes his point rather forcibly but don't you think he *has* a point?"

Macdonald nodded despite himself. "I know that pretty much everything he told me is accurate. Loads of people do. Hundreds of *thousands* of people in Scotland do. It's what we *do* about it that maybe separates us. Me and Charlie are used to handing out leaflets. What's Angus's game? Bombing post boxes?"

Bonnie's nose wrinkled in mild rebuttal leading Macdonald to think she was even more beautiful when riled.

"Not at all. He'd never spill blood, *Scottish* blood at least. He just wants to prepare the ground against the day when we have to deal with the inevitable English attempt to force Scotland to remain subservient to their interests."

Macdonald was about to respond that he still didn't understand the meaning of her words when MacDuff returned drying his hands on his denim trousers.

At least the big bastard washes his hands when he has a pee…unless he's had a wee accident at the urinal, he thought, less charitably.

Singh interrupted his thoughts by pulling up a chair between MacDonald and Bonnie.

"I'm definitely buying the next round…and I'm on the whisky now!"

"Jesus, Charlie. You Sikhs can fairly put it away when you want to!"

"Eating and drinking are pure, for the Lord has given sustenance to all." He hiccoughed and continued. "That's the teaching of Guru Nanak."

You're blootered!"

"I'm fine, Lachie. Just the very dab. I just feel like a wee whisky now." His voice rose to address the large table. I'm getting a whisky round in." He addressed the group. "What's your favourite malt?"

Various replies were lobbed at Singh who started looking for an implement to note them.

Bonnie intervened. "It's alright. I can remember them. You just help me carry them over." So saying, she walked round the six regulars taking their orders with Singh walking helpfully behind her lost in admiration of her taut backside every time she leaned over to collect an empty glass. Balancing several glasses she whispered to an unsteady Singh, "Angus always has a double. Is that okay?"

Singh managed to convey agreement without speaking and as his beautiful assistant took the glasses to the bar and reeled off the various drinks orders, Macdonald approached and growled quietly in Singh's ear, "Charlie you're absolutely pissed. You don't hold your drink at the best of times and this whisky idea is about as dumb as it gets."

"You were right," replied Charlie ignoring Macdonald's caution. "She's wonderful."

"Well, I'm glad you two got on so well"

"Her memory is amazing. She remembers complicated drinks orders. She was able to tell me back my mobile number without writing it down. She actually remembered my name without me having to tell her three times."

Macdonald started slightly. "Oh, so she's got your phone number now?"

"Aye. She needs it because I've agreed to help her in a wee undercover task tomorrow night. Angus asked her because she's got a car but it maybe needs a bit of lifting and she needed a strong man...like me!"

"What? You're helping *Seed of the Gaels* in a 'wee undercover task'?"

"I am that. It's harmless. We just go to the old Cathcart Cemetery after dark and bring back a wee parcel."

"Charlie, there are black holes in far distant galaxies that are brighter than you!"

Chapter Fifteen

The Cause is Everything

Boston Yacht Haven on the marina at Commercial Wharf exuded luxury. Andrew Buchanan thanked his driver as he left his Cadillac XTS stretched Limousine and hurried to his yacht past security guards sufficiently familiar with him to offer an informal salute rather than asking for ID. The sturdy floating boardwalk gave slightly under his weight as he closed.

"Sam!" He hailed the carpenter who had overseen the building of the yacht's interior and was seated on the wooden-framed power source on the boardwalk.

"Sorry I'm late. I was hoping you hadn't left. Are you well?"

"I'm fine," responded Sam Mahon shaking the hand of the man who had made him wait an hour and cause him to delay his first drink of the day in order to accommodate a client who, he would have to admit later in the bar, paid well; very well.

"We don't have much time, Sam. Just show me the compartment we discussed. The boys arrive tomorrow morning and I want a final check."

Both men retreated into the bowels of the yacht and Mahon talked him through the adjustments and improvements he'd made since Buchanan' earlier instructions.

"Now, Sam. Have you completed my secret whisky hold?"

Mahon, taciturn at the best of times, nodded almost imperceptibly and took him forward where he showed him the ribs of the boat where, in a design compromise, each side of the yacht had a run of six-inch wooden batons.

Mahon spoke slowly and in a low tone. "Now let me say that anyone looking at these might ask themselves why they're there. There's no obvious function to them. In a yacht designed for racing they'd be looked on as an unnecessary frippery. However…"

He moved towards the third of the batons and twisting it clockwise, did the same to the baton that was towards the other end of the section. Grasping two of them he lifted a segment of his installation revealing a compartment.

Buchanan peered into the hold.

"Jesus, this is excellent, Sam. I'd never have guessed there was so much space down here."

He made a calculation of the capacity of the compartment and the extent of the weaponry he'd be able to secret there and attempted his continued deception. "My whiskies will be safe there, Sam. Safe from the tax-man."

Explaining unnecessarily to Mahon who'd little interest in the future contents of the space he'd created, Buchanan spoke of bottles of very rare whisky costing fortunes which he intended to re-introduce to Scotland - the very land which had created them many decades previously. He laughed, hoping to present as a collector of antique whiskies who had found a way to beat the customs and excise of a foreign nation. Mahon cared little.

"Works for you, boss?"

Buchanan reached into his back pocket and withdrew a clutch of dollar bills and pressed them into the Mahon's palm.

"I'm delighted, Sam. Would you buy yourself and the misses a drink on me?"

Mahon made a quick estimation of the few thousand dollars' worth of drink that could be purchased as a consequence of the additional and unexpected munificence of his client and smiled for the first time that day. *That whisky he's hiding must taste gooood,* he thought.

The men shook hands and parted.

"We'll keep this to ourselves, eh, Sam?"

"Goes without saying, boss," said Mahon meaning it sincerely.

Buchanan walked Mahon to the boardwalk and bid him farewell, negotiating a further series of maintenance tasks upon the return of the yacht from the race.

Waving his departure from the marina, he took his phone from the pocket of his jeans and punched in a number on speed dial.

"Murdo! We're good to go. Get these cases down here now. We've some unloading to get done. This yacht is joined by your crew in the morning and we'd better be finished by then. The press will be everywhere. I'm leaving now. See you as arranged."

Only a minute later a black jeep appeared at the end of the dock and parked just as Buchanan reached his limousine. He walked to the rear of the Jeep where Monteith was awaiting the automatic opening of the boot and offered his hand.

"Good luck, Murdo. See you shortly."

"Thanks, Andrew. Now you make yourself scarce and I'll get these two canvas bags into the hold."

Buchanan converted his handshake into an uncomfortable hug and left.

Monteith lifted the two heavy canvas bags containing ammunition and three rifles each from the rear, unfolded a sack truck and placed them atop. He lifted a lighter third bag and slung it over his shoulder. Carefully he manoeuvred the device along the walkway towards the trimaran and carried them into the hold where he found the concealed space described earlier to him by Buchanan. Returning to the entrance door of the hold, he closed and locked it before going back to the recessed cache. On one knee he removed his smartphone from his rear pocket and punched a Bluetooth code that unlocked the padlock that secured the top canvas bag. Unzipping it, he moved the weapons aside and placed leaflets encouraging support for the Ulster Volunteer Force. *Very brittle. But it might give a decent lawyer an argument in court that this had nothing to do with Scotland.*

Reaching over he pulled this third bag towards him and unloaded two collapsible orange pods which he proceeded to flatten and open. He placed a bag of rifles in each one, closed it via a substantial zip, sealed the closure and blowing into an inner tube, inflated the pod until it looked similar to the other cushioned fenders employed by the yacht upon mooring. Lifting each in turn, he placed them within the false hold.

He placed the baton over the contents and twisted the wooden spars as instructed. He stood back and considered the lines of the vessel. *Jesus. No one would ever know there was anything behind those panels. Impressive!*

***

An hour later Monteith entered the Highlander Bar in Boston's Dorchester Heights. Buchanan sat alone at the bar. He half-turned upon seeing Monteith and finished his whisky in one swallow.

"I was only going to wait five more minutes. Five minutes or I figured you'd been captured by Homeland Security or some-such."

"I was careful, Andrew. I've been careful since I arrived. I don't want to end up in an American prison any more than you do."

"Two big Glenfidichs," ordered Buchanan of the underemployed barman. "And a cup of water."

"You can relax, Andrew. I've not been followed since I arrived on American soil. Guaranteed. The goods were placed in the hold without any problems. Now, your job is done."

Buchanan permitted himself a smile of relief. "Well, if I'm honest, I did allow my thoughts to stray over that last whisky. What if it was to be my last one?"

Monteith looked around the dark interior of the bar. "Didn't figure you for a bar like this. Thought you'd be more the country club type."

"I like both. I picked this one today as I knew it'd be quiet and it's also in Dorchester Heights here in South Boston where George Washington routed the British Troops during the American Revolutionary War. Thought that was, well…apposite, eh? The whole area's being gentrified as we speak. Not the same Irish enclave it once was. But it shows that the Brits can be defeated."

"Well, that consignment hidden in *The Butcher's Apron* will certainly help."

Buchanan took delivery of the whiskies and, bringing one closer, merely touched its surface with a splash of water, before sliding the other gently along the bar surface to Monteith. "You're an interesting guy, Murdo. I like the cut of your jib. Always have. You could have been a success in any walk of life yet you forego a big salary, wife and kids...." He halted, realising his presumption. "I'm sorry. Perhaps I just assumed..."

Monteith lifted his glass and raised his eyebrows before explaining. "No ballast. I'm an only child. Parents both killed when I was a baby. Adopted by a couple from Helensburgh. Dead now. Managed to make my way in life without any attachments."

"No family at all?"

"The folk who adopted me were childless. They adopted another kid; an older boy and we were close growing up but I've not seen him in twenty years." He raised the glass to his lips and took a long sip. "The cause is everything. I've lived the life many do when they don't have family roots. Bummed around. Learned how to play guitar and mandolin. Got good at it. Spent some time crewing on a yacht. Got good at it. I've pulled pints, flipped burgers, sold fruit in the market. Got good at it. But nothing you could call a career."

Buchanan placed his right hand on Monteith's arm and squeezed affectionately. "Murdo, if you'd decided to put down roots here in the States rather than go back to the old country to continue the struggle, I'd have been proud to invite you to become my personal assistant or something."

Monteith grinned. "A butler?"

"No. Nothing so servile. A guy who takes care of things for me. Speaking to people I want spoken to, negotiating deals, acting for me in my absence…playing Scottish jigs on the mandolin when I'm feeling maudlin or patriotic. Just a good guy who was close to me and mine."

They both laughed. Buchanan ordered two more big Glenfidichs and Monteith reminded him of his career ambition, such as it was, "The cause is everything!"

Together and in silent concord, each raised their glass and toasted his cause…*their* cause!

Chapter Sixteen

Rachael

Cavendish lifted the receiver tentatively. His secretary had informed him that a Mister Kelso had asked to speak with him. He cleared his throat and spoke in what he hoped would be an authoritative voice.

"Cavendish!"

"I now have an associate. You don't need to know his name. I will have further expenses. The account we set up will need a further ninety thousand."

Cavendish's attempted demeanour escaped him. His voice was almost a squeak.

"Ninety thousand?"

"If you repeat that one more time it goes up to a hundred thousand!"

Cavendish swallowed. "Look, Kelso. We don't like one another but I have to account for every penny you spend and just listing ninety thousand pounds sterling because a chap phoned and asked me for it won't go down very well with the Permanent Secretary."

"These guys are only interested in results. The Civil Service can find umpteen different ways to hide money."

"I think you'll find that the Civil Service requires a greater degree of precision than"...he decided to deploy the *lingua franca* of the irritant he saw as his subordinate..."*umpteen*!"

While Kelso enjoyed his bullying of Cavendish, he'd promised himself that the call would last little more than thirty seconds and would result in agreement of an additional fee and confirmation of access to the weapons cache he'd earlier agreed. Frustrated, he sighed and used his trump card.

"Look, you fucking feeble excuse for a human turd. Were you, or were you *not* instructed by Brigadier...?"

Cavendish, admitting defeat yet again, interrupted him, "Okay, okay...I'll confirm it with him. The money will be in the account within the hour. I've also organised your rifle request. It'll be where you want it when you want it."

On the other side of the phone, Bryson watched rather than listened with increasing incredulity to the phone conversation. Kelso caught his eye and smiled.

"Oh, and one more thing, Cavendish."

Wearily, Cavendish acceded to what he'd come to understand was Kelso's way of saying 'goodbye'.

"I fuckin' *hate* cunts like you!"

Bryson took a moment to process the information he'd just heard.

"You squared an additional ninety grand just by bad-mouthing that guy?"

"He's easy meat, Jackie-boy. These people down south are so feart of Scottish Independence they'll pay top dollar to see it ended."

"So that's what all this is about, Kelso. Scottish Independence?"

"It is, Jack. But I have a plan that'll upset that applecart. The cash is pretty much in the bank already… and that's yours on the way as well."

"You asked for an additional ninety thousand. The fee you offered me was fifty grand?"

Kelso looked nervously at his friend as he tried to manufacture a smile that exuded confidence. "Well there's expenses…"

"Aye, but by my reckoning and your earlier comments everything was bought and paid for until you took me on." His brows narrowed. "So just by taking me on you score an additional forty thousand quid?"

Kelso's upper teeth scraped his lower lip as he sought resolution. "Naw, naw, naw, Jackie-boy. I didn't think he'd go for the ninety. That was meant to be my opening gambit…but he *bit*. Like I say, he's easy meat, so…well, I mean I'm a businessman now Jack. Suppose we go fifty-fifty and say seventy to you, twenty to me?"

Bryson rose to his great height. "Ah remember the days when it was 'One for all and all for one!' Suppose we say you stick your arrangements right up your sizeable arse and I just find another way of gettin' more whisky?"

Kelso's legendary aggression boiled as he attempted to control his impulses.

"Look, Jack. I didn't want to tell you this. But the people I work for…they'd like you on board…which is why this kind of money is flying around. They want your involvement so much they've…"

"They've what?"

"They've…taken steps."

"Oh? And what might these steps lead to?"

Kelso showed his discomfort, further unsettling Bryson. A moment passed.

"Your daughter, Rachael."

A silence of some further seconds reigned while Bryson registered the significance of Kelso's comments. He gathered himself and spoke slowly.

"Kelso! You *know* me! If anything were to happen to my daughter, nothing would stop me killing you, killing that tosser you just spoke to, killing anyone I felt had harmed her."

Kelso interrupted angrily.

"Sit back down and listen. You don't even know what she fucking looks like. You don't know who she married. I *do*. I did my homework on your entire fucking family. She's married to a lawyer; a guy called Peter Kelburn. Lives in a house in the countryside. She's in no harm. In fact she's having a great time at the minute...but you need to cooperate. You need to take my offer of seventy grand...my *final* offer of seventy grand...and get your life back together so you can meet the lassie and her man once they're back in England."

"How? Where is she?"

"See, this is the bit I didn'y want to tell you." He moved surreptitiously closer to the small cooker where pots and pans might assist should Bryson not react well to his information.

"Rachael and Peter are having a great time in Dubai. They won a competition along with another couple for a three-week all expenses holiday staying in the *Burj al Arab* Hotel...they say it's a seven star hotel...best in the world..."

Bryson's puzzlement was evident. "So what's the catch?"

Kelso moved closer to the cooker. "Look Jack, this isn'y my doing. These people…they'll stop at nothing to make sure our mission is successful."

"What…is…the…*catch*?"

Kelso held his hands out before him, fingers to the ceiling, in what he hoped was a reassuring gesture. "Well, the competition was a fix. The other couple? They're undercover people. *My* people."

"And?"

Well, the worry I'd have is that Rachael would maybe be fitted up on some daft charge that would see her thrown in an Emirates prison if I don't get back to them by after speaking with you and let them know that everything's kosher."

Bryson placed each of his hands flat on the table and looked down as slowly he prepared to stand.

Anticipating Bryson's reaction and sensing his opportunity, Kelso grasped the handle of the heavy cast iron frying pan which had first been used six decades earlier and swung it with great force against his erstwhile friend's skull. The trauma to Bryson's brain was intense and stimulated an overwhelming number of neurotransmitters to fire at the same time, overloading his nervous system and sending it into a state of temporary paralysis. As he lost consciousness, he fell to the ground, his bulk breaking the wooden chair on which he'd been sitting.

Kelso breathed heavily and for the second time that day placed his three middle fingers on Bryson's neck to check his carotid pulse. Satisfied he hadn't killed him, he sat in his remaining chair and thought. *Let's hope my investment in sending his daughter and her man on an expensive holiday is going to pay off! I need a fucking patsy and big Bryson is perfect.* He lit a cigarette and reflected further. *I'd better restrain him before he wakes up.*

While Bryson was unconscious, Kelso went through his pockets. A few coins, a receipt from the local store in Ballantrae for a loaf of bread and two bottles of Scotch, and a bank card. *I'm betting it's an empty account.* He thrust everything into his pocket and awaited Bryson's recovery.

Chapter Seventeen

Fuckin' John?

"*My* place?"

Macdonald and Singh had found space in the Mitchell Library's café where they'd often stop off after university for further study over a coffee on their way back home.

"Well, yeah! There's no way I'm going alone. It was you who got me into this so I thought Bonnie could pick us both up at your flat. I gave her the address."

Macdonald fizzed in indignation. "I was just trying to see more of…"

"Her *patakas* …"

"No! Not her boobs! I thought she was lovely."

"Aye well I thought she was lovely too and when she asked me for a wee bit of help I couldn't help saying 'of course'… but I always assumed that you'd be in it with me."

Macdonald placed his cup down heavily on its saucer. "Charlie! We don't know any of these people. We know Sim wanted us to find out what they were up to so it's pretty safe to assume that they're up to no good in some fashion. We don't know what they want us to collect. It could be a gun or something!"

"Don't think I've not thought about it, Lachie but we promised Bonnie."

"*You*! *You* promised Bonnie."

"You were there too," Singh said weakly knowing instantly how easily his argument would be rebuffed.

Macdonald looked at him through narrowed eyes that displaced the need for a verbal response and turned his attention to the collection point.

"Charlie, my flat is an absolute mess! My radiator is covered in drying underwear."

"So what, Lachie?"

"It's not my *best* underwear. It's my daily underwear. Not my dating underwear!"

"You have *dating* underwear?"

"Never mind." He rubbed his eyes. "Okay. Look. We both go to my flat right now and tidy it up. When she arrives. No coffee, no nothin'. We hurry her out of the flat into her car." He thought further. "Do we know anything about what she wants us to help with?"

Singh pursed his lips. "Just said she'd tell us in your flat when she picked us up. She's coming at half-seven but we've not to leave until half-nine so it'll be dark when we get there at ten."

* * *

At seven thirty, Macdonald's bell rang indicating that a caller was standing outside in West Graham Street awaiting the opening of the door to the common close typical of the red-sandstones properties of the West End of Glasgow. He pressed the buzzer to permit entry and half-opened the door, listening to the footsteps on the stair becoming louder.

"Bonnie," he exclaimed warmly as she reached the top of the second floor flight. His reward was a peck on the cheek as he admitted her to his one-bedroomed flat.

"C'mon in and sit down."

Bonnie offered her cheek to a delighted Singh as she took in the room. Peeling wallpaper, rugs over the settee to cover torn fabric and a desk laden with books and notepads.

"Well, no one would figure that this was a student's flat, Lachie," she said grinning.

"All the rent I can afford," he grumped gesturing at Singh to sit, seating himself on the armchair whose missing front castor wheel propelled him forward each time he moved position. Coffee was organised in three unmatched cups, Macdonald ensuring that he took the chipped mug.

As the evening unfolded Macdonald turned the conversation to the task in hand inclining his body forwards assisted by the missing castor, hoping to signify seriousness. "Look, Bonnie, we're a wee bit worried about…"

"Och, Lachie! Don't fret. You neither, Charlie. This is just a wee bit of nonsense. We've to collect a parcel that Angus has hidden. It's his way of seeing if we're prepared to take care of a wee task without mucking it up. He's trying to find out if we're reliable."

"Well, if that's the case, what's in the parcel we've to collect?"

"Some old clothes, he told me." Her cheeks dimpled. "I wasn't meant to tell you that. He wanted to you think it might be something like a weapon or a bomb but you'd still collect it." She looked at the two students who were each meeting the other in eye contact, seeking reassurance.

"Old clothes?"

* * *

A sky that both warned and delighted farmers saw the three students sitting in Bonnie's car, a year-old Volkswagen Golf whose interior appeared to have been valeted in the recent past. They drove through the city centre, along Pollokshaws Road before heading towards Cathcart and its old cemetery.

"Angus was quite clear," replied Bonnie to Macdonald's questioning her directions. "We've to enter from the South Gate on Netherlee Road. The cemetery gatekeeper has a lodge at the other gate and would no doubt wonder at a car entering when it's dark. We've to enter the cemetery, turn first left along the wee roads that edge the graves and stop a few yards along at a fork where there's a big headstone commemorating the remains of someone called Patrick. That's their surname. Behind the gravestone Mother Nature has reclaimed the graves and Angus says it's like a jungle. We make our way through the under-growth to a gravestone marked 'James Shaw Carmichael' and just in case there are more than one of them buried there, it's the chap who pegged it on the first of February nineteen-seventeen."

"Well I hope your recollection is bang on," said MacDonald. My grannie used to live right next to Cathcart Cemetery. It's massive and has miles of wee roads and paths. We used to use it to make dens. It's like bloody Sherwood Forest…all overgrown. You could hide there undetected for weeks. In the darkness you'd get lost in a minute."

Singh ignored MacDonald's recollections and focussed instead on Bonnie's memory. "Wow, your memory for detail is fantastic!"

"I'm observant and I remember things." She glanced at Macdonald who had claimed the front seat beside her. "Your neighbours from the ground floor up are Strang, Philips, Chan, and McCreadie and across the landing from you is Barnes. The books you had on the shelve above your Samsung television included a Sony radio and were mostly history books but you had a section at the end devoted solely to Scottish history. You're methodical. Tidy. The electric fire was a Hotpoint and the entire flat was in need of a deep clean."

Singh clapped his hands. "Amazing!" He nudged Macdonald playfully on his shoulder. "Well, was Bonnie right, Lachie. Were the neighbours in the right order and does your flat need a deep clean?"

"It's a student flat and I wasn't blessed with parents who left me a fortune," protested Macdonald.

Bonnie was unfazed. "Life's not fair, Lachie. I can afford things and your flat is perfectly fine."

"That's Netherlee Road," interrupted Singh as darkness enfolded the city. "See, my memory's good too!" He laughed as he nudged Macdonald's shoulder again. "But my house doesn't need a deep clean."

"That's because you've never freed yourself from mummy's apron strings and live in a Pollokshields' mansion with your dentist parents who probably have a deep clean lady who comes round every Tuesday."

"Thursday, actually," giggled Singh. "Sometimes Friday too!"

As the Volkswagen entered the park, Bonnie stopped and turned off the headlights. "Let's wait a moment, get used to the darkness and remind ourselves of our job". She counted the tasks off on her fingers. "We find the grave, shove aside some undergrowth behind it, lift a piece of corrugated iron and retrieve a parcel wrapped in plastic covering. We then leave it in my car overnight."

She ran out of fingers and closed her hand in a fist. "…
and bring it to Angus in *Failté* tomorrow night."

Slowly she drove the car the few yards to the first left
turn and stopped at a row of gravestones.

"Let's find 'Patrick', she whispered.

All three exited the vehicle. Bonnie played a torch on
the gravestones and leapt back with a shriek when it
illuminated an elderly lady standing with her right arm
shielding her eyes.

"Don't hurt me", she cried. "I'm just out walking my
dog."

Singh was first to react. "It okay Misses. We…we're
only looking for *our* dog. He's gone missing."

The old lady walked towards them along the last few
yards of an old desire footpath that had long been used
by dog-walkers. "Oh, I got a fright there! I don't usually
meet people in here when it's dark but wee Bailey here
needs her walks. She runs my life so she does. When she
needs to go, she needs to go." A small dog sat obediently
listening to the conversation. "But what is *your* dog?"
she asked. "The one you've lost. What kind is it?"

Singh struggled for a breed name. "Eh, just a
mongrel. Nothing special."

"What colour?"

"Hmm, Black"

"And has he a name?"

"Eh, yes…his name's…eh… John!"

"You have a wee dog called John?" asked the old
lady.

Macdonald grimaced in the darkness and cursed
quietly. "Fuckin' *John*?"

Singh looked round at his two friends in the
moonlight aware that he'd bruised their pretext. "Yeah.

Daft name but it was my mother's idea." He recovered some composure. "Anyway we'd better get looking."

"Oh, let me help."

Macdonald intervened. "That would be great. Any chance you could look for wee John, down towards the bottom of the hill there. We'll spread out and cover this top bit." He attempted to disguise a look of considerable disdain directed at Singh before returning to the friendly dog-walker. "Is that on your way home?"

"It is actually. I'll go and help look for him. She took out a whistle. Wee Bailey always responds to this. I'll keep blowing in case your wee dog hears it."

Macdonald realised the import of a whistle being blown whilst they were engaged on a covert mission. "Ah, no, misses. Wee John is afraid of whistles. It'd scare him."

"Okay," the whistle was pocketed and she left midst a profusion of 'thank yous', her dog walking contentedly beside her, her winter-white hair soon the only sign of her as she ambled down the hill. Every few steps she'd call in a sing-song voice, "John?....John?..."

As she walked off into the moonlit graveyard, Macdonald turned to a silhouette of Singh. "You are the *biggest* eegit I've ever met."

Bonnie could suppress her laughter no longer. "*John*!"

Despite himself Macdonald found a smile forming on his lips. "Fuckin' *John*!"

"Sikhs don't have dogs so how am I meant to know what's what?"

Macdonald frowned. "How do ye no' have dogs?"

"Cause most Sikhs are vegetarian. Dogs aren't!"

Gathering themselves they followed the beam of the torch as it led them into thick undergrowth alongside the desire path. Bonnie was disconcerted at the profusion of vegetation. "These trees and bushes have completely devoured these gravestones. The ivy covers everything and means that these poor people are now invisible. It just shows you, eh? Mother Nature's the ultimate winner!"

All three fought their way up the slight incline, trees and gravestones blocking their way until Singh let out a loud whisper. .

"Here it is. James Shaw Carmichael. Nineteen-seventeen."

With some tripping and cursing, Macdonald and Bonnie made their way to Singh who was standing before a still-erect gravestone marked James Shaw Carmichael.

"Found it," said Macdonald. Now let's see what lies behind it."

The gravestones on either side were too close to permit them easy access so further tripping and cursing ensued as they made their way to the rear of the stone. Macdonald pulled at the ivy and stamped until he heard a loose metallic response.

"Think we've found it!"

The three students pulled at the surrounding ivy until the corrugated lid was exposed. Again Macdonald took the lead pulling it upward and uncovering a white package sitting in an inch of water. He heaved at it, pulling it from its own small grave and despite Bonnie's protestations, tore at the covering."

"Lachie, what are you doing?"

"I want to see what we're collecting. Anything dodgy and I'm putting it back in the hole. If it's old clothes like Angus said, well, we'll just tell him that it got ripped while we were removing it."

The plastic covering, tightly bound in cable was tough but a nearby sharp stone allowed a hole which soon stretched into a tear that allowed Macdonald to see its contents.

"Clothes right enough. Looks like camouflage gear." He stood. "Looks safe enough, eh?"

Bonnie stooped and waited until all three had a hold of the large package.

She counted. "One, two...*three*." The package was lifted and carefully they manoeuvred it back towards the car.

***

Twenty yards away, Tam Sim lowered his camera. "Good piece of work there, eh Big Man?"

Next to him, the gap-toothed smile of Angus MacDuff grinned his agreement.

Chapter Eighteen

A Proposal

A wave of intense pain caused Bryson to raise his hands to his head realising as he did so that they'd been tethered before him with a plastic zip-tie. Slowly he opened his eyes and considered his predicament. He lay on the floor of his cottage with Kelso seated and holding a large knife he'd removed from his back-pack. He cradled his throbbing skull.

Kelso spoke first.

"Bryson, I'm really sorry about that. I didn't want to do it but we both know that in a hand fight there's no way I'd be able to cope with you so I had to take you down…just so I could explain and talk some sense into you. You know the score."

Bryson raised himself onto an elbow and painfully, sat himself against the wall.

"You broke your other chair when you fell, big fellah….here," he handed Bryson a cup, "I made us both some coffee."

Bryson's continued glare had him withdraw the cup after it became apparent that his peace offering hadn't been accepted.

"Jack…I swear I had nothing to do with Rachael. These people in London, they're counting on you."

"Aye, sure. I'm the one man in the entire British Army that could pull off whatever lunatic plan you've got in mind...an alcoholic, out of shape hermit."

Kelso halted his intended sip of coffee. "An alcoholic, out of shape hermit that I *trust*! It's *me* they've hired for this. I just told them that in my opinion you'd be the man I'd most want at my side. They decided to treat Rachel and her man to the holiday of a lifetime to make sure you cooperated."

Bryson seethed inwardly. There was silence for some moments before he broke the stillness.

"Leave me that cup of coffee. Step outside. I want to think without you irritating me."

He rolled onto one knee and stood, leaning against the wall to ensure his balance. "You must have missed the session we did on restraints." Slowly he raised both arms above his head and stepping forward from the wall, brought both arms sharply downwards, his elbows swinging behind him, severing the ties instantly. "A ten year old girl could do that if she knew the technique."

Kelso raised his knife only to be rebuked by Bryson.

"No need for that. Step outside for ten minutes and let me think."

* * *

Outside Bryson's cottage, Kelso sat on the old bench, smoked another cigarette and considered his next moves. If Bryson was against his proposal he'd have to negotiate a way of walking out on the situation without a scrap. Even in his weakened condition, Bryson would be a formidable foe in a hand fight. That had to be avoided. If he didn't have his patsy he'd only be out the cost of a holiday for four in Dubai. He could carry out the tasks himself but then...

"Kelso! You still there?"

Kelso ground his cigarette on the paving stone, extinguishing it and entered the small cottage where Bryson stood at the table.

Taking one step forward, Bryson unleashed an uppercut that caught Kelso unaware as it landed square on his jaw. He fell instantly, his sense of self-preservation still keen enough to attempt some measure of recovering the situation. This ended as Bryson kneeled on his chest and spoke in a growl.

"I've been thinking alright. You and I were never best buddies when we served. You were always on the make and I never had the feeling that you had my back - or anyone else's for that matter. But if I'm *forced* to deal with you, I'm not fool enough to ignore a deal if there's seventy grand available. That could change a lot of things for me and for Rachael if I can fix things there. But I have my conditions."

He rose to his feet and noticed Kelso's shirt pocket containing a pack of cigarettes and a lighter. "Gimme a smoke!" he instructed.

Kelso sat slowly upright, placed them on the table and shoved them across to Bryson.

Carefully, he lifted his large knife from the floor and stood, preparing for a further fight. Bryson sat on the edge of the unlit stove, lit a cigarette and inhaled deeply. A coughing fit ensued followed by him reaching to his still throbbing head. After a few moments of quiet cursing, he returned to his dealings with a Kelso who was now on the balls of his feet in readiness for combat.

Bryson lowered the tension.

"I want to hear what you have in mind. If I think I can do it, okay. But before I lift a finger, you deposit my seventy grand in a bank of my choosing. Once I have confirmation that it's in place you then phone your pals in my presence using speakerphone and tell them that everything's fine and that Rachel and Peter can enjoy their holiday." He took another drag of the cigarette with the same consequences as before. "But I tell you this, Kelso. If you renege on the deal, or make a second phone call to Dubai, if Rachael is unhappy with so much as the fucking *weather* out there, if anything is done to hurt her I will hunt you down and kill you in ways I'd enjoy inflicting. For your sake I'd hope that nothing ever happens to her. You've made your move and it's too late for you to back out. You've threatened my daughter and I don't give a flying fuck if it's anonymous men down in London or your devious self who dreamt this up. I'm holding you personally responsible. So you live or die according to how you handle this."

"Jack…"

"I've not finished. When I served, my reputation was built on my abilities as a sniper and my close combat fighting. Don't know why you think I'm the only guy who can assist you but I won't shoot civilians if that's what you had in mind."

"Jack…"

"I'm still not finished. In my career I fought for causes I figured were probably okay even though I didn't have much confidence in the politicians and top brass who were deciding which bunch of towel-heads we were to shoot on any given day. This seems different. If it's about Scottish Independence…"

"Jack if you'd let me explain!"

"Okay. Explain."

In order to engender some confidence, Kelso placed the knife back in the back-pack taking care to leave the handle available should it be necessary. He leaned over, recovered his pack of cigarettes and joined Bryson in smoking.

"Listen. You've been cooped up here for Christ knows how long but out there in the big wide world there's a raging debate on Scottish Independence. Frankly I don't give a monkeys' one way or the other. This is just business. For the past five years the Security Services use me when they need to have deniability. I'm expendable so I get big money to do bad or deceitful things to people and organisations that may or may not deserve it. That doesn't keep me awake at night. The nation's spooks give me cash and resources and I go about things in my own way. I've always delivered and never been caught. If I was, I'd be described as a nut-job or a terrorist or whatever suited the suits or the brass. But I'm good at what I do and now they're scared shitless that there's a mood in Scotland that would see them take their natural resources and tell England to go fuck themselves. They want to do a number of things that stop this happening." He took a long drag of his cigarette. "They've put a lot of energy into media and stuff like that but they tried all that before and this time the polls are saying that it won't work a second time because all of the promises they made then were broken. So they need a new strategy and this time they want circumstances to arise where they can mobilise the police and military to stop what they'll argue are the illegal actions of Scottish patriots and present the Jocks as little more than the IRA; like tartan terrorists. They get to militarise Scotland and appeal to existing Unionists and the persuadable middle classes that an independent Scotland would be like the Wild West."

Bryson frowned, rubbing a thoughtful finger down the bridge of his nose. "The IRA shot people."

"Aye but we *won't*, Jack. That's why I wanted you. I need a rifleman who can ensure that he *misses* his target – but it's a near miss or a slight wound! The fact that individuals are just being shot at gives them the reason they need to increase security. I've already made a list of people who'll make great targets, bring the place to a boil and allow the media to do its stuff." He paused. "You're not a Nationalist are you?"

Bryson shrugged. "Never thought about it much. I'm a proud Scotsman but I've lived most of my life in England with other Englishmen as my closest comrades. Sure there were Jocks but…" his voice trailed off and he shrugged again. "Don't suppose I'm fussed…but seventy grand and no killing?"

He awaited Kelso's consideration. "Yes and Nope!"

"Okay. I agree your conditions, Kelso."

Bryson interrupted his flow. "You got any booze in that back-pack?"

Kelso weighed his answer. "I've the remains of a half bottle of whisky. But you need to get yourself together to deal with all of this."

"Well why don't we toast the fact that I'm seventy big ones up and that I've not ripped out your throat tonight?"

Kelso couldn't allow himself to be intimidated. "That would be a far from certain outcome."

"Well, pass me that bottle and let's hope we never have to discover the truth of the matter."

Kelso peered into his small rucksack and withdrew a half-bottle of Grouse whisky. He threw the remnants of his coffee into a small sink full of unwashed crockery and poured himself a stiff whisky, passing the bottle over to Bryson.

"If I didn't pour myself a wee straightener first I don't think I'd prise that bottle from your hands." He reflected for a moment. "D'you want a splash of water with that?"

Bryson unscrewed the top and put the bottle to his lips. "That's only for malts. Let's get dressed up and walk down to the hotel in Ballantrae. You're on the bell and mine's a big Macallan! I'll take water with *that*!"

Chapter Nineteen

MI5 cannot be compromised!

Originally used as offices by Imperial Chemical Industries, Thames House is a Grade Two listed building on the north bank of the River Thames close to Lambeth Bridge. Since 1994 it has served as the headquarters of the UK Security Service, MI5. On its fourth floor a group of intelligence officers and analysts gathered awaiting the arrival of Brigadier Sir Jonathon Pennington who arrived in buoyant mood, patting colleagues on the back as he passed them prior to taking his seat at the head of the table.

He scanned the room. "Ah, first let me welcome Commander Henry Cavendish to our weekly meeting dealing with Scottish Affairs. Henry is from the Home Office and is dealing with some covert work we needn't go into here but it will be of value to him I'm sure to hear of progress being made on other fronts." He turned to his secretary, Miss Evans. "Don't minute the Commander's presence or any comment he might make, Emily," before opening a folder he'd brought with him. "We're all busy so let's begin." He turned to his unnaturally tanned senior intelligence officer Jeremy Ogilvie. "Jeremy!"

"Been a busy week, boss. We've made contact through political sources with each of the key editors and fed them the information we've gleaned about the Police Investigations and Review Commissioner and left it to them to sandpaper the truth in ways that bruise the Scottish Government. We've requested support from the 77th Brigade which has teams of social media people dealing with Facebook and Twitter. They've established what I believe are called 'bots'; short for 'robots' and have developed a range of an advanced type they call a 'chatterbot' which can respond to messages in plain English, appearing to be an actual person. They're being a bit snooty at present and it might take a personal intervention on your behalf to see matters progress. It's important because the Independence movement in Scotland is frankly very impressive as a grassroots organisation. They completely dwarf the numbers of people who are communicating on-line in support of either of the large parties and without the use of our people in the 77th Brigade their digital messages of support for Scottish Independence would go relatively unchallenged."

"Television?" asked Pennington.

"Spoken with the Director-General, and our Permanent Secretary to the Scottish Government had an informal chat with the BBC Head of Nations and Regions Division as well as the Chairman of the STV Board when he was attending our regular London meetings. Matters going well. There's a groundswell of opposition to how news is presented in Scotland and a group gathered in protest last Saturday outside BBC headquarters at Atlantic Quay on the Clyde but the numbers were small and the PA system less than adequate to disturb those inside the building."

Pennington thanked him and turned to one of his analysts.

"James!"

"A minor setback in respect of our support for Scotland In Union, Boss. They've been fantastically successful recently in having over five thousand letters posted under assumed names in Scottish newspapers all arguing the case for the Union and denouncing nationalism. Unfortunately a senior member wrote to the group writing the letters and, in praising them for their work, reminding them to keep their mouths shut about the cloaked and veiled writing they were doing." He returned his spectacles to the bridge of his nose. "Specifically, the email reads, 'We all know the fantastic results you are having but your praises will have to remain unsung.' It goes on to make the point that if news editors were aware of the closet work of Scotland in Union, they might be more discriminating in the views they publish, although frankly I rather doubt that. Unfortunately the email was leaked to a pro-Independence activist called Stuart Campbell, a resident of Bath, who owns a popular blog site called Wings Over Scotland. He published it immediately and with great glee. It has rather become something of an own goal, I'm afraid."

Pennington sighed extravagantly. "Bloody amateurs!"

Directly across from him sat Michael Will, the youngest and most gung-ho member of the Caledonian Committee.

"Michael, something for you. Can you get yourself up to the Shetland Isles?"

Will raised his eyebrows in enquiry.

"Take a couple of agents with you. We're not hearing enough of what I'm sure is the pent-up enthusiasm of the Orkney and Shetland islanders for independence for Orkney and Shetland. I'm entirely certain it's about to consume the entire island given the fact that almost all of the oil that the separatists go on about is in their waters. If they were independent each islander would be richer than bloody Croesus. At least, your job is to manufacture that notion. It'll deflect some of the energy of the Scottish movement. Pay some people, attend some meetings, letters to the editor, and dig up some dirt on the protagonists, that kind of thing."

He directed a thumb at an old map on the wall showing much of the world coloured pink.

"Over the centuries our colonial project of *divide et impera* has met with considerable success. Of course, our detractors would argue that for the past two hundred years we suppressed, exploited, imprisoned, tortured and maimed people but they then refuse to celebrate the fact that we frequently left a working democracy at the end of it. I see no reason why we should deny the Scots this benefit."

He turned again to the map behind him.

"In Nigeria, India, Pakistan, Bangladesh, Ireland, the Middle East, Cyprus and elsewhere we broke up existing power structures, and prevented smaller power groups from linking up, we created rivalries and fomented discord among the people." He tapped his pen on the desk. "Over to you, Michael."

Michael Will grinned his acceptance of the task allocated him.

He turned to his most senior analyst. "Harold. What have you?"

Harold Duffy dressed as he'd done since leaving Cambridge, his tweet jacket with leather elbow patches being an ever-present garment as far back as anyone could remember. "Nothing dramatic but overall it appears that we may have a problem trend we have to consider."

"How so?"

"Over some decades now we've managed successfully to infiltrate the separatists and the left in Scotland. The right wing in Scotland has remained pretty unified. UKIP don't have much traction north of the border so things have rather consolidated around the Conservative Party. What's changed and changing fast is the coalition of all the groups on the left we've managed to splinter in the past."

He passed round a sheet of paper.

"Here's a map...it's not comprehensive...of the left and nationalistic groups in Scotland. We've managed to place agents over the years and encouraged splits whereby one group would find within itself a faction which opposed some element of the programme being adopted by the leadership and after some wrangling the faction removes itself and sets up a new organisation. It worked very effectively." He placed his spectacles on his nose and considered the representation he'd passed around. "For example you can see that the Scottish Republican Socialist Clubs were formed back in 1973 during the administration of Edward Heath in order to introduce socialism to the Scottish National Party and grow support for Scottish independence among the left. However, following some suspensions, the Scottish Republican Socialist Party was formed which then affiliated with the Scottish Socialist Party reforming as a cross-party movement called the Scottish Republican Socialist Movement."

Ogilvie intervened. "Wasn't that the organisation led by someone who was jailed for robbing banks and post offices?"

Duffy shook his head. "No. One of its leaders, indeed, its Honorary President, Donald Anderson was suspected of some skulduggery but the verdict on both occasions was 'not proven'.

Ogilvie was puzzled. "What on earth is 'not proven'. Some peculiarly Scottish verdict?"

"Precisely so, Jeremy. Local parlance has it defined as 'not guilty - but don't do it again'. He's actually quite a character is Mister Anderson, a retired history teacher now in his eighties but he remains a force within the margins of the left and nationalist politics in Scotland. Inveterate letter writer to newspapers that'll publish his views." He consulted his map once more. "Anyway, as you can see. They disaffiliated from the Scottish Socialist Party and…"

"I get the point, Harold. You mentioned a trend?" Pennington's legendary impatience rose to the surface.

"Well, yes. Over the last few years pretty much all of these groups…with the notable exception of the Labour Party in Scotland, whose membership has been dropping like a stone, have coalesced around the notion of independence and have, if not *buried*, their differences, certainly re-prioritised them and gathered around the flag as it were. So we see the Yes Campaign and the All Under One Banner movement, indeed even the Hope Over Fear grouping driven by Solidarity gathering as one. It's very evident when we analyse social media activity that there is a clear amalgamation going on. Regular marches in support of independence are being attended by increasing numbers of people…many thousands of people. A Saturday march in Edinburgh recently organised by All Under One Banner was attended by around one hundred thousand people. Police reported numbers to the media that were much lower but it was a genuinely impressive showing."

Further reports were made around the table which appeared to satisfy Pennington including one from Intelligence Officer Alfred Fender who informed the group that MI6 had received a signal from the FBI that the person they'd asked about, one Andrew Buchanan, a billionaire supporter of Scottish Independence in America, was benign if noisy. After some forty minutes he was about to wind matters up but turned instead to Cavendish. "Henry is there anything you'd like to add or have you any questions you'd like to ask anyone gathered here?"

"Eh, not really Sir Jonathon. Although I must say I yearn for the days when I was able to report on meetings with other civil servants or senior people in the media." He half-smiled in an attempt to convey his frustration. "I mean this probably isn't the place but I find myself as the accounting officer for activities that aren't costed properly and have to give approval to the activities of particularly incautious people engaged in surreptitious pursuits…"

"Welcome to the shady world of MI5," offered Jeremy Ogilvie grinning.

"Yes…probably best you and I discuss this after this meeting, Henry," said Pennington. He looked round the table a final time. "No other competent business?"

Ogilvie closed the files he'd brought with him as a prelude to departure. "Perhaps only to remind us all that despite our efforts, the poll of polls this week saw the separatists gain yet another point!"

Pennington nodded, more solemn now than when he had commenced the meeting. "I noticed that." He stood. "However let's take succour from our favourite Communist, Uncle Joe Stalin who pointed out the reality of life when he said as I recall, 'It is enough that the people know there was an election. The people who cast the votes decide nothing. The people who *count* the votes decide *everything*,'...and thanks to our capacity to assist the electoral process by managing certain of the delicacies of postal and proxy voting, that remains within our purview!"

Ogilvie countered. "But that won't help much, boss if polls show a consistent and sizeable lead and if the actual vote is as overwhelming as the European Referendum in Scotland."

Pennington smiled a cartoon smile at Cavendish. "And that's why we're counting on you, Henry." He pushed back his chair. "Thank you, gentlemen." He turned again to Cavendish. Henry, perhaps you'd stay on?"

He waited until all had left before moving to sit opposite Cavendish , took a beat and opened by advising him of a recent interaction.

"I wanted to inform you that Kelso telephoned me."

Cavendish's frustration overcame his natural timidity. "Honestly, Sir Jonathon...Brigadier...Really... *I'm* meant to be his..."

"Henry, we must face facts. Kelso sees me as a fellow warrior as a consequence of my military record and you as something of a desk jockey. It must be difficult dealing with a subordinate who has little respect for you. However, we need this man's expertise. He brought me up to speed on progress. He's recruited additional support…like you I have no knowledge of these men and have no interest in their identities or wherewithals. I seek deniability more than a successful outcome. MI5 *cannot* be compromised! Now, he's no fool and made the very sensible point to me that although what we consider the terrorist wing of the SNP, *Seed of the Gael* to have been proscribed, we each agreed that the media and the general public will understand the obvious consanguinity between both - much in the way we managed to associate the IRA with *Sinn Féin* for many years. He proposes some robust activity that would link the SNP to what Unionists will argue is their terrorist wing. Secondly, it's important that the Scottish Government are made aware of Scottish terrorist activity so they can't hide behind ignorance of the fact. Leave that part to me although keep me informed so I can plant some information as necessary. Now"…He smiled another of his most insincere smiles. "Be a good chap and support Kelso in any which way you can, would you?"

"Being honest, Sir Jonathon, I'd rather eat peas from a knife…" He hesitated. "But of course I'll do everything in my power to ensure that he has all the support he desires."

Chapter Twenty

The Drinks Are On Me

Buchanan was in his element. Camera crews, journalists and TV anchors holding microphones interviewed him and some of the crew. Every single interview included questions regarding the name of the boat and why he'd name it thus. Atop the mast, the Scottish Saltire flew alongside the Stars and Stripes; a lacklustre wind barely troubling them.

A small flotilla of yachts and other vessels waited just outside the marina awaiting the appearance of the trimaran. Before she cast off, Buchanan stepped aboard and shook the hand of every crew member giving Murdo Monteith an especially warm handshake and an additional firm clasp of his forearm. He met Monteith's eyes for a second longer than was afforded other crew. "Good luck, Murdo!"

He completed his tour of *The Butcher's Apron* and stood waving at the cameras, smiling broadly.

The sea was calm as the trimaran slipped its berth at the marina and headed for Boston Harbour skirting Spectacle Island and set off for the Atlantic Ocean and Scotland.

Buchanan and many of those who had attended his meeting in the Algonquin Hotel in New York stood in a mutually-congratulatory group on the quayside until the craft was distant before breaking up as Buchanan shouted, "The drinks are on *me*!"

Chapter Twenty-one

Shit Creek

Macdonald and Singh sipped at their lager in the small and dowdy Renfield Bar in Glasgow's city centre prior to meeting Bonnie in *Failté*.

"Ah mean, just what are we gettin' into here, Charlie? asked Macdonald.

"Och, it's a bit of nothing. When we meet Sergeant Sim again we tell him that we've done our best but no one would talk to us." He shrugged his shoulders. "Nothing to report."

As the words left his mouth, a shadow fell over their drinks as a customer leaned against the bar and addressed them.

"Hi guys. Nice to see you again." He caught the attention of the barman. "A big Macallan, pal. Nothing for this pair. I've bought them enough drink." Tam Sim placed a ten pounds note on the bar surface. "Tips jar," he informed the barman as his drink was being poured intimating that the change could be retained.

"A wee chat, eh?" He nodded towards an unoccupied table contained within a booth. "Over there?"

Macdonald was first to recover his composure as they convened.

"Sergeant Sim," said a still-surprised Singh. "We were just talking about you."

"What the fuck do you want now?" asked Macdonald irritably.

Sim didn't respond to Macdonald's question but put his hand into his inside pocket and laid out photographs one at a time in front of the twosome.

"Number one. Your knife covered in blood and your fingerprints Mr. Macdonald...'course, no one knows it's you yet. Serious assault. Young man from Springburn. He'll live!" Macdonald's normally glowing complexion paled. "Second photograph. A parcel being assembled. A number of camouflaged items commonly worn by military types...or terrorists! In the middle of these items you can see what *I* think looks remarkably like an improvised explosive device or IED generally used by terrorists in asymmetrical and unconventional warfare...you know, like *Seed of the Gaels*? Fourth photograph...uniforms and bomb all wrapped up and bound nice and tidy. Fifth and sixth photographs... looks very much like you two and your girlfriend are either trying to bury or remove said contents from a concealed place." He added some water to his Macallan and addressed them directly. "I asked you two to get to know an underground terrorist organisation. Not lead them in fucking battle!"

Both Macdonald and Singh protested noisily causing Sim to hush them.

"You two are up shit creek!"

Macdonald seethed. "I've read about corrupt cops before. But you're lower than a snake. You blackmail us into getting involved and then accuse us of collaborating with this mob..."

Sim shook his head. "I don't remember it that way. I think you two are just mainstream SNP members who've been misled. Two guys who are more used to delivering leaflets but who were tricked by big MacDuff into doing something you'd no reason to believe was associated with terrorist activity."

Singh gestured his excitement. "That's exactly what happened, Sergeant. That's exactly how we became involved. We were tricked!"

Macdonald's head shook almost imperceptibly at Singh's naivety. "You might just be the most sleekit big shite I've ever met, Sim."

He caught Singh's uncomprehending gaze and addressed him. "I'll give him this, Charlie. The bastard's good at his job!" He lifted the remnants of his pint. "A toast! A toast to a bent cop who will stop at nothing, including the illegal intimidation of two innocent students to help him penetrate what I understand is a perfectly legitimate organisation… just one of which he and his bosses disapprove." He took a sip of his lager. "So what's next, boss? Clearly you want us to get more involved. Who are you after? Big MacDuff? Don't tell me you're after Bonnie?"

Sim finished his Macallan and rebuked him. "Don't play with fire, Macdonald. Right now I'm your best friend. I decide whether you both end up in serious, serious trouble or whether you walk free having rendered Scotland a service."

"Somehow I very much doubt the service bit!"

Singh sought clarification. "What do you want us to do, Sergeant Sim?"

"Charlie. You're doing great. All of this can go away. I just need you to continue doing what you're doing. Keep close to MacDuff. Do whatever he asks and allow it to be known that you want to remain solid, conventional SNP members but that you're happy to help *Seed of the Gaels* now and again because you're frustrated at the lack of movement towards independence in Scotland right now."

Singh, as ever, looked for common ground. "Well that's *almost* true." He looked at Macdonald for reassurance but found none. "We *are* mainstream SNP and we are a *bit* frustrated…" He tailed off as he read Macdonald's anger.

Sim grasped his empty glass as a prelude to returning it to the barman. "I hope I've made myself clear. Say nothing of this. Keep close to your new pals in *Failté*." He stood and looked at his watch. You're going to be late. It's after eight. Make haste lads. I'll be in touch."

As he walked to the door Macdonald lowered his head to the table and rested it on his folded arms. "We're fucked, Charlie-boy. Well and truly!"

"But if we just do what he says, Lachie? What's the harm?"

Macdonald regained his posture. "So how did he know we were going to be late? The only people who knew we were to be at *Failté* by eight tonight were us two and Bonnie."

Singh's eyes widened as he realised the import of his friend's insight.

"So we can't even trust Bonnie?"

"Right now I'd bet even her boobs are falsies!"

* * *

Walking down Renfield Street, Sim pushed number four on his speed dial.

"MacDuff! They'll be down in a few minutes."

Chapter Twenty-two

The Desk Jockey

"Cavendish!"

On the other end of the phone Kelso smiled. "You do know I fuckin' *hate* cunts like you?"

Cavendish's frustration boiled over as he recognised his tormentor.

"*Enough* of this, Kelso! I've spoken at length to Sir Jonathon and although you may not have much in the way of respect for my military record it does occur to me that I'm still the man who signs off on all your expenditure and I'm past caring how successful your little operation is. If I don't get more regard round here and a better understanding of my need as accounting officer to justify these sums you're spending then I'll just close up and make things as difficult for you as possible - and that includes any payment that's due you."

Kelso recoiled momentarily at Cavendish's attitude.

"Well, it appears that my boss has found a new set of balls!" He changed his tone. "Very well, Commander, sir. I need a rifle delivered early tomorrow. It must be a L42A1, bolt-action Lee-Enfield as used in Northern Ireland back in the day. I need it delivered with some twenty rounds of ammo to the top right flat at number twelve Hughenden Road. I will be there to collect it.

The name on the door will be Wallace. It needs to arrive precisely at six o'clock pm."

"Anything else?"

"Is that your way of inviting me to say 'please'?"

"That would be childish, Kelso. Have you any other requests?"

"Are the seventy thousand and twenty thousand sums I asked to be deposited in the Swiss Bank now there?"

"They are."

"Then would you be good enough to send the transaction confirmations to my phone. I need proof."

"As soon as our conversation ends."

"Then it's ended!" He grinned widely. "You *do* know…"

"Don't try my fucking patience," said Cavendish, delighted at his new-found assertiveness.

He placed the phone on its cradle and pressed a button that connected him to his secretary. "Miss Anson, would you be good enough to come through? I've an equipment request that's rather urgent but before you do, would you get me on the first available flight to Glasgow following my meeting at eleven tomorrow morning. He released the button. *Thinks I'm a desk-jockey, does he?*

Chapter Twenty-three

Sergeant Sim

Singh and Macdonald entered *Failté* and were immediately welcomed by Bonnie who chided them but with warmth in her voice.

"We said eight o'clock. It's half-past. I thought you were going to stand me up."

"Wouldn't do that in a million years," replied Macdonald sourly.

"Wow, someone's got out of bed on the wrong side. Charlie, are you as touchy tonight?"

Singh reverted to his normal affable self despite them each bemoaning their situation as they'd walked down the short distance from the Renfield Bar to *Failté*.

"He's like that sometimes, Bonnie. Probably just needs lager."

"Now that's something we can fix."

As the three stood at the bar, MacDuff rose from his seat and approached them carrying his ubiquitous pint of Guinness. Towering over them he embraced all three in a light bear hug designed to show affection without risking a spill of his pint.

"Bonnie tells me the package is outside in her car. Well done all three of you." He hesitated and scanned the bar. "Let's have a wee chat over there." He indicated an empty table that was surrounded by other empty tables.

"Bonnie told me you'd be here half an hour ago," he said sternly. In this man's army punctuality is important. We're engaged on important matters and you aren't to know whether eight o'clock is of crucial importance, so in future when you're engaged on any wee task that's supportive of Scotland's Independence in any way and a time is agreed. We turn up on time. Okay?"

"No one told us it was important to be on time. We thought we were just turning up for a drink. We did everything you asked of us last night," growled Macdonald.

"Aye. You did. And it was appreciated."

Macdonald was still feeling aggressive and angry. "So what was in that fuckin' parcel anyway?"

"Sorry, all. Can't tell you that. But it was important." He lowered his voice. "Now I need you to do something else for the cause."

"Another graveyard in the dark?" enquired Macdonald sarcastically.

"No. It's a meeting. Tomorrow evening at five-thirty. Twelve Hughenden Road. West End. Top flat. The name on the door will be Wallace."

"And what's the purpose of this meeting?" asked Macdonald.

"Secrecy is important to *Seed of the Gaels*, Lachie. You only get told what you need to know. Just be there if you still believe in helping us achieve an independent Scotland."

He placed his arms over Bonnie and Singh. "Are we all in?"

Three heads nodded. No one smiled.

* * *

MacDuff returned to the rear of the bar leaving Macdonald, Singh and Bonnie to their drinks and their conversation.

"So you told Angus when we'd be arriving tonight, Bonnie," asked Macdonald.

"Sure. I phoned him earlier today to tell him that everything went well and then the three of us would be here at eight o'clock tonight." She looked puzzled. "Isn't that what we agreed?"

Macdonald and Singh looked at each other. "Yeah. We were just puzzled about how he knew when we were coming."

A stilted and awkward conversation continued for a further two rounds of drinks, Macdonald refusing any offer of Bonnie to buy a round. Bonnie addressed the change in mood.

"What's the matter with you two? You've been in a weird mood all night. I thought we were getting on well and that we had a bit of a laugh last night."

"Did ye, aye?" glowered Macdonald.

"We just had a wee surprise before we came down here," explained Singh.

Macdonald decided to clear matters. "Tell me somethin', Bonnie," he said abandoning his previous attempts at pronouncing the 'g' in any given present participle, noun or pronoun. "How long have you been involved with this mob and why did you get involved?"

Bonnie leaned her elbow on the table and rested her chin on the palm of her hand.

"Perhaps six months. I was a member of the SNP. Joined at university and it was fine but *Seed of the Gaels* seemed to offer a bit more action. To be honest it's really only involved a lot more drinking. I enjoy their company and I love hearing Angus talk. He knows so much about Scottish history and when he talks so passionately about the ways in which Scotland has been exploited by the Westminster establishment, I find myself really caught up. So when he asks me to do wee things like last night I'm happy to oblige."

"So he's not asked you to blow something up or anything like that?" asked Singh.

"God, no!" Her hands flew to her mouth to stifle a giggle. "See, that's because the media paint this picture of *Seed of the Gaels* as borderline terrorists." She swirled in her seat and nodded in the direction of the rear of the bar. "Do these people look like terrorists?"

"Don't know what terrorists look like," grumbled Macdonald. "For all I know, *you're* one. You could be as fake as a fake bank manager with a fake heart."

Before Bonnie had a chance to reply, Singh allowed his fourth pint of lager to skew his judgement.

"Lachie thinks your boobs are false!"

Macdonald raised his gaze to the ceiling in whispered reproach. "Jesus Christ Almighty!"

Bonny screwed her face trying to make sense of Singh's revelation. She angered.

"Well, I can tell you. They're real, they're absolutely spectacular and the only time either one of you two will see them is when they're covered by a bloody duffle coat!"

She lifted her drink and made to leave. Macdonald half-stood.

"Bonnie! I didn't say that. Well, I *did* but I didn't mean it in a disrespectful way. I was just thinking that I'm not sure that everyone here is on the level."

Bonnie slowly re-took her seat as did Macdonald. After a moment during which she regained her composure, she quizzed Macdonald further.

"Then what *did* you mean, Lachie? Explain yourself," she continued, still angry.

"Look you've been great and both of us have enjoyed gettin' to know you. It's just…well…a few days ago we were just two guys on a march. Regular SNP foot-soldiers and a few days later we're in a graveyard at night with someone we've just met doin' God knows what for a big guy that looks like he's an extra from a movie about the aftermath of Bannockburn." He lifted his glass an inch from the table in a mock toast. "So…I'm sorry I didn't mean to offend."

Bonnie smiled. "Apology accepted."

"That goes for me too!" agreed Singh.

Macdonald focussed his frustration on Singh. "Jesus, Charlie. When you have a drink you don't have a filter. You just open your mouth and get me into trouble."

"What about you two guys? How did you get involved? Was it just chance you came along here when we were meeting?"

Both responded almost in unison with a barrage of 'ayes', 'of courses' and 'for sures' before, after a hesitation, Singh drunkenly offered supplementary information.

"Well, we met a guy on a march to Glasgow Green and he suggested we come along."

Macdonald's face registered a disbelief that was missed by Bonnie.

"Same thing happened to me. I met a guy in the bar at an SNP Conference at the SECC, a car salesman. He was SNP. Tried to sell me a car but told me about

Seed of the Gaels and encouraged me to come along and meet Angus. Never seen hide nor hair of him ever since, mind you. Big guy. From memory, his name was Tam Sim."

* * *

It was most unfortunate that both Macdonald and Singh had chosen that precise moment to enjoy a sip of their lager. Upon hearing Bonnie's mention of their persecutor, it took all of their powers to retain their drink without spitting it over the table.

"That guy's a cop, Bonnie!" Singh couldn't contain himself.

"Huh?"

"He's a cop!"

"He's a *corrupt* cop, Bonnie," amplified Macdonald. "He's blackmailing me and Charlie here…and you too, for that matter!"

"Tam Sim? Describe him!"

Macdonald took the wheel. "Six foot tall. Solid build. Short black hair. Maybe late forties, early fifties. Glasgow man."

Bonnie looked puzzled. "Seems like the same guy"

"Well, the reason we were late tonight was he kept us back in another pub. He has a knife with my fingerprints on that he says he planted at a crime scene. He's got photographs of last night's parcel being assembled and inside all of that camouflage gear is some kind of small bomb." Macdonald leaned towards Bonnie to emphasise his point. "And he's got photographs of the three of us lifting the parcel out of that hole last night."

Bonnie lifted her hand to her mouth in horror. She didn't speak.

Singh attempted some balance. "But he might help get me into the police when I finish my degree."

Macdonald became animated. "What d'you think, Bonnie? We go to the police?"

All three sipped at their drink as they processed the information and considered options.

Bonnie took the lead. "So Sim wants us to go to a West End address tomorrow night? He must be in cahoots with Angus, eh?"

"Looks that way," agreed Macdonald. "He must have told Sim what time we were meant to be here tonight."

"It's up to you guys. But I think I'm going to go along. It might be better if you two don't show in case there's trouble."

"Don't be daft, Bonnie. Sim's got us dead to rights. If you go, we go. The question is, should *any* of us go?"

"Well, no one's going to harm a girl. Maybe we're making a mountain out of a molehill. Perhaps the meeting that Angus talked about is just that…a meeting of like-minded people." She thought further. "Maybe there'll be cheese and wine!"

"Get serious, Bonnie. Sim has incriminating photographs of us doing something that Angus told us to do. Either he's bugging everything that Angus says, the two of them are in this together or you are in it with Sim and for some reason are trying to see Charlie and me in the jail."

Bonnie opened her arms wide. "Look at me!" She caught Singh's gaze. "Up a bit, Charlie. You're looking at my boobs. I'm trying to ask if I've got an honest face."

Singh was quick to confirm. "It was just a glance!" Seeing Macdonald's disapproving look, he attempted recovery. "Yeah. Your face is very honest. Eh, Lachie?"

"Yeah. I'm okay with you. But if you're square, it means that big buggerlugs at the end of the bar is being deceitful. Now why is that?"

Bonnie rubbed her chin in thought. "If we go to the police and Sim really *has* fixed things we could be in trouble." She came to a decision. "I vote we go along to the meeting tomorrow night and see what's what. We go with our eyes wide open. We now have an advantage because we know they're up to something but they don't *know* we know!"

Singh had begun to slur his words. "I'm drunk. I didn't understand any of that but I agree with Bonnie whatever she said. Also Sergeant Sim might help me get into the police. I don't want to let him down."

Macdonald finished his pint. "I'm going home. We meet first in the Renfield Bar tomorrow night at four-thirty."

"I've not been drinking because I'm driving. I'll give you both a lift home but first you two help me get that parcel out of my car boot. If it contains what you say it does, big Angus can deal with it but I'd bet anything it's not an active bomb. Angus is too relaxed about the parcel being in my car only yards from his Guinness. We'll soon see when we bring it into the pub!"

Finishing their drinks, they stepped outside and together collected the parcel, walking it into the bar, carrying it up to the rear table.

"Where do you want this, Angus?"

MacDuff looked up from a conversation he was having with another group member. He waved his hand dismissively.

"Just leave it where you are. I'll get it later."

Clumsily they set it on the table next to where MacDuff was seated, their eyes meeting in confirmation of Bonnie's theory of the bomb's impotence. A series of smiling goodbyes followed as they left the pub.

Bonnie halted and stood thoughtfully for a moment.

"One question. Did this guy…this Sergeant Sim… did he ever show you his warrant card?"

Chapter Twenty-four

Hughenden Road

In a minibus heading towards Hughenden Road Kelso took the opportunity at a red light to punch the numbers ten sixty-six on his smart phone in order to gain access. Bryson, seated in the passenger seat noted the number. *He might have been a warrior in his day but the man has zero imagination! Ten sixty-six! I ask you!*

He held the phone so Bryson could see the screen. "Look, Jack! Here's digital confirmation from the *Banque cantonale de Genève*," he struggled to pronounce its name. "Here's a pen. Write down the account number. It's your seventy thousand, safe and sound."

Bryson noted the number and pass code. "Now delete the screen!" he instructed.

Kelso made a face and with an elaborate gesture he pointed his finger and slowly descended his digit until it pushed the 'delete' button. "You'd better not lose that piece of paper," he counselled, driving on before pulling up on Hyndland Road just before Hughenden Road.

The men stepped from the vehicle and entered the common close leading to the apartment three flights up. An obviously temporary piece of card on the door offered, 'Wallace' as the occupant. Kelso handed Bryson a pair of latex gloves, "No prints!" opened the door and both men entered a large but tawdry hallway.

"Well, it's not the Waldorf!"

Kelso showed no slight at the comment. "Better than your dump down in Ballantrae. It's been rented for a month." Both men walked into an equally down-at-heel living room.

"So why are we here?"

"Shortly, that bell will ring and a man in motorcycle gear will deliver a long parcel. Inside will be a L42A1, bolt-action Lee-Enfield just like the one you used in Northern Ireland back in the day when you could hold your drink."

It was Bryson's turn to ignore the gibe. "The Enfield's a fucking pea-shooter!"

"It has a muzzle velocity of two thousand seven hundred and fifty feet per second, an effective firing range of eight hundred yards and a ten round feed system."

"The weapon I used in Afghanistan was a DAN.338. I could stop a moving car, penetrate armour and kill a man with a head shot from more than a mile away."

Kelso disagreed. "The Dan would remove the fucker's head from his shoulders. Tonight you'll merely shoot a woman's handbag from across the road."

"A handbag?"

"Yeah. That's why we're using a pea-shooter. Also it's a common weapon with common rounds but with your skill you can make sure no one comes to any harm. Remember? We agreed, no killing!"

"So what's this all about?"

"There's a female newsreader the Nationalists don't like. She lives across the road. A bullet takes out her handbag and it'll be all over the news. They'd be the obvious suspects."

Bryson nodded his understanding but raised questions. "And this woman...Is she strong enough to cope with the thought of an apparent assassination attempt? She got kids with an exam in the morning?"

"Who gives a fuck! If I had my way it'd be through her fucking skull!"

The bell rang and Kelso admitted the caller. Moments later a parcel was wordlessly handed over. As he slowly unwrapped the tough, taped covering, the diminishing engine noise of a motorcycle could be heard outside as it left the street. Perhaps twenty minutes elapsed as Bryson checked and adjusted the rifle, bench checking and testing each of the gun's controls and functions until he was satisfied that he'd be able to shoot accurately.

"Without having a few test shots, I can't guarantee it'll shoot straight."

"It'll shoot straight enough for our purposes. The only problem is that it's a night shot but the distance is only about fifty yards. You should be able to hit a pin head at that distance."

Bryson looked out of the window onto an already darkening street courtesy of black Scottish storm clouds. He raised and lowered the window several times to ensure it had no impediment to its opening. "I need to shoot so that there's no ricochet. At this angle the round might hit the pavement and end up in the house behind her." He made further assessments. I'll shoot just as she turns into the close mouth. That way the bullet penetrates the bag and ends up in the earth behind the hedge."

The bell rang again startling Bryson. "Expecting anyone?"

Kelso removed a Glock 17 pistol from the waistband above his hip pocket. "Yeah. Be prepared to be surprised." He listened again. "Don't use any surnames!"

Kelso closed the door silently and continued to listen to the light chatter of people climbing the stairs. As they reached the door, he opened it just as they prepared to knock and waved the Glock at them.

"Inside!"

* * *

Macdonald, Singh and Gabriel sat together on a large couch, each very obviously anxious about the two men who faced them; one with a pistol, one with a rifle.

"You three are here for a purpose." He nodded at Singh. "I'm betting you're not Macdonald!"

"My name's Charan Singh, sir. People call me Charlie." He fought for something to say. "We're here for a meeting."

Kelso glared at him fearsomely before turning his attention to Macdonald. "And I'm assuming you're not the beautiful Bonnie Gabriel because you're a right ugly bastard!"

"Lachie Macdonald."

He turned his gaze to Bonnie. "Jesus. The big chap was right. You're a looker."

Bonnie was silent. The doorbell rang a second time."

Kelso turned to speak with Bryson. "Would you get that? It's my two friends."

Bryson moved into the large hallway, pressed the buzzer admitting the callers and stood against the door. Without opening it, he leaned against the door frame listening to steps becoming closer. The door was knocked. Bryson opened the Yale lock and stepped back in astonishment as the two figures entered the hallway.

"Wh...what the...Sim? MacDuff ? Wh...what...?"

Both men laughed and much handshaking and hugging took place with Bryson, largely at their instigation.

Eventually Bryson found his voice. "Don't tell me you're involved with that fucker through there?"

"We are," said Sim.

"We're kind of sub-contractors!" laughed MacDuff.

"Jesus I've not see you two since *Desert Storm*." He thought for a moment. "You've both hung up your rifles, I'm supposing?"

Sim placed his hand on Bryson's upper-arm guiding him towards the living room. "We'll answer all of your questions later. It's just good to be working together again. When you left to join the SAS after Iraq we stayed in for a bit before chucking it and getting in tow with Kelso through there."

The three men entered the room. Bonnie found her voice first as she recognised Angus MacDhuibh.

"Angus! What's going on here? You said this was to be a meeting tonight and now we've got armed men..."

"Hi there, Sergeant Sim," said Singh. Sim nodded in recognition.

Macdonald held his own counsel.

Kelso took control. "Right. You three! Phones!" He held out his left hand, palm upwards inviting them to part with their phones. His right hand still held the Glock. He placed the phones in his pocket and waved at Singh. "You! Into the hallway!"

"Fuck sake," said Macdonald now freshly fearful. "What are you guys up to?"

Kelso ignored the question and accompanied Singh into the hall where he spoke quietly but menacingly.

"Listen sonny-boy, we're serious people. You need to believe it wouldn't cause me much pain to put a bullet in your head so you're going to do exactly as I say." Singh nodded vigorously. "Now, my understanding is that those two in there live alone and won't be missed if they don't go home tonight, eh?"

"That's correct, sir. But I live with my…"

"Yeah. That's why you're out here." He pulled the three phones from his pocket. "Which one's yours?"

Singh pointed to a top of the range smart phone.

"Take it and phone your folks. Tell them you're staying at your ugly friend's house because you're leaving early in the morning to…" He thought…"To go hillwalking."

Singh nodded. "Bb..but sir…"

"Fucking phone them!"

Singh managed to speak coherently. "There'll be no one in. They're at a dinner party tonight!"

Kelso was satisfied. "Even better. Leave a message and tell them you've a weak battery but you'll phone them later…after the hillwalking stuff!"

Singh complied and was ushered back into the living room minus his now re-confiscated phone.

"Kelso checked his watch. "Okay, Jack. She should be here in about ninety minutes. It's apparently a pretty unbreakable routine."

Bryson gestured at the three students. "Why are they here?"

"Sorry, Comrade. No can tell. You have a job to do." He leaned closer to Bryson. "So *do* it!"

He turned to the five other individuals. "Now listen. There's going to be a shooting."

Bonnie responded as ever to shock by covering her mouth with her hand!

"No one's going to be hurt!" Said Kelso in what he hoped was a reassuring tone. "Now once my friend has fired a shot, we're all going to walk smartly and *silently* down the stairs. At the end of the road there's a white minibus. We all get in it. I drive. No one runs. No one talks." He looked at the threesome on the couch. "Am I clear?"

* * *

The three students listened as Kelso stood guard at the window while the other three ex-soldiers stood in the hall and exchanged memories of their time in the service of the Crown.

"What the fuck are you two doing with an arsehole like Kelso? asked Bryson. "He was always a bit strange when we were in uniform."

"He pays well," replied MacDuff.

"This is all just a bit of business, Jack. Makes a change to be operating in Scotland. We're usually down in London. That's where the action is."

"So you two big Unionists, eh?"

Sim answered. "I am but big MacDuff here is a major bore on Scottish Nationalism. 'Freedom!' eh, big chap?"

"Exactly so!"

Bryson's puzzlement got the better of him. "So why get involved in this stuff with Kelso?"

"Bills to pay!"

Kelso called Bryson to the window. "It's time."

Bryson inspected the scene outside. "Turn all lights off." He raised the window some eight inches.

After some minutes, a Mercedes pulled up in a space outside the property identified earlier by Kelso.

"This your friend?"

Kelso peered down at the street. "Yeah, right car… right time." A woman stepped from the car. "Right sex. Take the shot."

The car lights first dimmed and then flashed to signify it being locked. Gathering a briefcase under her arm, the woman fished in her pocket. *House keys not with the car keys?* thought Bryson. She found what she'd been looking for and walked slowly towards the pathway that led to her close-mouth. *These sights better be accurate or this woman's going to get a bullet up the arse*. Letting his breath out and holding steady, Bryson squeezed the trigger. The NATO 147 grain full metal jacket projectile sped towards its target with a loud crack and severed the strap holding the woman's bulky handbag sending it to the ground. The bullet continued and buried itself in the small garden outside the red-sandstone building. A second bullet aimed for good measure only at the garden followed its partner into the earth.

The woman screamed and after fumbling for some moments at the outer doorway, ran into the protective covering of the close.

"Downstairs everyone. Remember. No running. No talking. Everything quiet." He turned to Bryson who was in the process of closing the window. "Great shot, big man. You're still the best! Now…downstairs!"

Bryson left and Kelso paced the room, checking for anything that might inadvertently have been left behind. The shell casings lay beneath the window. He left them where they lay. He walked to the hallway and satisfied himself that everyone was on their way downstairs. Turning back he moved to an armchair. From his pocket he took the receipt and bank card he'd removed from Bryson's pocket when he was unconscious in his cottage. He took one of the phones surrendered by one of the students. These he left on the chair before walking swiftly to the door and, leaving it ajar to avoid the noise of a closing door, stepped swiftly downstairs where he rejoined the others at the minibus.

Chapter Twenty-five

Cavendish Arrives

As Kelso drove the vehicle towards Byers Road and the city centre, a taxi turned the corner of Hughenden Road and deposited Cavendish on the pavement outside number twelve. Finding the front door at the common entry unlocked, he gingerly climbed the stairs until he reached the door marked, 'Wallace'.

Across the road, having dialled 999, feverish attempts were being made to persuade the civilian call-handler that a shooting had just taken place in Glasgow's sedate and leafy West End.

Cavendish carefully pushed at the open door timidly asking if anyone was at home. Finding the accommodation empty, he tried a light-switch and upon entering the living room, was rewarded with his discovery of the shell-casings, receipt, phone and bank card.

"I'll have these!" he said quietly to himself. "They just might help me understand what's going on here." He pocketed them and after a brief investigation of the other rooms left the flat and walked downstairs. *Wonder where Kelso's got to?* he asked himself. On reaching the street he walked the short distance to the much busier Hyndland Road where he flagged a taxi.

"Eh, Central Hotel, please."

The taxi pulled away as two police cars and an ambulance travelling at speed turned into Hughenden Road.

Chapter Twenty-six

Further Duplicity

Pennington watched the BBC news tell the dramatic story of one of their employees being the target of a shooting. Reference was made to a Member of Parliament, Jo Cox MP who'd been shot and stabbed in 2016 as she prepared to hold a constituency surgery in West Yorkshire. Her murderer was an unstable far-right member of the neo-Nazi group, National Alliance and speculation was rife that the bullets fired at the newsreader were from a gun held by someone supporting independence for Scotland. Various spokespersons from the Scottish Government urged restraint until the police had completed their investigations. Scottish Conservative politicians looked grim and tried to find statesman-like words that did everything but accuse those minded to see Scotland independent of armed revolution.

Pennington pressed the buzzer on his desk and asked Miss Evans to arrange that Jeremy Ogilvie join him immediately.

* * *

"Hi, boss!" Ogilvie's sunny disposition was at odds with Pennington's more thoughtful demeanour.

"We may have them on the back foot, Jeremy, old chap. Probably time to move in for the kill so to speak."

"Saw it all on the news, boss."

Pennington sat back on his chair lightly drumming his pen on his knee.

"Why don't we let the splendid Police Scotland get on with their investigations but in the meantime, you send Harold an e-mail intimating that you have sources that suggest that this attempted assassination was undertaken by mainline SNP members and that you seek a discussion on any information he might have on radical influences within the party - whether members or elected representatives." He leaned forward and positioned himself as it to continue writing in order to indicate that the meeting was over. "I shall arrange that our agent, '*Treasure* will take steps to bring this leaked information to the attention of the Scottish Government. They need to have no room to deny their early knowledge of the culpability of their membership."

Chapter Twenty-seven

The Three-ring Circus

As *The Butcher's Apron* skimmed across the surface of the Atlantic, Murdo Monteith took a much-needed rest in the hull of the boat near the control section where all of the data necessary to make a transfer-Atlantic Crossing was processed.

"Penny for your thoughts? Murdo," smiled the Skip, Sam Ferguson.

"Eh, just wondering if we're making good progress. Skip."

As Ferguson replied, Monteith's gaze fell back on the secreted horde of arms lying only some twenty feet from him, disguised by the clever work of the trimaran's carpenter. A knot of anxiety formed in his stomach as he pondered his arrival at Stranraer; a host of photographers snapping his arrival or officers of the law snapping hand restraints on his wrists?

"…excellent, unless we overturn." Monteith tuned back into Ferguson's response.

"Oh! Eh, terrific, Sam!"

* * *

Harold Duffy lifted his phone and dialled the numbers to connect him to Jeremy Ogilvie some two floors below.

"Jeremy! Harold. Got your e-mail. You wanted a chat about radicals within the SNP?"

"Yes and no, old chap. Boss wants an e-mail to exist that says everything and nothing so he can stir things up a bit by leaking it innocently to the Scottish Government so there's a record of them being aware of these guerrillas within their ranks."

"But we haven't the slightest bit of evidence that there are any dangerous radicals; *violent* radicals anyway... The incident last night, as we know, was of our own making!"

"Yeah. We know that, old son but the boss says he just needs something that points to our presumption. We'd deny any information on grounds of national security but it'll stir things up!"

"I suppose so." He shook his head remorsefully. "This is why I'm an analyst and you're gadding about causing trouble."

Ogilvie laughed in recognition of the truth of Duffy's remark.

"One thing perhaps, Jeremy. I've just had a signal from the Homeland Security in the USA. It's a long shot but they've used photo ID to identify two gentlemen who've bought a collection of arms in various State gun shows using false papers. There's only a sixty-five percent positive identification on either one but it's possible due to them each being known associates." He placed his spectacles back on and peered at a piece of paper in front of him. "Cornelius, known as 'Cornie' Donaghey and Struan McAllister. If it's confirmed, they seemed to have amassed rather a haul of assault rifles. Probably unremarkable," he mused. Donaghey's Irish as his name might imply. McAllister's Scottish, as might his. Both close to Andrew Buchanan, President of *Friends of Scotland*, billionaire friend to all politicians on the East Coast and owner of the rather provocatively named *'Butcher's Apron'* sailboat currently crossing the Atlantic." He placed the paper on his desk. "The question arises whether these weapons are being transported to Scotland in the face of huge international media interest. It's all rather improbable, mind you. Buchanan is a pillar of society over there...bit of a peacenik by all accounts... and a racing craft needs additional weight like a hole in its hull!"

Ogilvie was silent for a moment as he thought.

"Improbable or not, we could probably make it into something. When's this boat going to make landfall!"

"Imminently, I gather. It's due to arrive at Stranraer in Scotland tomorrow if it maintains its current momentum."

A further silence ensued.

"D'you know, this might be something for Henry Cavendish's 'Third Direction' friend. After taking a pot-shot at that newsreader last night he might now be looking for some other delinquency and may be able to turn this into a three-ring circus. I'll check."

Chapter Twenty-eight

The Butcher's Window

The Glasgow Ship Bank was Glasgow's first bank, founded in 1750 by a group of Glasgow's wealthy Tobacco Lords. The bank subsequently removed to new premises in nearby Glassford Street and the three-storey building it occupied was subsequently used for shops and living accommodation. In 1845 a pub, the Old Ship Bank, opened on the ground floor. It was outside these premises, in Glasgow's Saltmarket that Kelso pulled up.

"Upstairs, quietly everyone." Kelso threw a set of keys to a surprised Macdonald.

"Second floor. Name on the door is Bruce. Everyone get settled. I'll park this mini-bus out of sight. Sim and MacDuff are in charge." He caught Macdonald's eyes in his rear view mirror. "Remember they're armed!"

Macdonald sat motionless holding the keys until urged again by Kelso who drove off as soon as all had vacated the vehicle.

The building they entered was similar in construction to the one they'd left only twenty-five minutes earlier but in a considerably less desirable aspect. The corner pub was still busy as the six passengers entered the adjacent close-mouth and made their way up to the second floor. They entered and were ushered to a living room furnished with a three piece suite. Sim withdrew a handgun from his waistband and gestured to Macdonald, Singh and Gabriel to sit together on the large sofa.

"Kelso said there would be provisions in the kitchen," said MacDuff going off to investigate.

Sim turned his attention to Bryson and beckoned him to the front window.

"There's tomorrow's target…"

Bryson peered into the darkness. "Nothing to see. Just a street."

Tomorrow at around ten o'clock there'll be several flute bands marching under the colours of the Orange Order. Your job is to take out the big drum…the big Lambeg drum when they're giving it laldy on the flutes."

Bryson inspected the street view before him for some moments before pronouncing his disinclination.

"Nah! Wouldn't work. The perspective we have here means that I'd be shooting towards an oncoming march. Any bullet fired at that trajectory would inevitably travel onwards and hit someone directly or ricochet. It's too dangerous."

"You'd better reconsider or Kelso'll be furious. He's put a lot of work into this. First we target a much hated journalist then we go after the Orange Order and bring them out on to the streets in opposition to the Nationalists."

Bryson didn't adjust his focus on the street before him and spoke quietly.

"You'll forgive me if I don't give a flying fuck what Kelso thinks. He promised no bloodshed and the shot proposed would certainly result in death or injury so it's a no-go." He intensified his attention on the shop-fronts, concentrating on one in particular.

"Hold on. Lights out and lift the window. Pass me the rifle."

Sim did as requested and handed Bryson the weapon. Stepping back from the window into the middle of the room, he knelt and trained his sights on a shop window scanning the frontage. After some further adjustment of the telescopic sight he lowered the Lee-Enfield.

"It's a butcher's shop!"

Sim was puzzled. "So what?"

"Well if there's a big lump of meat, say the hind quarters of a pig or something in the window tomorrow morning, I might be able to take a shot that does the business but which ends up safely in the butcher-meat." He handed Sim the rifle and stepping forward, lowered the window.

"I'll give it some thought and maybe take a wee look at the shop up close." He turned to the three students seated on the couch and selected Macdonald. "You! What's your name again?"

"Lachie Macdonald."

"Right Lachie. Make yourself useful." He turned to MacDuff. "Was there coffee in the kitchen like you were told?"

"Aye."

"Okay, Lachie. Boil some water."

Taking charge he invited the rest of the company to relax until Kelso rejoined them and followed Macdonald into the small kitchen. Checking to ensure that no others had followed him, he grasped Macdonald by the collar and leaned his face close to the student's.

"How do you three fit in here? What's your story?"

With Bryson's bunched fist pulling the neck of his jumper around his neck and his scowling visage inches from his own, Macdonald's fear was compounded by his inability to speak clearly.

"I'm fucked if I know. The three of us are just students but that fellah Sim has got us involved in this by blackmailing me. He's got my fingerprints on a knife and he's going to drop me in it if I don't do as he says. That big guy MacDuff was meant to be in *Seed of the Gaels* but I don't know what to believe now and we're all scared shitless now that you and your pals are shooting the fucking town up!"

Bryson considered the obvious fear and candour of the youngster and loosened his grasp.

"You're in no danger from me, son." He looked back into the living room where the others now sat in an awkward silence. "Stick some coffee on." A thought occurred. "Listen, son…Lachie…do you have any cash on you?"

Macdonald reached into his back pocket and withdrew three banknotes. "Sim gave me and Charlie fifty quid each to buy drink if we gave him information on the people that were drinking in the *Failté* Bar in St Vincent Street. I've thirty quid and some smash left."

"Could I borrow it, son? I'll pay you back."

Eager to indulge the large man who'd promised no harm would befall him, Macdonald parted with the money hastily.

"Thanks." He pocketed the money. "Coffee for the troops?"

Macdonald nodded and moved towards the kitchen cabinet whose glass front allowed sight of crockery.

Bryson shouldered himself off the wall against which he'd been leaning and re-entered the room. "I'm just going to have a quick look at that shop window to see if there's an angle that might allow the shot." He walked again to the living-room window and gazed outwards for a few moments before pronouncing. "Won't be long, people. Explain to Kelso if he's back before I return."

* * *

Having taken a sip of her coffee, Bonnie placed it on a side table and addressed the man she'd known as MacDuff.

"So is your name really Angus? I'd feel stupid calling you by your stage name."

"You call me Angus MacDuff or Angus MacDhuibh. That's how you know me!" he replied gruffly.

"And are you a member of *Seed of the Gaels*...a supporter of Scottish Independence like you claimed?"

"Bonnie...just drink your coffee and stop asking questions."

"Don't you think I've a right to ask questions of a man who sends me and my two friends on a moonlit traipse round a graveyard, gets me involved in some kind of shooting then forces me at gunpoint to wander the city in their company?"

Before MacDuff could answer, Singh interrupted.

"And are you really a sergeant in the Special Branch, Mr. Sim?"

"*Sergeant* Sim to you, Charlie!"

Singh looked wounded. "It was just you'd said you could help me joining the police."

Both Sim and MacDuff laughed as the door opened and Kelso entered closing it behind him. He addressed MacDuff. "Everything okay?"

"Aye." He decided he'd better offer Bryson's assessment of the shot that was to be asked of him the following morning. "Bryson thinks the shot's too hard. He'd probably hit someone!"

Kelso's face contorted. "Who fuckin' cares if someone gets shot. We're trying to start a war here." He looked around. "Where *is* he?"

Sim began to feel uncomfortable as he answered, anticipating Kelso's wrath.

"He's away to look at a butcher's window."

Kelso's face, previously distorted, took on the aspect of eager inquisition. His voice rose an octave. "Eh? A butcher's *window*?"

"He said he'd be back in a minute. He's away to look at the butcher's window up the road there so he can maybe take the shot tomorrow morning."

Kelso pursed his lips in frustration and lowered his gaze to the floor so avoiding the looks of bewilderment on the faces of those in the living room. He spoke quietly.

"Did Bryson have any money?"

There was a silence. Macdonald sat, hands clasped, saying nothing. Kelso continued.

"If that big bastard has any cash on him he will not be back in a few minutes. He'll be in the nearest pub and will be attempting to swallow so much alcohol that he won't be able to make a decent shot next Tuesday week never mind tomorrow morning." He pulled the Glock from his waistband, released the safety catch and pulled the slide to its rearmost position then releasing it to chamber a round. He spoke to Sim.

"You stay here and look after these three. MacDuff, you come with me! Sim, lock the door after us."

Chapter Twenty-nine

London Prices

Cavendish looked at the card advertising the prices to be charged if any miniature bottle of alcohol were to be removed from within the mini-bar for consumption in his hotel room.

"Dear God in heaven! These are London prices!" He opened the fridge door to see a tidy array of miniature whiskies, vodkas, gins and brandies. "Sweet Jesus!" He rubbed his chin thoughtfully and reflected upon his new, self-appointed role as an investigator and reflected on the expected behaviour of the frontline agent he'd decided to become. "Needs must!" He removed two miniature bottles of rum and poured them into the glass he'd removed from the bathroom so as to avoid drinking from the clear plastic glasses provided by the four star hotel and returned to the fridge to remove two packets of cheese-flavoured biscuits.

The Glasgow Central Hotel in which Cavendish was resident forms the front of the Glasgow Central railway station on the city's Gordon Street, directly adjoining the station concourse. It was one of Glasgow's most prestigious hotels in its heyday, hosting residents as famous as Frank Sinatra, Winston Churchill and on one celebrated occasion, Roy Rogers in company with his horse, Trigger which proceeded promptly to defecate gloriously and liberally in the hotel lobby. In more modern days it had attempted to recover some of its past glory and had been awarded four star status.

Cavendish sat on the edge of his bed reading the brief history of the hotel which accompanied the price list for the contents of the mini-bar. His phone rang. He answered.

"Cavendish!"

"Dear boy! Jonathon Pennington. Are you well?"

Cavendish attempted to minimise his fluster and tried to accelerate the swallowing of the over-generous mouthful of dry biscuit he'd attempted as a first *repas*.

"Brigadier!" He took a moment to ensure that he'd completed a satisfactory proportion of his mastication to permit an intelligible reply and continued, still chewing a mouthful of dry biscuit. "Sho good to heee faum oo!"

If Pennington was aware of Cavendish's fine dining, he didn't comment.

"Sorry to trouble you, old boy but I thought you might like to hear of a ruse our chaps have come up with in respect of our 'Third Direction' activity as is currently being made flesh in Scotland by your Mister Kelso."

"Certainly, Brigadier. I'm giving it my complete attention and would welcome any guidance you might care to offer." He continued chewing the remnants of his cheese biscuits and sipped half-heartedly at his rum in an attempt to cleanse his palate, deciding mid-sip not to intoxicate himself any further lest he disturb his confident assessment of Sir Jonathon viewing him as a thorough professional.

"Excellent! Your little initiative with that newsreader has gone down very well here. The media is fully engaged. More of the same I say!"

"Well, thank you, Sir Jonathon. I fully intend that that be the case!"

"We've had a signal from our friends in Homeland Security that there's an outside chance that a yacht, a trimaran called *The Butcher's Apron* will berth later tomorrow in Stranraer in the south of Scotland. We've now identified one of the crew as thirty-two year old Murdo Monteith, a member of *Seed of the Gaels*. It's possible although unlikely that the yacht contains some weaponry bound for paramilitary use in Scotland. Down here we wondered if your Mr. Kelso might take an interest. Some intervention leading to these suppositions being taken up by the media would aid the cause."

Cavendish had been attempting to make ink flow from a hotel pen and had had to multi-task in the initial phase of Pennington's comments as he scribbled frustratedly while trying to remember then write the key points. He attempted a summary.

"So...use Kelso, engage with a yacht called *The Butcher's Apron* tomorrow...in Stranraer...guy called Murdoch Monteith..."

"Murdo."

"Murdo Monteith...possible arms cache on board... but unlikely...*Seed of the Gaels*." He reviewed his scribbled notes. "Okay, got it. I'll get in touch with Kelso directly."

"Good chap. I'll be in touch."

Cavendish ended the call, finished his large glass of rum in two long gulps and moved to the mini-bar where his options had reduced to whisky, vodka or brandy. He removed two brandies and emptied them as one into his glass. Sitting on the edge of his bed he gave thought to his next move. *I'll phone Kelso once I've thought this through…but I'd better head down to Stranraer myself tomorrow morning to make sure everything goes well.*

A thought occurred. He moved to his jacket and removed the card and receipt he'd taken from the flat in Hughenden Road. *Thought so…the receipt's from a grocery shop in Ballantrae. That's probably the nearest civilised plot of earth up the coast from Stranraer.*

Interesting!

Chapter Thirty

In Flagrante Delicto

It was late evening but the lights in the Scottish Parliament still burned.

Mirren Maugham was deep in conversation with the Scottish Cabinet Secretary for Justice.

"Not looking good. But I believe it's survivable."

"Perhaps. But there are photographs...some years old I'll grant you but the media would make great play of the fact that she was barely nineteen...barely legal. And here we have an MSP...one of our own...caught *in flagrante delicto!*"

Treasure was more sanguine.

"That translates from the Latin as '*in blazing offence*', Minister. The photographs are ambiguous and certainly do not meet the standard of '*in blazing offence*'.

"Perhaps...have we received a complaint? Is the media aware?"

"No complaints and the media are unaware as far as I'm aware but once they get a sniff they'll be on to opposition parties to manufacture outrage."

"Quite!" He looked again at the four photographs of a thirty-something man and an obviously much younger woman in a state of *dishabille* each smiling at a camera lens. The date stamp on the photographs showed them as having been taken four years previously. "Mike was single then, eh?"

"Divorced a year."

"Did the relationship between these two last?"

"A few months, during which they took a holiday on the Costa Something. These shots were taken there. She looks young but I gather she was nineteen at the time."

He placed the photographs squarely on the desk before him.

"We're going to have to take our lumps." He thought for a moment. "Mirren, you get on well with Mike. How about you explain that it makes sense for him to answer to an internal investigation in the present absence of complaints? We don't want him going off at half-cock. The purpose of the enquiry will be to establish whether there was anything illegal, anything improper or anything that brings the party into disrepute. If we take the initiative we head off the worst of press comment. They'll doubtless interview the young lady and manufacture a lascivious story whether or not it was a most enjoyable holiday with the nicest man she'd ever met. Can we keep this quiet until we get our ducks in order?"

"I'll see to it."

Treasure collected the photographs and returned to an office only four doors away. Closing and locking the door, she laid out the papers and photographs on a table near her desk and taking a blank piece of A4 paper, wrote the word '*livid*' in ink in the centre of the page. A smart phone captured the images and with a few words identifying the individuals and their newsworthiness, Maugham pushed a virtual button which sent them to the screen of MI5 Analyst, Harold Duffy. Satisfied they'd been sent and received, all trace of the transaction was instantly deleted.

* * *

Three hundred and thirty-two miles away in his office in Thames house in London, Duffy looked at his computer screen and made sense of the images. *Doesn't amount to a hill of beans but I suppose I'd better send them on to the boss with a copy to Jeremy Ogilvie. He can become quite excited by these apparent transgressions.* He looked at the image which merely contained the word '*livid*'. *How peculiar,* he thought. *Still, it'll doubtless make sense to the boss.*

In Edinburgh, a newly-flustered Mike Hudson, the List MSP for Central Scotland was contacted by *Treasure* and asked to make an early appointment to meet the SNP's Chief Whip.

* * *

An hour later in her Leith apartment as she prepared for an early bed, Mirren Maugham opened an encrypted digital missive from London; a copy email from Jeremy Ogilvie to Harold Duffy marked '*Secret*' and advising that sources had confirmed that currently unsubstantiated evidence suggested that three young members of the SNP had been involved in the attempted shooting of the BBC newsreader. It advised that Police Scotland be informed and that a meeting be convened to share information held by the security services.

A phone call she received moments later from Ogilvie to check her safe receipt of the document invited her to hold this leaked missive to herself until a formal version had been sent to Scotland's Cabinet Secretary for Justice - but to ensure that just as it is received, her media contacts also receive a copy.

Maugham read the email again and further encrypted it for later use. Tired, she pulled the duvet over her and in minutes was asleep.

Chapter Thirty-one

The Saracen's Head

Sim and Kelso walked downstairs to the Old Ship Bank pub. It was quiet and there was no sign of Bryson; the barman, John subsequently testifying in response to Kelso's enquiry that no one of his description had sought custom that evening. Nodding his acceptance of the information, Kelso gestured to Sim that they should move on. Close by at Glasgow Cross beckoned the bright internal lights of the Tollbooth Bar, Glasgow's oldest Irish Bar if the banner above the doorway was to be believed. Kelso gently shouldered the door and entered its portals, scanning the busy bar for any sign of Bryson. The occupants, a lively bunch, were all eyeing a recording of a previous evening's match featuring Celtic and were shouting imprecations at a referee who had denied what they obviously viewed as a stonewall penalty. The crowded bar required his greater inspection and he slowly made his way through the throng apologising with a quiet insincerity as he went. Finding no one, he returned to Sim who had been guarding the doorway lest Bryson had managed to elude him. The Whistling Kirk was next visited but again there was no evidence of his quarry. His frustration mounting, Kelso snapped his fingers as a realisation dawned on him.

"It's the fuckin' Sarry Heid." He slapped the palm of his hand against his forehead in a comic gesture of cartoon astonishment. "The Saracen's Head Bar! Of course! He took me there a few years back. It was full of flat caps with wee drunk men walkin' about inside them. It's only a few hundred yards round the corner. Let's go!"

They walked briskly up the Gallowgate towards the pub, Kelso recounting Bryson's tales of the pub they were about to visit.

"The pub's got the skull of the last witch to be executed in Scotland. They've got it in a glass case on the wall, for fuck's sake! From memory, a sign on one of their pillars says, 'No Dancing on the Bar'."

"Sounds like a nice drinking environment, eh?"

"Well, it's been serving bevy for two hundred and fifty years. They've learned something about the trade in that time. Last time we were there we sat round a blazing coal fire all night. Good pub. Let's see if he's gone back."

* * *

In October 1773, Dr Samuel Johnstone and Mr. James Boswell returned to Glasgow from their tour of the Hebrides and stayed at the Saracen's Head Inn. Robert Burns took rooms there. Celebrated philosopher and economist, Adam Smith, the author of the economist's bible, 'An *Enquiry into the Nature and Causes of the Wealth of Nations',* drank there and poets William Wordsworth and Samuel Coleridge also took refreshments under its roof.

Alas, over the years the facility had begun to enjoy less celebrity and had become more of a community pub, it's dark brown, wooden slated seats and stripped down interior offering a functional and not particularly comfortable amenity; it's high ceiling afforded more wall space for tributes to Celtic players and in an exceptional nod to modernity, small televisions on which to watch their efforts were also to be found. Consumption had changed from mature malts and elegant cognacs to cheaper wines, then fortified wines and local lagers. It was to this hostelry that Kelso and Sim advanced.

***

Both men instinctively felt their rear waistband to ensure their handgun was secured. Bryson's reputation as an aristocrat in unarmed combat was well known to both and a pistol butt might assist if a confrontation ensued. Even at two on one, each man knew the odds would be against them coming out on top. Gunplay, or the threat of it, might be necessary even at the risk of alarming the lieges sufficient to have the police notified.

Exchanging wary glances, they entered the pub, pushing its narrow swing doors inwards allowing them to step inside only one at a time. It was busy enough but there was no need to search for Bryson as was necessary in the Tollbooth as at the far end of the bar, a tall man towered above other topers. He held aloft a glass of whisky in his right hand and, eyes closed, was singing loudly;

"Take these chains from my heart and set me freeeee,
You've gone cold and no longer care for meeeee"

"Here goes nothin'," whispered Kelso.

Both men slowly approached. Kelso started smiling and clapping along. He joined in loudly, capturing Bryson's attention.

"All my faith in you is gone but the heartaches linger onnnn"

Bryson's smile widened as he beckoned Kelso towards him, embracing him as they closed. Together they completed the verse, eyes closed, faces contorted in shared musical torment.

"Take these chains from my heart and set me freeeee!"

They hugged and laughed in recollection of the many sing-songs they'd shared in bars all over the world. Kelso continued as if the years were undimmed.

"Tam, get a round in. Whisky for me and Jackie-boy. A gentleman's measure for the both of us. Whatever you're havin' yersel'." He placed his hand on Bryson's neck and squeezed it affectionately.

"Your singing hasn'y improved, big chap! You're still the worst singer in every pub you've sung in!"

Bryson smiled goofily. "I was just gettin' a wee snifter before tomorrow, Kelso. I've been out checkin' the lie of the land so to speak!"

Kelso was experienced and practical enough to realise the need for an amendment to his plans were he to exhort Bryson to take the shot the following morning. Bryson was drunk but he'd seen him consume oceans of booze on many occasions then appear on the following morning and carry out his duties as if he'd been sleeping soundly after drinking nothing but hot chocolate the night before.

"We'll share a wee glass or two…" He held Bryson's gaze. "But then it's up the road, eh?"

Bryson's smile broadened and he poured the remnants of his whisky down his throat."

"Fuckin' right, Kelso!" He turned to Sim. "Get them in, Tam!"

Chapter Thirty-two

The Orange Walk

Cavendish rose early and breakfasted on a full Scottish Breakfast as detailed on the menu calculating that the greatest proportion of its contents would make their way almost instantly to his left ventricle. Rebuking himself for not asking for the much healthier porridge that was on offer he reviewed his tasks that day. First, he really must contact Kelso and instruct him to meet *'The Butcher's Apron'* as it docked in Stranraer. He removed from his pocket the items he'd picked up from the flat and consulted his iPhone where he pulled up Google Maps and dialled in Ballantrae. *Too much of a coincidence,* he told himself as the screen showed the close proximity of Ballantrae to Stranraer.

Perhaps if I hired a car, he thought. *I could be down there later today just to check that Kelso has fulfilled the task as required. I'll show him who's a 'desk-jockey' and incapable of front-line action!* His natural caution overtook him. *But first, perhaps I'll give this more thought in my room. I don't need to check out until eleven.*

***

Hundreds of members of eleven Orange Lodges had congregated early in Glasgow's George Square, their members resplendent in their traditional bowler hats, dark suits, orange V-shaped collarettes and white gloves. Some several scores of drummers, accordionists and flautists practised their repertoire before being called to order. Most Lodges held aloft banners proclaiming the name and number of their Lodge. Union Flags and the Ulster Banner flew proudly as the match formed prior to proceeding to Glasgow Green down Saltmarket where they proposed to swear further allegiance to the United Kingdom, Queen Elizabeth, her heirs and successors and commemorate the Siege of Derry back in 1689.

Police officers lining the perimeter of the square were looked on askance by some members as a consequence of their oath being to 'uphold fundamental human rights in Scotland and accord equal respect to all people, according to law' rather than pledging allegiance to the Crown.

"Fucking Fascist Papist bastards," volunteered one marcher to his friend.

A young constable overhearing the insult looked on stony-faced and dismissed the insult. More difficulties lay ahead. No point engaging too early.

Billy Cummings stood beneath the Cenotaph in Glasgow's George Square with forty-four of his fellow Orangemen from Govan and with some effort, fastened the neck harness of his large Lambeg drum and lifted it before him, obscuring the view of everything in front of him and much above him.

In concert with the bagpipe, the drum is one of the loudest acoustic instruments in the world, reaching over one hundred and twenty decibels. The shell of Billy's drum, handed down by generations of his family, was made of oak, its skin of stretched goatskin, pulled tighter than other drums to produce a bright and hard tone.

Billy struck forcibly the drum six times with his Malacca canes, producing a thundering pulse that echoed *fortissimo* against the walls of the nearby city chambers and had others in the flute band cheering.

"Not long now, boys. Flutes at the ready!"

* * *

In the tenemental property in Glasgow's Saltmarket occupied by Kelso and the others, only Bonnie and Kelso had awakened. The rest slumbered on the sofas and armchairs on which they'd been directed the previous evening. Bryson snored loudly in a small bedroom he'd shared with Kelso next to the tiny bathroom.

In the kitchen wearing disposable latex gloves to protect her skin, Bonnie cleaned the coffee cups from the night before and had set the kettle to boil in anticipation of further cups being sought.

"Don't you think this has gone far enough, Mr Kelso?" asked Bonnie. "You've been dragging the three of us around town, you've obviously got plans for further mischief and I can't for the life of me understand why you want three students in tow. Isn't it…"

"For God's sake be quiet woman," said Kelso irritably. "I have no need to explain why you're needed as part of my little 'mischief' as you call it. All you need to know is that no blood will be spilled but that I'm quite prepared to use violence to keep you three quiet and in line. Now be a good little housewife and get some coffee going or you'll get the back of my hand. I'm going to wake people up. It's 'go' time."

From the darkened hallway a voice growled at him.

"Kelso, I can just about cope with you when I'm blind drunk! You're decent fun in the pub but as soon as you have to deal with civilised people sober you become a complete arsehole!"

He shouldered himself off the wall and entered the kitchen, continuing his snarl.

"That's no way to talk to a young lady!"

Kelso intuitively stepped backwards and prepared himself for a strike that wasn't forthcoming although Bryson's criticism was.

"You always tried to make out you were a hard man but you and me both know that you couldn'y punch your way out of a wet paper bag. Here's you threatening to slap a young woman. Fuckin' behave yourself!" He turned to Bonnie. "Sorry about him, hen. You shouldn'y have to hear a conversation like that."

Kelso decided that rapprochement was a better bet than confrontation and produced a smile.

"Christ, who got out of the bed on the wrong side this morning, eh?"

"Just as well I did, or this young lady might have been assaulted."

"Aw, c'mon Jackie-boy. It just takes me a wee while to come to in the morning. I need a coffee before I'm sociable."

Bryson was in no mood to accommodate him. "I'd be surprised if there was enough coffee in Brazil."

Listening to their exchange, Bonnie had continued making coffee and directed her question to Bryson. "Milk? Sugar?"

"As it comes, thanks."

"And yourself, Mr Kelso?"

"Just straight, Dear!"

Taking the cup with the sarcastic hint of a courteous bow, he turned and entered the living room, all of whose residents had already been awakened by the argument in the kitchen.

"Open the curtains," he ordered MacDuff.

Light filled the room as its occupants rubbed their eyes and accommodated the heightened lambency. Bonny followed on carrying a tray of cups containing coffee and busied herself in customising them as requested. As everyone sipped silently, Kelso considered the view out of the window, beckoning Sim and MacDuff to his side. Placing his cup on a side table, he pulled the curtains further to permit a wider view of the road.

"Once these bands start coming down Saltmarket, there'll be one hell of a racket. These tenement buildings on both sides are high, the road's quite narrow and these boys kick up a shit storm. However, we don't have the liberty of hanging around to take the perfect shot. If we're to get out of the close-mouth and into the van, we need to shoot as the first boys turn past the Tolbooth at the top of the road. They'll run everywhere except towards us."

Bryson insinuated himself into the conversation.

"There'll be no shot today!"

Kelso's brows furrowed. "Eh?"

"Any shot...*any* shot at this trajectory would certainly ricochet and once a bullet hits the hard surface of the road or the wall, there's no saying where it'd end up. Someone is bound to be hit. You promised no blood would be shed. Take a shot from this window and blood *would* be shed."

Kelso stepped back and retrieved the pistol from his waistband. Taking a further long step backwards, he held the gun before him, folding it into both hands and spread his legs to balance himself, adopting the conventional position when about to shoot a handgun.

"Oh, you'll take the shot alright, Bryson. You were brought here to take a few shots and someone in that Orange Walk this morning is about to get the fright of their life."

Bryson looked at him steadily, apparently untroubled. "Nah. I've made my mind up!"

"Really? What about me shooting you? What about you taking my money? What about your daughter? Want to see her jailed on a trumped-up charge in a cage in Dubai?"

Bryson shook his head not in disagreement but wearily.

"You've never been good at reading people, have you Kelso? You and I both know you won't shoot me. You and I know that once I've made my mind up I won't change it. You and I know the money you refer to has already been transferred to my account and you and I know that just by threatening my daughter however insincerely, you've ended any relationship you thought you had with me."

"If that's the case why don't I shoot you here and now and just fuck off never to be found again. Spend my life in the Seychelles?"

Bryson crouched slightly and moved one foot backwards to offer his body propulsion should he need it.

"I'm fucking warning you, Bryson, I'll pull this trigger!"

As the stand-off escalated and neared a conclusion, Bonnie, standing behind Kelso, cursed the fact that she'd dressed the previous morning in a tight woollen skirt she'd anticipated wearing to a cheese and wine party. In one smooth movement, she stepped sideways, hitched her skirt an inch to provide a greater measure of freedom and athletically swung her right leg its full measure until her instep met fore-square and with great ferocity with Kelso's testicles. Priding himself on being among the toughest of men, Kelso was nevertheless reduced instantly to astonished and crumpled disability, folding from the waist like a wet towel and allowing Bryson to step forward and remove the pistol from his grasp, throwing it towards Macdonald. His left hand held the tortured face of his adversary at the chin and pulled it upwards, positioning it slightly to the one side where it met with a ferocious blow from Bryson's right fist. Kelso was rendered unconscious instantly.

Satisfied that his adversary no longer posed a threat, Bryson retrieved the gun from Macdonald who'd collected it with some small measure of apprehension and faced Sim and MacDuff.

"Your shout, boys. If you've a problem with me taking out Kelso, tell me now or forever hold your peace."

Both MacDuff and Sim, each seated deep in the upholstery, raised their hands from their laps and positioned the palms to face the ceiling indicating that they intended no contrary notion.

Macdonald's astonished face contorted into a silent question as he caught Bonnie's gaze, inviting an explanation of her assault on Kelso.

She smiled. "Right-winger for Glasgow University's Woman's Football Team. If I'd been wearing shorts I'd have crossed his bollocks to the far post!"

Bryson stood over Kelso and checked him roughly for any other weaponry. Grimacing in a fashion that evoked, *'I just knew it,'* he removed a small-bore Beretta M 92 FS pistol from Kelso's right ankle and a sharp *sgian dubh* stabbing dagger from a small scabbard attached to his left calf. Continuing his search within the pockets of Kelso's grubby combat jacket, he removed his wallet, car keys and three phones and began to check his upper body when one of the phones rang.

* * *

Billy Cummings was a proud man. Before him, a man expert in baton-twirling or 'throwing the stick' as others might have it, went through his gyrations sending the weighted mace high into the sky and catching it perfectly as it fell from heaven before repeating the procedure - this time to even greater heights. But other than the stick man, no other stood beyond. To all intents and purposes, Billy Cummings, master butcher, captain of the golf club, Secretary of the local Chamber of Commerce, was Leader of Govan and District Orange Lodge Flute Band, the office that gave him most satisfaction in life.

As the band was waved off from George Square, no man was more proud. Cummings thumped his Lambeg drum with increased vigour and an ace too quickly requiring that the flautists join in playing a slightly more *allegro* version of *'The Protestant Boys'* than the one rehearsed.

* * *

Bryson considered the three mobile phones in front of him and decided immediately that the two modern, clean and up-market phones were those Kelso had confiscated from the students. He stared at Kelso's ringing phone in puzzlement. Never overly concerned about the appearance of his appliance, Kelso had allowed grime and scratches almost to obscure the surface requiring Bryson to make best use of his twenty/twenty vision to read the name of the caller. He had to read it twice to ensure that he'd understood it as it actually read. It said, *'Cunt'*.

Confused, he pushed the accept button and placed the phone to his ear, standing as he did so. Calculating that his and Kelso's dialect were the same, he answered, keeping his utterance brief.

"Yeah?"

"Cavendish here, Kelso. Just calling to ensure that you're still alive and that you've evaded the forces of law and order after last night's shooting."

"Yeah."

"All good. Still in Glasgow?"

"Yeah."

"Excellent! Now listen here old chap. I've been informed that there's a boat docking today down in

Stranraer. It's called *'The Butcher's Apron'*. Bit of a flying machine. It's funded by a wealthy Scots/American chap called Buchanan and there's a possibility that it might be carrying arms. We've not troubled the authorities with this information as it seemed to us that you might pay a visit and cause some commotion. If there *are* arms on board and a few shells start to fly it'd make headline news. Think you might swan down there and deploy your usual skills?"

Bryson eyed the others in the room, each of whom were staring at him intently.

"Sure."

"Now there's some likelihood that the crewman on board who's responsible for any arms smuggling is a Scotsman. One Murdo Monteith, a thirty-something member of *Seed of the Gaels*. Identify him and involve him in an incident and we have our headlines."

Bryson didn't respond as his mind raced.

"Kelso! You still there?"

A further silence ensued before Bryson found the wherewithal to reply.

"Yeah!"

"Super. One final thing." He hesitated and swallowed hard, anticipating Kelso's wrath. "Circumstances find me in Glasgow myself so I may wander down to Stranraer myself later on. Watch from a distance. That kind of thing."

Bryson, his mind still trying to absorb what he'd just been told, had no objection.

"Sure."

Relief and delight fought for supremacy as Cavendish ended the conversation. *Well, my new-found military assertiveness seems to have worked a trick with our Mr.*

Kelso. Perhaps now that our relationship is on a more proper footing, the Brigadier might not be quite so disdainful about me being a desk-jockey as he terms it.

* * *

In the Saltmarket tenement, the thud of Billy Cumming's Lambeg drum could be heard reverberating down Glasgow's High Street as the Orange Walk approached the Tolbooth. The piercing tones of the score of flautists also grew louder although at this distance, the tune they were playing wasn't identifiable. Soon they'd be visible at the top of the street. Traffic had been stopped and a crowd of followers lined the streets awaiting the spectacle.

Bryson took in the room. Three students. Two old soldiers from his days in Desert Storm back in 1990. One unconscious comrade-in-arms from the Special Air Squadron and an Orange Walk approaching. Three thoughts dominated his thinking. Should he fulfil his contract with Kelso and fire on the approaching marchers? One shot might have Scotland in flames. How might he place his daughter in a place of safety in Dubai…and how might he protect his young fellow-adopted brother, young Murdo Monteith; the man he'd not seen for twenty years and the man he'd just been told was about to disembark from *The Butcher's Apron*?

He made decisions.
"Sim, MacDuff, into the kitchen. I need a word."
He looked at the three students who sat silently together on the settee.

"Don't know what to make of you lot but *you*?" He looked at Bonnie. "What you did took courage. Thanks!" He bit his lower lip in thought. "What's your name?"

"Bonnie. Bonnie Gabriel."

"Okay, Bonnie. Sit here a minute with your pals while I deal with this pair next door."

He collected all of the items he'd taken from the still unconscious Kelso and handed the small-bore pistol to Bonnie. "We need to trust one another, Bonnie. If this eejit wakes up while I'm next door, shout me. If he makes even the slightest move before I get here, shoot him in the leg. It's only a peashooter but it'll slow him down a bit."

Bonnie accepted the small pistol, her mouth agape. Macdonald and Singh exchanged a glance which implied complete disbelief in what they were observing. All three sat motionless and silent as Bryson left the room and entered the kitchen.

Sim and MacDuff each leaned their bulk against the kitchen worktop as Bryson entered and took command.

"You guys carrying?"

Sim slowly produced the handgun he'd kept in his waistband and offered it butt first to Bryson who accepted it before emptying the chamber and placing the bullets in his pocket. MacDuff stooped and removed a *sgian dubh* from his right boot.

"That it? Do I need to search?"

Both men shook their head. Bryson returned the empty pistol to Sim.

"What's the deal you have with Kelso?"

The men eyed one another before Sim spoke.

"We do bits and pieces for him. Low-level. We never know the big picture. We just take care of jobs. Some break-ins, occasional threats, surveillance work. He pays well. Government stuff they don't want their prints on."

"How much are you being paid for this?"

MacDuff spoke first. "I'm being paid a thousand a week to infiltrate *Seed of the Gaels*.

Sim couldn't help his outburst. "Fuck off! I'm only getting six hundred a week to shepherd these students towards your fucking drinking sessions."

Bryson allowed both his irritation and puzzlement to surface. "Speak to your union representative, boys. Why the fuck has he picked on these three next door?"

Sim sighed loudly. "Kelso wanted their fingerprints all over the flat in the West End and here. He wanted clues left so that they'd be implicated in both shootings. He figured that them being around when you were taking a pot-shot at the BBC Newsreader and an Orange Walk would make it look like it not only *Seed of the Gaels* but also mainline SNP members were taking up arms. He reckoned that it'd set back the cause of Scottish Independence - which it's pretty obvious was what he'd been asked to accomplish by whoever's paying him."

"Bet he's getting more than six hundred a week," grumped Sim.

"You think?" retorted Bryson sarcastically. "And tell me, why does he need me to do his bidding here? He could take a couple of pot-shots at an Orange Lodge without the need to make use of a sniper?"

A silence lingered as both men looked uncomfortably at the ground.

"Am I considered disposable? Eh, Simmy? Am I the drunk, depressed down-and-out who was to be found dead or compromised with an unexpectedly large bank-account?"

"Don't know the answer to that one, Jack," replied MacDuff reluctantly.

"I wonder if *I* know the answer, boys?" he offered rhetorically.

He considered them both evenly. "Look guys. We fought together in Iraq. I know that Kelso was there with us before he and I left for the SAS but I need to trust you. Kelso has put my family in peril to try to make sure I was involved. I need to make sure my daughter is unharmed. You both know that in our code, blood comes before money. I expect you both to honour that. I also expect you to understand that Kelso has forfeited any allegiance he might have thought he'd receive from me." He paused for thought. "So here's what we're going to do. I'm going to take these three students from here. They can help me before I set them on their way. Now we have to figure that they'll want to visit the cops to protest their innocence before they're fingered. But it still gives us some time. I'm taking Kelso with me once he comes round so he can have my daughter released. He's an evil, twisted bastard and whatever happens he won't prosper. You two? You decide if you want to be associated with him if he survives our encounter. I'm going to lock you in when I leave. You'll soon force the front door but take it leisurely before you do. Clean the place and make sure there are no prints. All surfaces wiped."

He placed Sim's handgun he'd been holding in his waistband as he brought the engagement to a close.

"Now you guys have decisions to make. Play it the way I've laid it out and we'll never meet again. Play it any other way and if it results in my family being harmed as a result I'll hunt you down and beat you before ending you. You both know I'm a man of my word in these matters." He allowed a silence until each man held eye contact with him. "Are we clear?" He waited while two nods indicated acceptance.

"When these three go to the cops, you'll be implicated and identified. I'd take steps to become invisible. You know how to do this."

Again two nods in unison.

"But before you disappear, Simmy. Drop your knife with that fellah's prints on it in the bin. I don't want them involved in any of this."

"It's okay, Jack. He thinks I'm a cop who can fit him up and…obviously, I'm not!"

Bryson nodded his acceptance and raised his right hand to his waist palm upwards, making a fingers gesture expectantly.

"Phones!"

Each man withdrew a mobile phone from their pocket and wordlessly handed it to Bryson.

"Hey! Hello in there!" Bonnie shouted her anxiety as Kelso began to show signs of life.

Bryson stepped from the kitchen doorway and went to her side.

"Point that pistol at his leg, Bonnie. If he gets troublesome, shoot him. Aim for a bone. Any repercussions and I'll say it was me." Kneeling on Kelso's back, he lifted his left leg upwards from the knee and with his free hand removed his shoelaces. He repeated the manoeuvre on his right leg. In one swift movement he brought Kelso's arms to his front and using the laces, tied his fingers together sufficiently tightly to advance his painful resurfacing.

He turned to find Bonnie pointing the pistol at him. Slowly he raised his arm inviting her to hand him the small bore handgun.

"It's okay, Bonnie. I'm the good guy. You three and me were to be expendable dupes. So we're on the same side. I've got things to fix but shortly I'll be able to let you go and protect you into the bargain"

Bonnie looked at Macdonald and Singh as if to canvas their opinion but found just blank stares on two frightened faces. Making her own calculation, she removed her finger from the trigger and handed the small gun to Bryson.

"Thanks, Bonnie. I won't let you down."

He patted his pocket and removed the three phones he'd picked up, placing them on the floor beside those of Sim and MacDuff.

"One of these phones belongs to this eegit." He looked at the other more modern devices. "Whose are these?" Macdonald and Gabriel raised their hand. "You have a phone, Charlie?"

"Yeah."

"So where's your phone, then?"

A further search of Kelso's person revealed no other items.

"A puzzle," deduced Bryson. "I could open a phone shop with all the phones I've retrieved but yours is missing, Charlie?" He became suspicious. "Do I have to search you, son?"

Singh became excited and started turning out his pockets. "No sir!" He pointed at the unconscious Kelso. "He took all of our phones in the last apartment."

Bryson lifted a phone and invited ownership. Bonnie claimed it.

"Open it, please."

Bonnie did as she was asked.

"Dial your number, son."

Singh dialled his number and awaited a ring tone from somewhere in the flat. None came.

"Okay son. I'll hold on to all of these for the minute."

Chapter Thirty-three

The 77th Brigade

Sir Jonathon Pennington's car closed on Denison Barracks in Hermitage, Berkshire, headquarters of the 77th Brigade. Formed by David Cameron's Government in 2015, the brigade was named the 77th in tribute to the 77th Indian Infantry Brigade which was part of a guerrilla brigade led by Major General Orde Wingate in the Burma Campaign during World War Two. Presenting itself in its modern form to the public as specialising in 'non-lethal' engagement, it was created by drawing together a host of existing and developing capabilities essential to meet the challenges of modern conflict and warfare - in particular psychological warfare, hacking and pro-active offensive and defensive operations dealing with the threat of cyber-attacks, espionage and sabotage.

Pennington was ushered in to an untidy office where a further orderly saluted him and brought him to an ante-room wherein Brigadier Alastair Aitken OBE rose to greet him with a huge smile on his face.

"Brigadier Pennington!"

"Brigadier Aitken!" Pennington affected a stiff bow. "Congratulations on Her Majesty's recent award to you of Commander in the Military Division of the Most Excellent Order of the British Empire. No one else deserves it more!"

They shook hands warmly.

"It's a fucking mouthful, eh, Jon? A CBE. One of those awards the State grants which means fuck all, pays fuck all and doesn't let me tell my superiors to fuck off."

"Well, I've never known you reticent at telling *anyone* to back off, Alastair but I gather that retirement beckons and the military community celebrates your glorious career. The Black Watch will remember you well."

"They'd *better* fucking remember me. Northern Ireland, Germany, Scotland, Hong Kong and Bosnia. Now this mob!"

He ushered Pennington into a comfortable armchair and accepted a whisky from his orderly who knew from experience that any meeting that started after mid-day would be commenced by a stiff glass of *Bruichladdich*.

"You'll join me?"

"Only if you have a Speyside malt hidden somewhere. That *Bruichladdich* that you prefer is undrinkable."

"Dear Jon, you just have no appreciation of the finer malts." He turned to his orderly. "McKenzie, pour a glass of something more palatable to this fucking amateur; this whisky dullard." He lifted his glass in a toast unhindered by the absence of a glass in Pennington's hand and consumed half of its contents."

"It's great to see you, old chap. Haven't seen you since we were together in Londonderry. And look at you now. A fucking spymaster, b'God!"

"You're wearing well, Alastair but this new award by the Queen seems to have gone to your head.

I remember the days when you'd refer to the city of Londonderry as Derry. You were quite the rebel in those days."

The orderly returned with a generous glass of whisky for Pennington. "Highland Park, Brigadier?"

Aitken pretended annoyance. "Fucking Highland Park! Next time give him low-fat milk, Mackenzie! And that's a fucking direct order! This man has no soul!"

Pennington swirled the whisky in his glass before presenting it to his mouth. "In MI5 we learn to leave our souls in the cloakroom before we're seated at our desks, Alastair. I suspect it's somewhat the same here."

"S'pose," responded Aitken, lowering the tone. "I've had to come to terms with our new world, Jon. No longer does the charge of the fucking Light Brigade feature as a military option. Nowadays it's about out-thinking fucking seventeen year old Russian and Chinese geniuses who have been ordered to hack our submarine procurement programme or fuck up the fucking council elections in fucking Hammersmith!" He brightened. "But we do get to view quite a lot of porn!"

"Indeed," replied Pennington in an attempt to maintain the earlier serious mood. "And I know that unlike me, you face the challenges of modern warfare using what the world would recognise as legitimate non-military methods to influence the behaviour of opposing forces and adversaries."

"That's what it says on the tin," replied Aitken finishing his whisky and holding his empty glass outreached awaiting the attention of his orderly. "Of course, it depends what you mean by 'influence' and how you define 'adversary'."

Pennington smiled and sipped at his malt. "Ahh, those are actually a couple of the questions I'd intended putting to you today, Alistair."

Aitken grinned as his glass was replenished. Pennington continued.

"Her Majesty's Government...the very one which bestowed upon you a well-deserved CBE, understands that your focus inevitably requires to be focussed upon external adversaries but they are increasingly concerned about *internal* dissent...about the growing enthusiasm in Scotland for independence. Despite our best efforts in the media, particularly the BBC, *despite* the widespread political support down here in England for the Union and thus far, *despite* our own efforts in MI5 to temper this enthusiasm up north, support for Scottish independence is growing and it has been made clear to me that the loss of Scotland to the United Kingdom would be an unimaginable political and economic tragedy. Quite simply, I've been asked to use whatever means are at my disposal to fix this and while I have a number of potentially successful operations taking place using *inter alia,* the Third Direction, there can be little doubt that we are taking a hammering on the social media front." He took a draught of his Highland Park malt as Aitken observed him closely, their earlier bonhomie discarded. Pennington developed his theme. "Over the years, what is now referred to as the 'Yes Movement' has put down social media roots that completely dwarf anything the other Scottish political parties can emulate. There's is a genuine bottom-up movement that has tendrils that reaches all parts of Scotland, all political viewpoints, all socio-economic classes and even finds a receptive if surprising audience with some supporters of Rangers Football Club...the fucking 'Queen's Eleven'! In essence, if I might paraphrase Emperor Hirohito at the *denouement* of World War Two, 'the situation has developed not necessarily to our advantage'."

Aitken interrupted. "Well, good fucking luck to them. *Fuck* the Establishment!" He held his glass high a second time, awaiting replenishment. "*Fuck* the United Kingdom. *Fuck* Highland Park whisky!"

Pennington was somewhat taken aback. "B-b-but Alastair?"

Aitken's brows furrowed. "I mean it, Jon. Good fucking luck to them. This fucking Union is a charade. You and I both have seen it up close and it's nothing but a vehicle to keep a coterie of well-off, entitled fucking London toffs swanning about attempting to ensure that the working class, the north of England, the Scots, Cornish, Welsh and anyone in Northern Ireland who doesn't play the flute knows their place. It permits them the ability to rob them blind!"

Pennington found only his earlier words. "But Alastair?"

Aitken finished his *Bruichladdich* in one long gulp. "Ach, don't worry, Jon. I'm a Scot but have long ago understood that I take the Queen's shilling in order to do her bidding, even if it's against England's last colony, Scotland. I can now sleep at night...although I don't very often. Too many good men and women whose families I know are each day and night putting themselves in peril to support politicians who care not one fuck about them despite their weasel words when we meet death and destruction in the field of combat."

Pennington recovered something of his *savoir-faire*. "My dear Alastair. Difficult day at the office today?"

Aitken's face broke into the broad smile with which Pennington was more acquainted. "Nah! Just sounding off to an old friend. The 77th Brigade stands ready to assist you in your colonial and imperialistic ambitions."

Pennington returned the grin before sipping again at his whisky in order to mark a pause in the banter.

"We are seriously outgunned in Scotland by those whose ambition is independence. The newspapers do what they can…"

"Aye, and as Napoleon remarked, 'Four hostile newspapers are more to be feared than a thousand bayonets!'"

"Regrettably, those days are no more as well you know. The average circulation of the two most popular daily broadsheets in Scotland hover around the twenty thousand mark and decline every year. Indeed, the only intelligent broadsheet to buck the trend and see a slight rise in readership is *The National*, Scotland's only pro-Independence newspaper. However, a well-judged tweet promoting nationalism in Scotland can reach almost a million pairs of eyes. Twitter, because of its inter-activity can actually show clips of Westminster politicians making complete clods of themselves or insulting the proud Scottish nation. It's no wonder their polling figures are remorselessly upwards. If you look at the electoral popularity of the SNP over a longer period, over twenty or thirty years, the graph is frightening. One more push and they're over the line and my superiors are completely determined that this outcome should be avoided at all costs." Another sip allowed a silence which Aitken did not fill. "My request is this; what measures might your band of men and women take to halt this progress?"

Silently, the orderly slipped a third *Bruichladdich* on the small table beside Aitken.

"Well, we have several warehouses across the country full of staff who are adept at creating new organisations, false identities, false flags and who can infiltrate other bodies and create dissent, cause confusion, change dates of meetings, insult people then switch identities and demand a retraction. We've become quite adept at hacking pollster organisations and, let's say, *encouraging* the result we've been asked to secure. Our main focus is Russia. The list is endless, dear boy."

"All of these engagements would help."

"Aye, they'd help but we've already looked at the Scottish situation some months ago in anticipation of a cry for help as matters deteriorate. In my view, no matter the efforts my people put in, they are no match for an electorate which has been engaged intelligently ever since the last referendum…a referendum that saw eighty-five per cent of those eligible to vote doing so, the highest democratic vote ever recorded in the UK. The European Referendum engaged with only seventy-two per cent. Both referenda were beset with flat lies and exaggerations from the winning side. Flat lies and exaggerations that have subsequently been exposed as such." The *Bruichladdich* almost disappeared in one mouthful as Aitken warmed to his topic. "People aren't daft, Jon. We'll do your bidding and give it our best shot but our contribution will at best be meretricious, apparently attractive but having no real value."

Pennington ignored his pessimistic assessment. "Anything you can do to assist would be looked on most favourably."

Both glasses were emptied as Aitken brought matters to a conclusion.

"We've outsourced some work to an organisation we've funded called the Integrity Initiative. It's set up in a large Victorian mill-house based in the Gateside Mills up in Scotland, near Auchtermuchty. The troops there are mostly English with a number of Commonwealth boys who are fucking geniuses on a keyboard. We've a large group out in Lithuania at present supporting key people in Vilnius in infowar techniques but the really clever boyos remain. Not only do they infiltrate target organisations but they can develop detailed surveys about voters in marginal seats and merge this polling data with information from electoral rolls and commercial market research to produce a comprehensive picture that allows us to focus our efforts where they'll do most good…or harm. But what needs to be understood is that although we can confuse, distract, and ultimately discourage certain voting behaviour, to have an effect it needs to be done over the long term. That's why the Yes people are so successful and why Westminster is so fucking maladroit!" He paused. "However, I'll have them look at this with their customary assiduity and will provide you with weekly updates on progress but hope that you'll remember my counsel. Too little, too late, too fucking stupid."

They shook hands warmly.

Aitken widened his grin. "Once I'm retired you can buy me lunch in your club if you're still a member."

Pennington nodded. "I am and I'll make sure they're well stocked with your undrinkable *Bruichladdich* !"

Aitken shook his hand with increasing vigour. "Then cry Havoc and let slip the fucking dogs of war!"

Chapter Thirty-four

The Sash My Father Wore

Bryson hauled Kelso to his feet and pushed him backwards. Still dizzy after the blow to his chin and unable to step to his rear, Kelso collapsed into an armchair as Bryson had intended. Outside, the passing Orange parade, now playing '*The Sash My Father Wore*', raised the decibel level such as to force Bryson to speak to Kelso in a manner approaching a shout.

"I've had it with you, Kelso. I'm going to give you very clear instructions. If they're followed instantly and to the letter, you might live. If not I'll certainly maim you prior to dispatching you. You need to understand that." Bryson sought eye contact. "Look at me Kelso. Do you understand that?"

Kelso nodded his acceptance, his face twisted in impotent rage.

Bryson held his gaze until Kelso blinked and looked away. Turning and kneeling so he was at the same eye-level as the three students, he wrestled momentarily with what he wanted to say.

"Look guys, you've been caught up in something organised by bad people. This arsehole behind me didn't care who you were, just that you were regular members of the SNP so that the mayhem he intended could be tracked back through you to your political organisation and impact upon your party's popularity. Trust me, you'll come to no harm now…but I'm afraid I can't just release you immediately. I need your help if I'm to fix things, I can't explain everything to you but I need you to trust me. Now, you don't know me from Adam and all you've seen is some tough guys duking it out and waving guns around. You'd be less than sensible if you weren't terrified out of your wits. Sim and MacDuff will leave. You won't see them again." He directed his left thumb over his shoulder. "This bastard has placed my daughter in danger and my first order of business is to make sure she's safe. I can't take the chance that you walking the streets might involve the police before I can take care of that and some other business that's weighing on my mind now." Aware that he could command their compliance merely by producing the pistol from his waistband, he chose another route. "I'd like to ask you for your help. You're free to walk out of that door unharmed but it would help safeguard my family if you stuck with me for a short time."

As Macdonald and Singh exchanged glances, Bonnie took the initiative. "Well, the way I see it, the three of us don't know if or to what extent we're in trouble. You've saved us from three men who wished us harm so you're in the good books. So long as you don't ask me to do anything that's illegal or puts me in danger, I'm happy to throw my lot in with you." She turned to Macdonald. "What do you say, Lachie?"

Before he had a chance to respond, Singh interrupted, directing his question to Bryson.

"See if we *did* help you, sir…"

"I answer to Jack or Bryson. Your shout."

"Well, Mr. Bryson, sir…I'm Charlie by the way…do you think it might be possible for me to phone my parents and let them know that I'm okay. It's not usual for me to be out overnight and they'll probably be worried."

"No problem, Charlie but I'd like to hear your story before you talk to them to make sure you don't raise their suspicions that something's wrong."

"Oh, I'd just say I stayed at Lachie's and we were studying. They'll just assume I drank too much last night…they don't like me drinking…but they'll not worry if I tell them I'll be home…eh, *tonight*?" The raised inflection at the end of his question suggested a certain misgiving over the time-frame he'd proposed.

"Sounds fine, Charlie. Would you be okay with me listening in to the conversation?"

Singh nodded his head vigorously in assent as Bryson turned his head towards his friend.

"I'm in," said Macdonald succinctly.

* * *

A jacket placed over his bound hands disguised Kelso's enfetterment as Bryson guided him towards the mini-bus parked audaciously the night before outside the nearby, now defunct Central Police Headquarters in St Andrew's Square. In the near-distance on Glasgow Green, the sounds of the now encamped Orange Walk continued to offer a soundtrack to their departure.

"Everyone in!" Instructed Bryson. "Bonnie, you take the wheel. I'll look after Kelso."

"Sure!" Said Bonnie as she slid her frame into the driver's seat. "Where are we headed?"

Bryson hesitated. "Go south. Head in the direction of Kilmarnock. While we're travelling I'll take time to sort out my thoughts." He strapped Kelso into his seat. "How are we for gas?"

Bonnie consulted the electronic data on the dashboard. "It says eighty …maybe ninety miles in the tank if I drive like an old lady."

"Well, I need you to drive like the young lady you are. Keep up with the flow of traffic…and keep your eyes out for cops. If we're pulled over, God alone knows how this'll end up!"

"Gotcha!" Responded Bonnie as she steered the minibus into traffic and hunted for signs indicating the M77 South.

Despite the fact that he was in a vehicle directed by a man who carried a guns in his waistband, two *sgian dubhs* and a rifle behind the rear seat and had a dangerous prisoner bound in the seat next to him, Macdonald's over-arching thought was of the stunning natural beauty of the woman who was driving them to an unknown destination for an unknown purpose.

Chapter Thirty-five

Emerging Doubt

Brigadier Pennington leaned back in his office chair, put his feet atop his desk and crossed his legs. He did his best thinking this way. Having been advised not to disturb him, Miss Evans nevertheless brought him his ten o'clock cup of tea as had been her practice since the day she'd begun working with him. His reverie disturbed without rebuke he decided to invite comment from his trusted senior intelligence officer, Jeremy Ogilvie and asked that he be brought to his presence.

As he placed his now empty cup on its saucer, his office door opened and Ogilvie entered, as ever smartly dressed, tanned and even at this early hour, a five o'clock shadow dusting his jaw-line.

"Morning, boss. You wanted a chat?"

"Yessss," he hissed, attempting to convey his uncertainty. "Take a seat."

"Problems?"

"Not sure, Jeremy old chap. Just had the Home Office on the blower. Usual polite chatter but looking for assurances that we're on top of this Scottish thing. I made the point that MI5 can have no fingerprints on this escapade but that we're trying to be helpful to his people…"

"This our Commander Henry Cavendish of that ilk?"

"One and the same. Thing is, The Home Office have no track record in this stuff. They seemed rather peeved that we'd not taken more of a hands-on approach and when I countered with our Charter, they were somewhat dismissive. They insist that Ministers want to see results and have high confidence in young Cavendish due to his naval career and his vanishingly distant connection to the royal family but you and I both know that he's a bloody amateur."

"But didn't you see him up close in that Manchester operation last year?"

"Yeah…but he was one of a team, quiet as a mouse. He always took tremendous trouble to remember everyone's name and ask after their family. Complete arse-licker! He had no discernible talent beyond making the odd infelicitous comment. Just sort of hung around the place and reported back to the Home Office. And now he's leading what the Home Office clearly see as a project of some fundamental importance."

"But you have Kelso working at the sharp end?"

"Indeed, but it would appear that Cavendish lives in abject fear of him and Kelso knows it."

Ogilvie stroked his dark chin thoughtfully. "What's the present state of play?"

"Miss Evens reliably informs me via Cavendish's Secretary that he's taken himself off to Glasgow to offer hands-on support to Kelso."

"Christ! That offer of assistance will go down like a plate of cold sick!"

Pennington held Ogilvie's gaze for some seconds. "We have to step carefully, Jeremy. Over-play our hand and we're sitting before a Parliamentary Enquiry explaining why we acted against the democratic wishes of our cousins from north of the Tweed using taxes raised by them...on the other hand, if we leave this to Cavendish and the Home Office..."

"Mind you, Kelso and the people he uses have never let us down in the past."

"Accepted but he's always been under my thumb. More than once I've had to temper his enthusiasm but with Cavendish as his overseer I can see two problems, First that Kelso acts without caution, disregarding Cavendish or secondly that Cavendish decides to become James Bond."

A further silence ensued broken by Ogilvie.

"Want me to go up boss? Fix things quietly?"

Pennington shook his head. "Can't spare you from your duties on Bosnia, I'm afraid. No...I was wondering whether we might introduce *Treasure* into the front line. The girl has potential."

"Has she ever been around when guns go 'bang'?"

"No. But she's smart and cute....not in the sense of... well she's cute in both senses."

"Sound just my type. Sure you don't want me to go up and..."

"Thanks but no thanks, Jeremy," smiled Pennington knowing his friend and senior intelligence officer's reputation as a ladies' man.

Pennington started tapping his pen on his knee, a sign Ogilvie knew was a prelude to an idea.

"When Kelso was out with the Special Air Service wasn't one of his great assets an ability to manufacture

Improvised Explosive Devices that actually bloody work? And don't we have a cache of Kelso's bombs scattered over a few secret locations?"

Ogilvie caught on. "Yes. And isn't one of those hidey-holes in the military barracks near Edinburgh?

"It certainly is, my son!" said Pennington becoming excited. "If memory serves, we've secreted one or more of his devices at Glencorse Barracks near Penicuik in Midlothian." He removed his feet from his desk and sat forward. "It seems to me that the best way of dealing with this mess is to make a swift move that places the Government of Scotland, the Scottish National Party and their followers behind an outrage and between a rock and a hard place. We simply must militarise this thing. We need police in riot gear, troops manning roadblocks, stop and searches on an industrial level." He recommenced the tapping of his pen on his knee as he took time to ponder his options. "Your earlier information suggested that there might...just *might* be some arms being brought ashore illegally at Stranraer. The assessment was that it's a long shot...but what if there was an *actual* explosion. I gather that Kelso has accumulated three members of the SNP in his little entourage. If they could be placed in a compromising position with an IUD, it wouldn't matter a damn if there were any arms or ammo in this flaming boat, the print media in particular would make mincemeat of them!"

"The Beeb wouldn't be far behind them."

"Indeed so!" He shared a smile of satisfaction. "I'll make contact with Glencourse Barracks and arrange for '*Treasure*' to pay him a visit today."

Chapter Thirty-six

Whisky and Bleach

As the mini-bus drove south towards Kilmarnock, Bryson, silent until then, leaned forward and asked Bonnie to take the next off-ramp to New Farm Loch, one of the town's estates on its north-east periphery. Obeying his directions, she travelled directly until forced by an intersection to turn right, stopping at his request outside a local grocery shop.

"Lachie, could you pop in there and buy a bottle of whisky and a bottle of bleach, son?"

Macdonald shifted uncomfortably in his seat. Despite Bryson's earlier reassurances, he remained apprehensive at being in a car with men comfortable with violence.

"Sorry, eh, Jack...er, Mr Bryson...but I gave you the last of my money last night. You remember...?"

"Oh, aye, son...Eh, Charlie?"

Singh almost leapt from his seat, reaching for the buckle of his seat belt almost before his name had been mentioned.

"Sure thing, Mr. Bryson. I'll get them. Have you a particular brand of whisky in mind?"

"Anything, son. That and a bottle of bleach."

Minutes passed before Singh emerged with but one bottle in his grasp. He opened the rear door and spoke to Bryson without entering the vehicle.

"The shopkeeper says he's not allowed to sell alcohol before ten o'clock. That's another ten minutes."

"Fuck's sake!" He grimaced. "Never mind. You get the bleach?"

"I did, sir!"

"Okay, skip the booze. Jump in."

Bryson gave further directions to Bonnie who found herself driving along a 'B' Road out of the town continuing south, this time with Stranraer as her destination.

Bryson consulted the map on Kelso's mobile phone. "There's an estate ahead on the right. Signpost should say, 'Coodham'. Head for it until I can see somewhere to park."

Some few minutes later, the mini-bus entered the country estate, previously the home of a religious order, now accommodating a few very expensive properties in its extensive rural grounds, the Fathers of the Passionist Order long having settled for the generous settlement offered by a local property developer.

Bryson observed the road ahead carefully and Bonnie reduced speed to a crawl at his request.

"Over there, there's a side road. Go down until we're concealed by the trees." He turned his attention for the first time since leaving Glasgow to Kelso, still trussed and immobilised in the rear seat. He spoke to Bonnie. "Me and Kelso are going to have a quiet word. Your job is to find a way of driving onwards. According to this map this road's a dead end. Turn round and make your way back here." He looked menacingly at Kelso. "This won't take long."

Leaving the vehicle, Bryson walked round and opened the door nearest to Kelso. Leaning over, he freed him from his seatbelt, simultaneously grabbing his collar and dragging him unceremoniously from the vehicle which trundled onwards around a bend until hidden by the hedgerow.

"Jackie-boy…"

"Shut the fuck up, Kelso. You threatened my daughter and I have one solution to this. You're going to resolve the matter right here, right now and I will not give you a second chance so don't even think about trying to negotiate or outwit me. If this doesn't work with instant effect, I'm just going to shoot you and fix things some another way." He pulled him over to the verge and placing his left leg behind Kelso's, pushed him backwards lowering him to his back. Instinctively Kelso pulled his knees towards his stomach, protecting his groin as Bryson knelt on his chest, pinning him to the ground.

"One chance, Kelso. One chance! You might calculate that you could withstand a beating but I've just decided just to blind you. One eye, then if you don't comply with my instructions, both eyes. That way you can still talk but you'll wander the earth thereafter with nothing but a white stick and some memories." He took Kelso's phone from his pocket. "You're going to phone Dubai and speak to your people. You're going to tell them that your mission has been accomplished and that my daughter and her man are free to return home at any time of their choosing." He thought for a moment. "How long do they think they're staying out there?"

Eyeing the bottle of bleach Bryson had settled beside him, Kelso swallowed and croaked, "Fuck off Bryson. Drown yourself in another bottle of oblivion."

Tightening his grip, Bryson lifted the bottle of bleach and shattered its neck on a nearby rock spilling some of the contents over his right hand, a shard of glass cutting it slightly. The bleach found the wound and he winced giving an added edge to his guttural rasp.

"You were warned!"

Kelso blinked first, "Wait! Wait…." He fixed Bryson with a glare. "Three weeks. They've two weeks left."

"Have you the authority to instruct your people to catch the next plane to London?"

Kelso nodded. "They'll act on my instruction."

"They MI5? Special Branch?"

He shook his head as much as was possible with Bryson's fist balling his shirt collar. "My people. Ex-Black Watch…Iraq."

Bryson bit his lower lip in thought. "Okay. Here's what you do. You phone them right now." He thought further, his grasp on Kelso's shirt tightening as he did so.

"I've changed my mind. Let Rachael enjoy her holiday. You tell them their mission's complete and that they explain to Rachael that they've a family bereavement or something and that they have to return immediately." He tightened his grip on Kelso's shirt collar. "Do you have Rachael's mobile phone number?"

Kelso's nod was almost imperceptible. Defeated, he mumbled, "Yeah", in a whisper.

Bryson placed the bleach on the ground nearby and brandished the phone which he then held above Kelso's face.

"I'll phone her later. First you phone your people. One chance, Kelso. If I think you've deviated from what I've instructed or if I think there's something coded going on, you're a blind man. Nod your head if you understand"

Kelso attempted a nod and Bryson shook his head in disbelief.

"Ten sixty-six! What a fucking dumb password for a phone. School-kids have better protection." He entered the security code and the phone sprang to life. He pressed contacts and a short list of names emerged, including, he noticed, one named '*Cunt*'.

"Who are you phoning?"

"Guy called Simpson...Eddie Simpson"

"Make this chat sound natural!" He pushed the screen enabling the speakerphone. The phone rang several times before it was answered.

"Hi boss. Sorry' bout the delay. I was in the pisser and had something else in my hand."

Kelso glared at Bryson, holding eye contact as he began his dialogue.

"How's things?"

"Great job boss. Sitting here in the sunshine drinking cocktails. I've had worse assignments. We're getting on like a house on fire. They've no idea we're anything other than fellow competition winners."

Kelso swallowed hard. "Well, the fun's over. Our work here is done so I need you back immediately. Both of you." He changed the subject. "Marlene okay?"

"Yeah. She's best friends with Rachael now. Shoes, handbags, make-up, all the bollocks."

"Okay. Next plane out. No questions."

Bryson mouthed a silent instruction, confusing Kelso.

"Hold on a minute, Eddie." His eyebrows invited clearer instructions from Bryson who attempted a silent stage whisper. "Leave cash for their expenses over the next two weeks."

Kelso grimaced reluctant agreement.

"You got cash left?"

"Tons, Boss. You gave us enough for three weeks."

"Leave a grand in cash in an envelope at Reception. Tell them it's for your friends. Put their name and room number on it and leave."

Bryson anticipated Kelso's attempt at concluding mischief and lifted the bleach as a discouragement.

"Can't persuade you to let us stay on a bit, Boss?"

"Back to London. Now. I'll be in touch."

Bryson pushed the red button killing the call.

"You might just *see* the next blow coming your way, Kelso. Now, remind me…what's the name of the hotel they're in?"

"The *Burj al Arab*…"

"Okay." He stood, removing his knee from Kelso's chest and pulled at his shirt until he sat upright. The minibus emerged from behind the hedgerow as Bonnie approached slowly. Bryson placed the bleach on the ground and held his palm towards her, stopping the vehicle some hundred yards away.

"We're not finished yet, Kelso." He lifted the bleach. "You did some fuckin' number on me, eh? Not only was I to be expendable but so was my daughter!"

Kelso avoided his glare.

"And now my wee brother is caught up in your nonsense."

Kelso looked at him, puzzled."

"I know sweet fuck all about *that*!"

"Really? Aye? Well your bosses in London know about him and are trying to nail him today in Stranraer."

He pulled Kelso to his feet. "I'm undecided, Kelso. There's maybe one chance in ten that you'll survive today. If things work out with my brother, who knows? But trust me, if I even get annoyed about the way you fuckin' breathe, I'll just shoot you in the head so if I was you, I'd behave and hope I'm in a good mood when this ends." He threw the bottle of bleach into the hedgerow and waved Bonnie towards him. He turned back to Kelso until their foreheads touched and pushed slightly.

"Savvy?"

Chapter Thirty-seven

The Improvised Explosive Device

Close to Glencourse Barracks Mirren Maugham eased her black Ford Mondeo into a space between two cars parked at the roadway before killing the ignition. Denied the musical accompaniment that had offered a backcloth to her thoughts, the silence was broken when the rear door of her car opened and a man slid into the seat immediately behind her.

Expecting him, if not so soon after her arrival, Maugham was nevertheless mildly surprised at his entrance.

"Keep facing forward!"

Maugham complied as a hand reached over her right shoulder offering her a small plastic appliance which she accepted and inspected.

"Do not turn it on," she was instructed. "This beside me on the rear seat is a command-initiated Improvised Explosive Device and is detonated by you merely by turning on the triggering mechanism you hold in your hand and pressing the 'open' button. Two simple movements. It's actually an automatic garage door-opener and was constructed some years ago by your Mister Kelso who favours those against the more common mobile phone trigger. Apparently it's his 'signature' and he's recognised as one of the best at assembling these things. We tested it earlier and everything's in good order. He pushed a small box towards the middle of the rear seat and lifted it on to the armrest on Maugham's left where she could see it.

"It's a taped shoe-box and contains a detonator, a receiver, a little thermite, some metal fragments, some literature advancing the cause of Scottish Independence and three hundred and seventy-five grams of Semtex 1A..."

Maugham interrupted. "And just how powerful a blast does this IED provide?"

"Well a lesser charge of three hundred and forty grams brought down the Boeing 747 over Lockerbie so it's a powerful enough punch." He tapped the box. "You shouldn't have to worry about that. As it sits, it's perfectly harmless. Semtex is very stable. There's a switch at the front of the box facing the dashboard. It's currently pointing upwards at a red indicator. To explode the bomb you merely switch down to the green which arms the receiver. When you click the device you hold in your hand it becomes live. Pressing the button then sends a wireless signal that explodes the device. It's standard practice to remove yourself from the scene before pressing the button," he said sarcastically.

Maugham ignored the jibe. "Pretty straightforward!"

"I've seen them go wrong when people get anxious in a live operation. You, on the other hand can deal with this in a relaxed way."

"What's expected of me? I'm more a background girl. I've not really been exposed to front line action."

"Needs must. We have another operative in the field. Guy called John Kelso. Very experienced. I gather you have his contact details in coded form. He's being supported by a Home Office wallah called Commander Henry Cavendish. Submarine chap who has no experience in this work."

"Well, neither have I!"

"Your task is pretty simple. There's a racing sea-yacht named somewhat provocatively '*The Butcher's Apron*' docking today at Stranraer. We have some information from our American cousins that there may be arms aboard. Long shot. Normally we'd just advise the local bobbies and let them sort it out with help from the urban cops with guns and loud-hailers but headquarters reckon there's an opportunity here to have some live ammo introduced in front of the cameras so it can be pinned on the Jock Separatists. We're not sure if Kelso can pull it off so your job is pretty simple. While all eyes are on the yacht and its crew, if there's no evidence of gunplay, place this box below a car. Arm it as I've shown you, step away until you're safe and when you're ready turn on the device I gave you and press the button. If it's beneath the car and you take care, no fragments should endanger life. The car will absorb all of the high velocity shock-wave although the fuel in the car will add some detonation fuel. There's a crew member on board the yacht. A person of interest called Murdo Monteith...there's a photograph of him in here." He placed a Manila folder on top of the box and tapped it lightly. "There's also a photograph of Kelso. He'll be your ally if you need him."

The rear car door opened slightly as a prelude to departure. "In all probability Kelso will take care of business. He's very able. You'll probably end up being bored watching a yacht dock and some bullets firing into the sea causing the media to panic and file the kinds of news reports we're looking to them to file."

Maugham sensed his departure and interrupted his matter-of-fact description of her task.

"Hold on! What if there are civilians around? School-children? Suppose…?"

"Welcome to the dark world of the security forces. You can't be squeamish. Always there are casualties in our battles and sometimes these are regrettable but these can't detract us from our mission. Front line staff have to accept that. Today you're front line staff. You are expected to perform just as would any other member…"

"But I've not been trained," she protested.

"Learn on the job!" he replied before adding as he departed, "I did!"

Maugham looked in her near-side wing-mirror but could only see the rear of a black-coated man, perhaps six feet tall, walk away. In seconds he'd turned a corner and had disappeared.

I'm sitting next to an explosive charge with three hundred and seventy-five grams of Semtex, she thought. *I've been a desk officer and an analyst since I joined the service and without so much as a by-your-leave I'm to place a bomb that might injure and kill people.* She shivered at the thought, her mouth suddenly dry. *And I've never even been to Stranraer before.* Lifting the surprisingly heavy box on to the front passenger seat of the car she spent a few moments looking at it, reflecting on its lethal power. Shaking her head as if disapproving of her own decision, she turned the ignition key, powered the satellite navigation device on the car and entered 'Stranraer'.

Chapter Thirty-eight

Contacts

"Turn on the radio, eh, Bonnie?"

Bonnie complied and after folk-rock duo, Simon and Garfunkel had sung of troubled waters, the announcer introduced the news on the hour. All listened intently but the shooting incident in Glasgow's West End had dropped from the news summary. The newsreader informed her audience that the SNP Government had intimated internal proceedings against Mike Hudson, the List MSP For Central Scotland, the First Minister was that day to open a new health centre in Dumfries and Bryson sat forward in his seat as the news concluded with the story that the large racing yacht '*The Butcher's Apron*' was due to arrive in Stranraer on the high tide at around six o'clock. He consulted his watch. "We've plenty of time."

He pressed Kelso's phone, bringing it to life before thinking better of it and turning it off. *Later*, he decided. A silence descended on the travellers until he broke it.

"So you want to be a cop, Charlie?" Bryson sat in the rear of the mini bus behind Kelso as Bonnie drove towards Prestwick *en route* to Stranraer.

"I think so, sir." He hesitated. "But this has been something of an eye-opener. I'm not sure I could deal with this sort of thing every day."

"Most of the time you'd be standing in the rain with yellow and black tape behind you while paramedics deal with an alcoholic couple who've been trying to avoid killing their wean when they were trying to kill each other. Usually it's boring. Wee adventures like this aren't everyday occurrences."

"I'd hope not, sir..."

"Bryson or Jack. No one calls me sir."

"Sorry...Mr. Bryson, sir."

Bryson turned his attention to Macdonald.

"Here, Lachie. You're nearest the door. Take Charlie's money and when we turn off into Ayr, Bonnie'll stop at the first shop and you jump out and buy a bottle of whisky and a bottle of bleach."

Singh reached into his pocket to comply as Kelso stared grimly at Bryson at the prospect of more bleach.

"Charlie. Your job is to search this fellah. Every pocket. He won't object."

To encourage Kelso's cooperation he playfully waved Kelso's Glock 17 pistol at him.

Kelso eyed Singh. "You touch me, son an' ah'll fuckin' kill you!"

Singh looked at Bryson for reassurance.

"You choose, Kelso. Right knee or left knee. After I've lamed you, I'll blind you once Lachie here gets me some bleach. You're of no use to me now. I'm still working out how to deal with you." He nodded at Singh. "Go ahead, son."

Licking his lips apprehensively, Singh uncomfortably removed the contents of Kelso's pockets as he offered neither restraint nor assistance. He placed everything on the seat between them; some coins, a wallet, an old rail ticket and a coiled wire that served to charge his phone.

"Empty the wallet, son."

Singh did as requested. Bank of England notes in the sum of eight hundred and seventy pounds, two bank cards each embossed with the logo of the Post Office and a piece of paper were laid on the seat.

"Gimme the cash, son…and that piece of paper."

He shoved the notes in his pocket and consulted the fragment of paper. The single word 'Ballantrae' was revealed.

"Looks like my home address, eh Johnnie-boy?"

Kelso, attempting disdain, looked out of the window.

Singh inspected the rail ticket. "Eh, there's one more thing, sir…eh, Jack…Mr Bryson, sir."

"And what's that, Charlie?"

Singh handed him the rail ticket upon whose rear was written five words;

- *Mix*
- *Civil*
- *Livid*
- *Mild*
- *Dill*

Bryson held the card before him. "So what's this, Mister Kelso? Crossword clues?"

Kelso shrugged and shook his head. "Fuck knows!"

Bryson consulted the ticket given him by Singh. "I'll think on this! Perhaps the bleach will help your memory."

Approaching the turn off into Ayr and its racecourse, Bonnie was invited to head on until an off-licence could be found which it was…almost immediately.

"Here, Lachie. Give Charlie back his money." He pulled two of Kelso's twenties from his pocket. "I've just realised that I'm rich. Make it a single malt, eh?"

The transaction completed, Macdonald exited, returning minutes later with a bottle of Glenfiddich whisky but no bleach.

"Fuck me! First a bleach shop with no whisky and now a whisky shop with no bleach." Bryson pursed his lips and shook his head. "There's a gap in the market here, people! Nonetheless…" He inspected the bottle, "Eighteen years old! I've not tasted this in a while. Excellent, young man. You are now the official purveyor of whisky for Mister Jack Bryson!"

He smiled and looked at Kelso. "Maybe you can blind people with whisky, eh?" Kelso looked away. "You never know until you try!"

Twisting the metalled cap, he exposed the corked bottle top which he pulled and took a long draught of the whisky.

"Pure gold, people. Pure gold."

He began to replace the cork but stilled his hand. He held the bottle at shoulder level.

"Anyone?"

No one was inclined to drink and Bryson closed the bottle.

"I've a wee task to take care of. I'll be standing right outside so any tricks from buggerlugs there and I'll deal with it."

He slid back the side door on the minibus and stepping outside, closed it and inspected Kelso's phone. He manoeuvred it to the 'contacts' page and scrolled down the few names until he found the name 'Rachael Kelburn. *So that's her man's name? Kelburn? Fuckin' Kelburn?*

He took a deep breath and pushed the call button. Holding the phone to his ear he recognised the dialling tone that implied a foreign call. It rang several times until he heard a voice he hadn't heard in years.

"Rachael Kelburn!"

The easy words he'd intended saying wouldn't come. "Hello?"

A strangled cough was all Bryson could muster.

"Hi. Rachael here!"

Further moments passed making a terminated call likely.

Bryson turned his back on the vehicle to conceal his emotional state.

"Rachael...."

"Hello. Who's calling?"

A deep breath and Bryson was off.

"Rachael. It's dad. It's your father."

A silence ensued as each tried to make sense of the conversation.

Eventually, Bryson repeated, "Rachael. It's your dad."

"Dad?"

Bryson's emotions forbade a response. He gathered himself.

"Darling...I've no right to drop in to your life like this but please stay with me while I say what I need to say..."

"Dad...are you drunk?"

"No Rachael. I'm as sober as a judge. Listen...." He tried to find a new seriousness in his voice. "I know you're in Dubai. I know you won a competition. Listen to me and don't interrupt. Are you alone right now?"

"…Balcony. Peter…he's my husband…he's inside."

"Look I know. Peter Kelburn. Your husband. Look, Rachael. The two friends you've spent time with…Eddie and Marlene…have they gone?"

The puzzlement was evident in Rachael's voice. "B..b..but how did you know…?"

"Have they gone?"

"Why, yes. They left suddenly because Marlene's mum had a stroke. They're flying out immediately. Left about an hour ago."

"Listen to me and don't…please don't react badly. You and Peter are in danger. I know you've a wonderful holiday organised. I know the standard of the hotel you're in but you must leave. Pack your clothes, don't sign out. At Reception ask for an envelope in your name. It'll contain a thousand pounds. That'll pay for new flight costs. Just leave. Have Peter take your cases outside. The deal you have is that everything has been paid for. Get a taxi and head straight for the airport."

"Dad…I don't hear from you in ten years then out of the blue you phone with this cock and bull story…"

Bryson angered. "Rachael! You know the work I used to do, eh?"

"I'm not…"

"Listen. I was in the Special Air Service. I did murderous things all over the world in the name of the British Government. I don't kid about things like this. Now I think that your two pals leaving Dubai reduces the threat to you both but a phone call could change everything so get yourself out of Dubai unless you want to spend some time in a Emirates jail."

"Why on earth…"

"Rachael...I promise I'll explain everything but right now I need you to leave." He thought further. "Can I speak with Peter?"

"You don't see me for a decade and now you want your first conversation with your son-in-law to be this nonsense?"

"Somehow I need to convey the seriousness of this. Perhaps Peter will appreciate I'm not messing about and that if he wants to protect his wife, he'd better do as I say!"

"D'you know what I think, Dad? I think you're drunk again." Her voice croaked with emotion. "I want to love you, Dad but you make it so difficult. Speak to me when you're sober?"

The line went dead.

Bryson's head drooped as slowly he lowered the phone from his ear and placed it in his pocket. Angered, he turned around and opened the sliding door of the vehicle.

"Kelso! You're going to regret ever crossing me and my family. He withdrew the Glock 17 pistol from his waistband and cocked it, for the first time noticing fear in the eyes of his adversary. Macdonald acted as intermediary, placing his hand lightly on Bryson's arm.

"He's no threat and we're here at least in part because you promised no gunplay."

Bryson's gaze remained locked on Kelso for some moments but his mood tempered and he replaced the gun before consulting his watch.

"There's still time. Bonnie, we're all going for a coffee at my place. Head towards Ballantrae. I need to collect my passport. I've a long flight ahead of me."

Chapter Thirty-nine

Shipping Lanes

Brigadier Pennington skipped up a few steps and took shelter beneath the Doric portico of the entrance to his London club, the Athenaeum relieved to escape the unexpectedly heavy rain which had descended on central London. He stopped at Reception to mention the name of his guest asking if upon arrival he could be shown to the Smoking Room for drinks prior to lunch. Lifting a copy of the Times, he consulted its front page as he walked slowly up the wide, central Egyptian staircase and took a seat in distressed leather armchair awaiting his old friend Admiral Coby Eisenberg; for some years, a senior figure in America's CIA.

A large Glenmorangie, its ice tinkling in the glass was brought to him by an attentive member of the waiting staff well aware of Pennington's predilections in matters whisky. It had hardly been touched due to Pennington's forensic examination of the day's news when Eisenberg appeared.

Pennington stood, folding the newspaper and greeted his guest.

"Coby, you old bastard! How the devil are you? It must be a year since last we spoke."

Wreathed in smiles, the tall Texan Eisenberg shook his hand warmly covering their clenched hands with his free hand, creating a cocoon he intended might convey a deeper level of affection.

"Great to see you, Jonathon. I bring best regards from our mutual friends in the Agency. Peter Dalton asked especially to have his best wishes passed on."

The waiter reappeared and was sent back to the bar with a request that he return with a large Jack Daniels Silver Select Tennessee Whiskey on the rocks; its characteristic and significantly higher alcohol by volume strength suiting both Eisenberg's palate and appetite. They sat.

"Your staff here tell me that I'm not allowed to smoke in the Smoking Room. That right, Jonathon?"

"Alas, no, Coby. But fortunately we can still dine in the Dining Room. I've booked us a table at one so we've time for a drink and a chat. It's also quieter in here before lunch. We can talk without interruption. You proposed we get together but Miss Evans was unable to guide me as to the nature of your enquiry."

Eisenberg raised his glass in a silent toast to his friend and sipped appreciatively at its contents.

"Jonathon, you and me both know that America's multi-faceted alliance with the United Kingdom spans two centuries. Together we have worked to prevent conflict and respond to disasters around the world. The US needs a strong ally which maintains its military, intelligence and cyber defence capacities."

"Sounds like I'm in for a lecture!"

"Not at all my old friend. We hold your efforts in the highest regard. You know that."

Pennington smiled. "Then perhaps you'd like to offer Her Majesty's Government some friendly advice?"

"Thought perhaps we'd run through a short history lesson. Call it 'Nuclear Arsenal 101'."

"Very well."

Both men sipped at their drinks, each now aware of the weight of their words.

"Back in 1963, our President Kennedy and subsequently that scoundrel President Lincoln Baines Johnson negotiated a deal with your Prime Ministers Macmillan...subsequently that scoundrel Prime Minister James Harold Wilson which resulted in the United States supplying the United Kingdom with Polaris missiles, launch tubes, and fire control systems on the basis that NATO would have access to your port at the Royal Navy Submarine Base at the Holy Loch in Scotland. We even towed the Dry Dock, USS Los Alamos to the loch and assembled it in six months to kick-start the facility and have since upgraded Polaris to Trident."

A new seriousness was now evident. "We remain eternally grateful."

"Yeah, yeah!" Eisenberg dismissed Pennington's light sarcasm.

"Well, I bring you concerns from both back at the Farm and over in NATO that the advent of an Independent Scotland, one which will break our agreement by closing the port to our boats, will have profound policy implications for America. The fate of fifty-eight Trident II D5 missiles you lease from the US which have functioned as the UK's most prolific deterrent against a potential nuclear attack since the close of the Cold War are at risk. The fate of four Vanguard-class submarines, which are used to carry these missiles, is also at stake."

Pennington bristled. "You are aware, of course that the British Government shares your views and is completely opposed to the separatists in Scotland and their ambitions."

Eisenberg nodded. "So I gather, my friend," before dismissing his reassurance and continuing, his tone now more aggressive. "You used to be the masters of colonialism. Now you're unable to contain unrest in your own backyard. Your colonial powers are on the wane. As a proud Republic we shouldn't have to give you lessons on this."

Pennington's thin lips compressed to near invisibility. He placed his glass very precisely on a small table-mat provided for that purpose, a sure sign he was engaged in marshalling his thoughts and paused before smiling his rejoinder, a well-practised attempt to present what he saw as a brutal truth in a way that attempted to make it more acceptable to his adversary.

"Dear Coby, the only difference between us is that you refer to your colonies as 'territories'. You live in denial. When have you ever seen a map of the US that had Puerto Rico on it? Or American Samoa, Guam, the US Virgin Islands, the Northern Marianas or any of the other smaller islands that the US has annexed over the years?" Eisenberg started to interrupt but was silenced by a slight hand movement by Pennington. "According to your own census count in the year before Pearl Harbour, nearly twenty million people lived in your territories…what we call colonies…the great bulk of them in the islands of the Philippines. That meant slightly more than one in eight of the people in the US lived outside of the states. For perspective, Admiral, consider that at that time, only about one in twelve was

African American. If you lived in the US on the eve of the Second World War, you were more likely to be colonised by America than be black in America."

Pennington's smile hadn't leavened the message. Eisenberg's temper surfaced.

"Enough of your history lessons! This Scottish business could shift the balance of power within NATO and a weakened Britain would have an impact upon America's security and economic interests. We're taking this very seriously, Jonathon! We are engaged in nothing less than full spectrum dominance. Military superiority over land, sea, air, space and information. This requires a compliant NATO."

"Quite so, Admiral. It's currently the policy of the Scottish Government that even in the event of their being independent of the Crown, they would remain members of NATO."

"Admitting a new state to NATO requires the unanimous agreement of all the other members and Greece blocked the Macedonian entry for several years."

"I'll grant you that but Scotland would certainly be seen as an exceptional case because it is presently the home of a nuclear arsenal central to the alliance's defence umbrella."

"But, Jonathon... five NATO states have already called for the removal of all remaining US nuclear weapons on European soil in a move intended to spur their ideas on global disarmament. Belgium, the Netherlands, Germany, Norway and Luxembourg have already made a joint declaration and have been working to influence a growing debate within NATO over the usefulness of nuclear weapons in alliance strategy. Scotland would be in that camp!"

"Now you are telling me all of this, why?" asked Pennington.

"Well, there is an awareness that anything that might be seen as US interference in a Scottish decision on its independence would almost certainly be counter-productive. So there's a desire to keep from doing anything that would undermine the case for keeping Britain together...but we need you to understand how much importance the US places on the United Kingdom remaining, well...*united*!"

"We welcome your support, Coby. And my comments are genuine. All I can do is reassure you that we take this matter as seriously as you do and..."

"And what of the shipping lanes around Cape Wrath? Two-thirds of the Russian naval forces are based on the Barents Sea coast around Murmansk. Their Northern Fleet includes about thirty nuclear powered submarines based at Zapadnaya Litsa where the fourth generation multi-purpose attack submarine of the Yasen class has its homeport."

He paused to summon up a greater level of seriousness.

"Jonathon, the naval ports of Vidyayevo, Gadzhiyevo, Polyarny and Severomorsk are located almost on the border of northern Norway and that's where all multi-purpose and ballistic missile submarines, as well as the surface warships of the Northern Fleet are based. All of these vessels...*all* of these vessels, pass through international waters off the coast of north-west Scotland. Right now we could detect a child's plastic bathtub boat if it sailed on or underneath these waters. However, the prospect of an independent Scotland, opposed to nuclear weapons, whose government are at least in some measure opposed to NATO, left-leaning elements of which are at least ambiguous about the United States of America…well, it horrifies us. There's no telling what they might do."

Pennington grinned mischievously. "Scotland's also an oil-rich nation. If it becomes independent you could just invade it like you've done all over the globe!"

Eisenberg had the good grace to smile in return.

"Unfortunately, Scotland along with Ireland is one of the more popular nations we hold in our affections back home. Many of the signatories on our Declaration of Independence were of Scots descent. We based the entire goddamned hallowed document on the Scottish Declaration of Arbroath and twenty-six of our forty-four Presidents were of Scottish descent, for Chrissake! Scotland is not Grenada, Panama or Iraq. It's the fucking home of *golf*!"

Pennington examined the bottom of his whisky glass and signalled to a waiter standing diplomatically out of earshot that a further two refreshments would be welcomed.

"Well, you see our dilemma, Coby. We take precisely the same view as you. Indeed, given the impact upon our balance of payments were Scottish resources to be denied us, we have even more reasons to be fretful."

Eisenberg reacted badly to Pennington's expression. "Fretful? We're a damn sight more anxious than fretful."

Brooks *sang-froid* was unimpaired as he accepted Eisenberg's challenge. "Perhaps it was a poor choice of words, Admiral." He leaned forward in his chair. "Look, Coby, much as it's a delight to enjoy a lunchtime refreshment with you, you didn't come all the way over from Boulevard Leopold in Brussels to tell me what I already know."

Eisenberg leaned his tall frame forwards echoing Pennington and lowered his tone.

"We want to know what you're doing to halt the progress towards Scottish independence. I noticed even in this morning's newspapers that some polls are moving against the status quo. We want to know what we might do to assist…without being caught with our fingerprints all over a botched operation."

Pennington was curt in his reply. "I think you'll find that Her Majesty's Government have no need to employ the services of others to assist in their covert activity."

Eisenberg was equally short. "Jonathon! In this morning's papers there's an article on recently declassified papers showing how the then Irish *Taoiseach*, Charles Haughey was targeted by loyalist paramilitaries 30 years ago because MI5 had ordered his assassination. Your people ordered the killing of a friendly head of state! The CIA are well aware that the Ulster Volunteer Force were being used by MI5, MI6, and British army special forces from 1972 through to 1985 but also that they refused this particular hit on the basis that they were not going to carry out work of this magnitude for what they called the Dirty Tricks Department of the British Establishment." He sat back, his tone now edging on scorn. "The files released recently show you even wrote to those fucking knuckle-draggers making the request on fucking headed notepaper. So…you use third parties when you choose."

Pennington admitted defeat. He smiled dryly. "Well… what are friends for?" before continuing. "We are taking active steps to link the separatists with violent acts;

armed revolution. It might allow us to raise the stakes sufficient to frighten the lieges and deter them from supporting the *Independentistas*. We have the media side sewn up although social media is somewhat beyond our reach." He hesitated as the waiter returned with two drinks on a tray, recommencing his reproof after both he and Eisenberg had partaken of a large draught. "We are making use of the 77th Brigade. They should redress the balance there. They're also influencing the publication of polling results that threaten to show trends we don't happen to like and finally, when push comes to shove, we have the count of any future Referendum under control. Postal ballots provide excellent opportunities to shape the final result."

Eisenberg nodded his satisfaction then murmured conspiratorially. "We might be able to assist in defaming their leadership."

Pennington raised his eyebrows inviting further explanation.

"We have quiet information concerning the sexual behaviour of two of their senior politicians. Now, to be frank, we have quiet information regarding the sexual behaviour of politicians of *every* party. Indeed these sexual encounters are often transactions that occur at our hand." He sipped again at his whiskey. "It makes for an easier life."

Pennington demurred. "These things often unravel. It may take time but these things often unravel. You didn't manage to keep your surveillance of the sexual exploits of the estimable Doctor Martin Luther King Jr. quiet for long, did you? That came back to bite you!"

Eisenberg raised his glass in acceptance of the point.

"Still got shot, eh! He was still removed as an immediate threat even if his death was counterproductive further down the line." More Jack Daniels disappeared as he warmed to his offer. "We'd like to make information available to your media that would mire two prominent SNP politicians in a sexual controversy. Whether there's any substance to these lurid allegations would of course be something the police, courts and news media would take time to understand. In the meantime, many right-thinking voters would certainly think twice about having their country run by sexual desperadoes. Mud sticks, Jonathon."

Pennington consulted his watch. "I suspect lunch will be ready. We should go on through. The waiter will bring our drinks." He rose. "I leave your suggestion open. I, of course have little time for office tittle-tattle but if lewd and lascivious behaviour of the kind you allege makes its way into the headlines, I say it's only fair on the victims, their families and the general public that this is made known. We must uphold the highest standards of private behaviour in public life. Don't you agree?"

Chapter Forty

Ballantrae

Gazing at the massive blue hone granite volcanic plug of Alisa Craig just ten miles off-shore, Cavendish sat in his hired Vauxhall having pulled into a lay-by just outside Ballantrae. His attention returned to the items left by Kelso he'd removed from the apartment at Hughenden and had placed on the passenger's seat for inspection. Shell-casings he couldn't identify, a receipt he could barely read, a phone whose password he didn't know and therefore couldn't access and a bank card...in the name of one Jack Robert Bryson. The crumpled receipt did allow him to read the word 'Ballantrae'. He put the car in gear and drove on.

The small Scotmid Cooperative shop in Ballantrae advertised its wares and opening times on a blue-banded soffit and was possessed of some useful parking space which Cavendish decided to employ. Slowing almost to a halt, he consulted the receipt again and satisfied himself that the almost indecipherable wording on it could, in a certain light read, 'Scotmid'. He parked the Vauxhall and entered the small store making a series of small purchases of biscuits and energy drinks.

As he approached the counter to pay he was welcomed with a broad smile by the shopkeeper who had watched his movements in a large mirror judiciously placed to allow observation behind aisles that would otherwise have had to be covered by a more expensive close-circuit television system.

The shopkeeper awaited his arrival. "Thanks, sir!" as Cavendish handed over his purchases to be scanned.

"Wonder if you could help me. I'm looking for an old friend...Jack Bryson. Lives round here. I was just passing and wondered if you knew of his whereabouts?"

The shopkeeper, coming from a long line of merchants who understood the meaning of excellent customer primacy, was anxious to help.

"Ah...Mr Bryson. Haven't seen him in a few days. Only usually see him when he wants his whisky." He leaned forward conspiratorially. "Likes his whisky, does Mr. Bryson."

Cavendish caught the shopkeeper's intention to be helpful.

"I was hoping to call in to see him. Lives nearby?"

"Six pounds, twenty please." He finished bagging Cavendish's goods. "Gowanbank cottage. Up on the hill." He pointed through the window at the hills which came down to meet the village. "Take a right along Main Road there, left along Arrol and left again along Church Road After the farm there's a bridal path; a public right of way, that'll take you directly to his cottage door. Bit of a climb!"

"Why thanks..."

"Might Mr Bryson appreciate a bottle of whisky, sir? He seems to enjoy our own brand."

"Good idea. Yes. I'll take a bottle." He withdrew further monies from his wallet and made the exchange. "Thanks."

* * *

To the west, the coast of Ireland could be observed through the spray as could the Isle of Man to the east as *'The Butcher's Apron'* skimmed the relatively calm waters of the Irish Sea as it approached the North Chanel and *'The Sheuch'*; those waters that separate the Irish Sea from those of the Inner Hebrides. Loch Ryan and the port of Stranraer lay ahead only a few hours' sailing away.

Murdo Monteith was tired as were his fellow crew members. The trans-Atlantic crossing had been uneventful, fast and had occupied every one of the crew throughout.

He signalled to Sam Ferguson, his skipper by waving his arm. "Skip! I'm going to the head. Leaving my position!"

Ferguson scanned the position of the other hands, looked forward and upwards at weather conditions and potential obstacles and agreed, giving Monteith a thumbs-up gesture.

Moving as carefully as his harness would permit, Monteith made his way below. At the rear of the craft a decent working toilet was clean and operational despite the sometimes urgent attentions of the crew during the crossing. He unhooked himself as he levered himself through the hatch and made directly to the cache of weaponry where, confident that the skipper would give no one else permission to leave their post until he'd returned, he opened the internal wall of the yacht. Pulling at the two orange pods, he placed them to one side of the others stacked in readiness for arrival at their next port of call. Quickly he returned the section of the enclosure he'd removed and twisted the batons to hold it in place. Charged in advance with dealing with the cushioned fenders upon arrival he satisfied himself that he'd be able to place the two pods carrying the rifles over the side unobtrusively so that they might sit side by side with others more capable of preventing damage to the hull upon docking. Reconnecting his harness, he returned to his post and gave Ferguson a reciprocal thumbs-up.

***

Mirren Maugham drove considerably faster than would normally have been the case, the twisting road south and west testing both her concentration and nerve. Despite her determination not to do so, she found herself intermittently looking anxiously at the shoe box on the passenger's seat, her mind conjuring up images of the explosion it might engender. Occasional farm vehicles obstructed her journey for periods but upon passing Strathaven the sat-nav informed her that she was scheduled to reach Stranraer by four o'clock. Reassured, she eased back on the accelerator telling herself that if she didn't intend to leave this world as a consequence of a bomb blast, she sure as hell didn't want to depart due to a mundane miscalculation on a bend made slippery by cow dung. Ayr slipped past on her off-side as she made her way through Maybole and past the edge of Turnberry.

Ahead, the few spires of the sea-side town of Girvan broke a horizon otherwise characterised by rural fields and woodlands. Thirty miles to go. Ballantrae, she noticed idly, was but twelve miles further on. She'd make her destination comfortably.

Then she just had to place a bomb beneath a car.

* * *

The Cabinet Secretary for Justice, Alan Lafferty stood behind his desk and prepared to meet Scotland's Chief Constable, Andrew Miller who entered along with Lafferty's Special Adviser, Chris Cunningham on matters to do with Justice and Parliamentary Liaison. He shook Miller's hand and offered him a seat.

"Thanks for coming Alan...and also for not coming team-handed. This is sensitive."

"Not at all, Minister."

"I've asked Chris to join us. As you know, he has a particular interest in the special measures you've put in place to deal with security."

Miller nodded.

"This shooting in Glasgow. Any news? Progress?"

Miller clasped his hands and placed them before him on the table.

"Our investigations are continuing, Minister. We know the shots were fired from a L42A1, bolt-action Lee-Enfield rifle. This weapon was used commonly by belligerents on each side of the divide in Northern Ireland back in the nineties. It's pretty easy to get your hands on one of these if you have a few quid and know the right people. The flat from which the shots were fired was rented on a short term lease. A cash transaction to avoid tax no doubt but the description of the man who rented it fits half of the people walking along Princes Street right now. We've examined the flat but whoever used it left no particular trace. We have some fingerprints but the boys reckon these will belong to previous owners. Six cups had been used and had been washed and dried but no prints and we don't know if it was six people using one cup each or one assailant who had an obsessive cleaning disorder. No witnesses so far. Both we and you have had a signal from MI5 that they may have evidence that links three mainstream members of the SNP to the shooting but we've seen nothing yet. I've asked for information to be provided as soon as possible. A meeting was scheduled but MI5 postponed it."

He opened his hands and spread his fingers intimating the end of his contribution.

Lafferty bit his lower lip in thought.

"What's your gut feel, Andy? It's headline news and I can't defend us."

"Difficult to say without hearing from MI5. It's possible that their assessment is accurate. BBC newsreaders aren't popular with certain sections of your party, Minister. But on the other hand…well, I've learned not to jump too quickly to judgment."

"Do you have any people from your special measures group dealing with security involved with this?" interrupted Cunningham.

"We're trying to cover all the bases, Chris."

The Minister intervened. "We agreed we wouldn't quiz the Chief on special measures, Chris. These are operational matters and I want to remain at arms-length." He returned to questioning Miller. "Is there anything you'd like me to do, Alan?"

"Perhaps one thing. Our sources suggest that the media had hold of the exact wording of the signal sent us by MI5. Now I accept that this could have been a cop, a leak from MI5 or someone in your department but it appears that someone leaked an extremely confidential document. I've already set in place an investigation within the force. You might want to do something similar here."

"That's all we bloody need!"

The Minister was displeased. He picked up the pile of six newspapers which had been to one side of him throughout the meeting and slammed them on the desk. The Minister was *most* displeased.

Chapter Forty-one

Up the Hill

"Fuck's sake!"

There had been silence for some minutes as the minibus headed south along the narrow thoroughfare that was the main road through Maybole. Scores of enormous articulated lorries recently disembarked from the Belfast-Cairnryan Ferry trundled along the hideously dangerous High Street towards Glasgow, Edinburgh and all points north forcing Bonnie to stop and await a break in the traffic.

"This is ridiculous! Take the turn-off there and go via Maidens...past Culzean," shouted Bryson as a huge and noisy six-axel behemoth sat motionless in a queue beside them spewing diesel fumes and compelling the minibus to mount the two-foot wide pavement and await its onward journey.

Bonnie manoeuvred the vehicle off High Street and on to surface roads which took them on to rural twisting lanes that slowed the vehicle but allowed steady progress towards Ballantrae where Bryson intended collecting his passport. He undid his seatbelt, turned to the seats behind him and addressed Macdonald and Singh, including Bonnie in his comments.

"I want you guys to know that I'm really sorry you've been caught up in all of this." He gestured at Kelso in the rear seat, his hands still bound. "This arsehole has placed my daughter in danger and now, given the circumstances that have unfolded, would certainly damage me and probably you too if he could." He was suddenly angered. "And now I find that a young brother I've not seen for years is also in danger." He wrestled with his next words. "Now, none of this has fuck all to do with you guys but I can't let you off the noose until I settle matters in Stranraer. You'll be in no danger. I promise you that but despite you obviously being good people, I can't take the chance that one way or another the cops might become involved. I've enough on my plate."

Singh interjected, worried. "I think we all believe you, Mr, Bryson but will we still be able to get home tonight? My mum and dad…" He tailed off.

Bryson smiled at the simple decency of Singh.

"Aye, you're fine, Charlie. This'll all be over by tea-time…at least for you guys." He lowered his head slightly and looked along the barrel of the pistol he held directly at Kelso. "Can't say the same for Mister Kelso here. Although if he displeases me in any way it'll all be over instantly!" He glanced at a road sign as they passed the grounds of Culzean Castle. "Not long to go now. We pick up my passport at Ballantrae, drive on to Stranraer and after a bit of business, you guys are free to go."

* * *

Cavendish had climbed the hill to Bryson's Gowanbank cottage but before approaching had stopped to catch his breath. He leaned on a gatepost and turned to take in the view. *Very beautiful*, he decided, *but this is a guy who wants to remove himself from society.* His thoughts turned to the cottage before him. It looked unoccupied. He pondered his next move. So...*I visit the flat in Glasgow and pick up evidence that suggests the involvement of someone called Jack Robert Bryson who seems to live here in this cottage.* He began the short walk to the front door of the cottage. *Pennington sees me as a desk jockey who doesn't command the respect of his field officer. Well, I'll show him I'm more than an office-boy!*

Cautiously he approached the cottage, listening for any activity. He hesitated as he prepared to knock on the aged front door asking himself how he'd introduce himself and what he'd hope to achieve if his knock was answered.

A timid tap on the door was followed by a more authoritative strike which suggested that the door wasn't locked as it gave slightly under his rap. A further knock brought no response and Cavendish pushed gingerly at the door which allowed itself to be pushed open with minor difficulty causing him to start slightly at the noise of the heel of the door scraping against the slabbed floor.

Inside, the cottage showed signs of habitation if not exquisite living. An internal door had been removed from its hinges allowing unfettered access to a living area which evidenced broken furniture. *A fight*? pondered Cavendish . Empty whisky bottles of the same brand as the one he carried in his Scotmid plastic bag lay strewn in a corner. *No food?* He searched the little cupboard space and found none. Cigarette butts filled an ashtray. He stepped back towards the front door and entered the small bedroom. It smelled of dampness and further numbers of Scotmid's cheapest whisky bottles lay emptied at the side of the bed. He switched on the light which illuminated the room if only slightly. *At least he pays his electricity bill!* Faded yellow floral wallpaper redolent of World War Two decorative chic covered each of the rooms. Next door a bathroom offered a toilet and an old white bath green in places due to copper staining and was being used to hold various pieces of Bryson's army equipment; mostly clothing.

Cavendish returned to the living room and sat at the table. He removed the items he'd taken from the flat and placed the shell casings, phone, bank card and receipt before him asking himself their significance. He decided that the phone held most promise. Clearly modern and evidently fully charged, perhaps there was a way in which he could by-pass the code needed to open it. He gave this his full attention.

* * *

Bryson had Bonnie drive the minibus up to the edge of the farm and had walked everyone up the hill to Gowanbank cottage, not wishing to leave Kelso under the supervision of his young friends.

As the group approached the gatepost, Bryson stopped everyone with a raised arm. Turning, he mouthed the words, 'lie down' and gestured with his hand that he meant flat, not just crouched. He laid the rifle he carried down by the gate and removed the Glock pistol from his waistband. Grabbing Kelso by the neck he hauled him to his feet and positioned him before him.

He spoke quietly. "When we left, I closed the door. Now, as you can see, it's open. You are the only person who knows I live here. Have you organised a welcome party for me, eh Johnnie-boy? Is this where I get to shoot you in the gut so you die slow just because you tried to trick me one last time?"

"I've not spoken to anyone about your place. It'll probably have been a fox or something."

"A fox or something," repeated Bryson sarcastically. "We're going in. Nice and quietly. If I find that you've arranged some kind of ambush, the first bullet goes in your stomach, the second in your spine. I hope you survive the injuries. Give you time to think on things."

Holding Kelso as a human shield, Bryson walked quietly towards the open door. Peering into the gloom he could see a man seated at the table, his back to him, facing towards his fireplace. He pushed the gun firmly against Kelso and stepped inside. In one swift move he sprang forward and brought the heel of the gun down upon Cavendish's head knocking him unconscious. As he fell to the floor revealing himself to Kelso, he engendered an unintended comment. "Fuck me! Not *that* cunt!"

Bryson was on his toes, unsure of what was transpiring. He spoke angrily to Kelso gesturing as he did so.

"Sit in that chair. He moved quickly outside and took Kelso's *sgian dubh* from his boot and swiftly cut a tired washing line which the previous occupant had strung from two poles outside the cottage. He returned in seconds to find Kelso almost free from his bonds. The Glock pointed directly at him stopped his attempt at escape. He raised his shackled hands as if in prayer. "Look, Bryson. You need to believe me. I know this fucker but I've no fucking idea how he managed to find his way here!"

"Well, we're going to find out aren't we? The gun was waved again. "Lie on the floor. He cut Kelso's bonds. Place your hands behind your back."

He stepped backwards and called to the three students still lying on the grass beyond the gate. "You can come in now! One of you bring the rifle, please!"

He cut the long-perished rope in half and used one length to secure Kelso's hands more tightly behind his back. Taking the second length he bound Cavendish in similar fashion before inspecting his head-wound and, determining he was not about to pass away, took an old feed bag that had hung behind the front door since he'd first arrived in the cottage and placed it over Cavendish 's head.

"First things first!" He stepped through to the bedroom and lifted a floorboard next to the bed. From its depths he lifted a small bag in which was his passport, one hundred and fifty pounds in Sterling and a small Russian 8mm Baikal self-defence pistol, originally used for firing CS gas but converted by removing the partially blocked barrel and replacing it with a rifled barrel so it could fire 9mm bulleted ammunition. The replacement barrel was threaded so that it would accept the silencer which was also in the bag. He returned the gun and accoutrements to the solum under the floor and made good the floorboard.

He returned to the table just as Macdonald, Singh and Bonnie entered the cottage, each of them taking in the *tableaux* before them and attempting to come to terms with the gloomy interior.

Bryson took the rifle from Macdonald and spoke directly to Kelso. "Who is this man and why is he here?"

Kelso looked to the ceiling of the cottage for inspiration and as a sign of his frustration.

"I call him 'Cunt'. His phone number is on the contacts list on my phone."

"And why is his number on your phone?"

"He's the guy who agreed your fee. He's a fucking civil servant and I've no fucking idea…" he repeated his words for emphasis. "I've *no* fucking idea…what brings him to Scotland."

Cavendish began to stir.

"Then we'll ask him." He pulled Cavendish roughly to his feet and sat him on a second stool.

Without waiting for Cavendish to clear his head, Bryson commenced his questioning.

"I gather you're called 'Cunt'. Tell me why you're here."

Disconcerted by the blow to his head, the question compounded his disorientation.

"Wha?…" He searched for meaning in the question and found an answer.

"Is Kelso here?"

Bryson glared at Kelso and leaning forward, conducted a search of Cavendish's person. Finding only a wallet, two phones and no weaponry, he turned his attention to the items on the table. Bryson opened one of the phones and was surprised to see it spring to life without need of a password or code. He checked previous phone calls and noted the time of the call made to Kelso's phone which he'd answered in the flat. Realising that it had been Cavendish who had phoned him assuming him to be Kelso, he kept his own counsel.

"What are these things on the table?" He leaned forward again as he noticed his bank card. "That's my fucking property. Where did you get this bank card?"

Kelso's head sank to his chest as he contemplated Bryson's likely reaction.

"Why...why, I found them in a flat in Hughenden Gardens.

Bryson nodded his understanding. "Did you now?" He paused for further reflection. And what else did you find?"

Beneath the head-cover, Cavendish's face was twisted in an anxious confusion.

"What...eh...a phone, receipt, bank card and some bullet cartridges."

Bryson activated the phone and observed a photograph of Singh wearing a silly hat. He held the phone up to Macdonald for inspection. "Yours, Charlie?"

He nodded.

Bryson held on to the phone and examined his bank card. "Care to offer an explanation, Kelso?" He continued his questioning as Kelso looked steadfastly at the uneven, slabbed floor of the living room. "This man..." He changed tack and questioned Cavendish. "You! Do you answer to 'Cunt' or have you another name?"

"Cavendish."

"And what does your mammy call you?"

Cavendish sighed. "My given name is Henry. I'm a retired Commander in the Royal Navy. Currently with the Home Office."

Kelso sat silently examining the floor as if looking for dust mites as Bryson returned his gaze to him. "I repeat...care to offer an explanation?"

The invisible dust mites continued to occupy Kelso's attention. Bryson picked up the receipt and screwed his eyes trying to make out the lettering before arriving at an understanding of Cavendish's visit to his cottage. He noticed the plastic bag and withdrew the bottle of whisky.

"This whisky. From the store at the bottom of the hill. A peace offering?"

Cavendish nodded although the loose hessian sack covering his head moved only slightly. Bryson unscrewed the cap and took a deep pull on the bottle's contents, replacing the cap and continuing.

"So you put two and two together...Did Sammy down at the store give you helpful directions to the cottage?"

Again the hessian sack fluttered slightly in agreement. Bryson weighed the evidence.

"So, Mister Kelso. These items left in the apartment from which a shot was fired were left to be found by the authorities which would have tied me in directly...and due to Charlie here having his phone planted, him, Bonnie and Lachie would also have been implicated."

He shook his head admonishingly at Kelso. "Some years ago you took an oath. Brothers in arms, eh? One for all and all for one? But you were going to drop me in it. I was to be a useful idiot. A man with a few quid now in his bank account so he must have been up to something. Oh, you had me good and proper."

He turned to Macdonald. "Back in the flat, Sim told me you three were just regular foot-soldiers for the SNP."

Macdonald demurred. "Members! Not foot-soldiers. Watching what's going on here I want nothing to do with soldiering."

"Fair point son." He returned to Cavendish. "And how come you happened upon the flat in Hughenden? Blind luck?"

Cavendish now adopted what he imagined might be the proper approach taken by a field officer. "I think I've said enough."

Bryson laughed. "Jesus! Name rank and serial number, eh? Top man. You're a regular James Bond!"

"Well, chums, it appears that we've stumbled across a dastardly plot to present the doubtless admirable political party to which you belong as having terrorists as members, eh?"

He stood from the table and took a piece of cord that hung behind the front door.

"Bonnie would you loop that string round this arsehole's neck and tie it slightly so it pins that sack to his head and doesn't slip off. Try not to choke him but I want him blinded to what's going on."

He looked outside the dirty living room window and established the weather.

"Everyone else, let's go. We're going to undertake a rescue then I'll disappear and you three can go home. This pair here", he cuffed a surprised Cavendish on the back of his head more firmly than he'd intended, "they'll likely end up in the drink!"

He patted his pockets to ensure that his passport and Kelso's cash were in his possession and, satisfied, nodded his head in the direction of the door indicating departure, stepping back momentarily to collect the bottle of whisky. Remembering the plastic bag on the floor contained comestibles he lifted it and threw it to Singh. "You guys must be starving. Biscuits, chocolates and crisps from what I can see." He indicated Bryson and Cavendish. "This pair don't want any. Wire in!"

Chapter Forty-two

A Safe Harbour

The Butcher's Apron skimmed the surface of Loch Ryan as it approached the sea-loch, its weary but euphoric crew waving to passengers on the large ferry leaving Cairnryan on its way to Belfast. Monteith looked at his watch and pursed his lips in appreciation. The skipper had said they'd dock at Stranraer at four-forty that afternoon and it looked like he'd arrive with the kind of precision usually associated with NASA were it not for a significant drop in wind conditions as they entered the shelter of the sea-loch.

He glanced at preparations that had been made for docking. Everything was as it should be. A blue sky above framed some feathery white clouds that meandered across the Scottish coast given the absence of any wind which slowed the craft but provided a wonderfully calm panorama of the tree-lined loch.

Sam Ferguson, elated by making the journey so smoothly, cupped his hands around his mouth and shouted to Monteith, "Your country is beautiful!" before raising is arms above his head in triumph and shouting to the rest of the crew. "We did it guys. We only fucking *did* it!"

Stranraer was still some way off. Eight miles of the sea-loch still had to be transversed and there was little wind propelling the craft onwards to its destination. Monteith remained on edge.

* * *

Bryson directed Bonnie to slow as they entered the port of Stranraer. In the rear seat, a hooded Cavendish sat next to a bound Kelso. In the middle seats, Macdonald and Singh looked out of the dark tinted windows at a seaside town in the southernmost region of Scotland neither had visited before.

"They won't dock there," said Bryson pointing at the long railway pier which jutted far out into the loch. "Keep on until we reach the harbour but watch your driving. It's immediately opposite the local police station."

Bonnie nodded her assent and upon Bryson's encouragement, continued to drive beyond the Ulsterbus terminal, past the police station and along and upwards along narrow streets so tight they enjoyed double yellow lines throughout. Small, douce terraced houses lined each thoroughfare. Bryson became excited.

"There, Bonnie. I need height."

He pointed to a church with no steeple but which was articulated by slender buttresses supporting a castellated parapet within which was a watchtower. Bonnie drove up Sun Street until she arrived at Stranraer's High Kirk. A modern wing had been added to the old sandstone church. Some cars sitting outside suggested occupancy but a far road-side entrance to the church allowed Bonnie to park out of sight immediately opposite the heavy oak doors which protected access to the rear of the church and the battlements tower above it.

Bryson lifted his rifle, removed its sighting mechanism and spoke to the occupants of the minibus.

"I need to use these sights. I want to see what's going on in the harbour." He thought quickly. "Let's see… Bonnie you come with me. Boys…he fished in his pocket for the Beretta M92 FS gun he'd found taped to Kelso's ankle and handed it to Macdonald. "Lachie, you and Charlie keep an eye on this pair. They're both tied up so there shouldn't be any problems. Okay?"

Both students nodded, Macdonald gazing at the pistol he'd just been handed.

"Now look guys. No funny business. I need you to take care of this. All I'm trying to do is look after my wee brother and my daughter. I don't care what happens to me afterwards. But first I need to check on a yacht coming in to harbour. Sit in the front seat so there's distance between you and don't let him away with any nonsense. Be careful. I'll be back in a minute."

He and Bonnie tested the heavy double doors which were locked. Its keyhole was much worn over the years and the locking mechanism was equally frail.

"Strong doors," said Bryson to Bonnie, "but they're only as strong as their lock."

Stepping back he kicked at the lock with the sole of his right boot. It swung open instantly.

"Okay. Stay close."

Together they climbed the ancient staircase until reaching the top where a further door barred their way onto the castellated turret. Again it yielded to Bryson's boot and they stepped onto the surface of the watchtower. Some champagne glasses suggested its earlier use as an entertainment venue for the holy.

Bryson knelt against the sandstone surround and brought the rifle sights up to his eye, adjusting them as he did so. Scanning the harbour to orientate himself, he raised the sights until he could view the loch. Perhaps one mile from the harbour was the unmistakable sight of the large ocean-going yacht on which his young brother was a crew member and who'd been fingered as a gun runner by Cavendish of the Home Office.

Lowering the sights he had an excellent view of the harbour where a large crowd had gathered to bid the yacht welcome. A flotilla of small yachts had sailed out of the harbour and was now attempting to return alongside their larger and more muscular peer, each looking for wind to assist them in doing so.

Bryson checked on the progress of the *Butcher's Apron. Slow*, he thought. *I've time to get down there.* Again he lowered the sights and checked on the crowd looking for police or other security personnel. *Difficult to tell*, he told himself. He scanned the roads leading to the harbour looking for any preparations for road-blocks or other signs of security activity and watched as a young lady carrying a box approached a red Vauxhall car, looked around then stooped and placed it below a car before returning to her own some hundred yards away.

"What the f…" He focussed the sights on the driver who sat motionless in her car.

He lowered the sights and spoke to Bonnie who was contemplating the situation at the harbour in terms of its newsworthiness. "I think someone's just placed a bomb under a car near the entrance to the harbour."

Bonnie was drawn back from her reverie. "A bomb? Are you sure?"

"Yeah. A woman placed a device under a car and returned to her own. Looks like a remote-control job. Either that or I'm going to make a complete arse of myself and have every cop in Stranraer on my tail for a mindless assault on an innocent woman." For a moment he forgot his mission. "I'd better get down there. C'mon."

Both ran down the stairs as quickly as possible given the absence of any light in the stairwell and emerged into the car park where both Macdonald and Singh lay unconscious. Cavendish lay in a heap next to an opening into the church graveyard, his hood intact and his consciousness or otherwise therefore indeterminate. The minibus was missing. As was the rifle.

"Oh, for fuck's sake!" He made a quick decision. "Bonnie, first things first. If that *is* a bomb it takes precedence. You look after those three. Keep Cavendish's hood on if you can. Don't let him see you or the guys. I'll be back shortly."

He leapt on top of the wall enclosing the graveyard and considered the quickest way to the harbour entrance. It involved cutting down through some domestic properties but Bryson moved quickly and shortly came down in to the road behind the car. Slowing, he walked towards it until arriving at the driver's door which he swung open surprising the woman. She hadn't engaged her seatbelt and was removed from the vehicle with ease, a sharp startled cry her only resistance.

Bryson's first move was to bring her hands before her and ensure that they weren't holding a triggering device.

Treasure recovered some of her composure. "What on earth…?"

Bryson walked her roughly round to the passenger seat, his eyes on activity around him lest someone had been alerted to his intervention. "Sit!" he ordered, pushing her onto the seat. "Do not fucking move. I'm armed." Reassured by her failure to scream for help or assume the prospect of sexual abuse, he patted the pockets of her jacket for any weapons. Finding none, he knelt beside the open door and spoke firmly.

"I watched you place a device under a car. Was I mistaken?"

He looked directly at Maugham whose eyes were glazed as if from a well-timed uppercut.

Before she could answer, he opened the glove compartment and saw the garage-door opener. For some time he looked at the mechanism. "Fucking Kelso! It's his fucking trademark!"

He removed it and ejecting the battery, placed both items in his pocket. "Now, you don't know me and I don't know you but you're going to walk back to that car and remove the device you've placed under it. I'll be driving your car right behind you and will have a gun trained on your back. Once you collect it you will return and sit in this seat. Do you understand me?"

Maugham, now very frightened nodded tearfully. This wasn't what she joined the service for.

Bryson moved into the driver's seat and followed Maugham as she did as requested. As she carried out his instructions, Bryson lifted a Manila envelope. Within it was a photograph of Kelso and of his young brother, Murdo Monteith.

"Back seat," instructed Bryson as Maugham asked wordlessly what she should do with the box. "Get in!"

As he drove his passenger slowly back towards the church to avoid any raised eyebrows, he couldn't help himself. He handed Maugham the envelope and held her gaze accusingly.

"I don't know who the fuck you are. We'll find that out. But I know one thing. That device you placed was designed and manufactured by one John Edward Kelso. So you're either Special Forces, a mercenary working for Kelso or an innocent woman blackmailed into conducting a terrorist act. Which is it?"

For a second Maugham considered his final option but decided saying nothing was a better bet until she'd worked out what had gone so wrong. This had been meant to be a simple act.

Bryson pulled into the church yard to find both students seated and alert. Bonnie was tending to a still-hooded Cavendish.

"You guys okay?' asked Bryson as he held Maugham by the elbow and guided her through the open door of the church. "What happened?"

Singh was anxious to explain. "Sir, we did everything you asked then that man just jumped over the seats and took the gun. He hit us both and knocked us out. I don't know how he untied himself. Don't know what happened to that guy with the hood."

Bryson leaned out of the entrance door to see Cavendish seated and obviously conscious being tended to by Bonnie.

Macdonald spoke tersely. "He escaped because someone tied him up with a rope that had been out in the weather for maybe ten years. It was as weak as straw."

Bryson didn't argue the matter. "Fair point, Lachie. I should have thought of that."

He shouted to Bonnie. "Bonnie! Leave buggerlugs and come over here would you?"

Doing as she was requested, she left Cavendish propped against the graveyard wall.

"These boys all right?"

"Charlie might be slightly concussed. He's a bit confused. Both are scared. Lachie's angry."

Bryson nodded his acceptance. "Look, Bonnie. Kelso can wait. I need to protect my young brother. He's coming in on that yacht. Can you hold the fort here? That young woman in the church planted a bomb. It now can't explode but she's no terrorist in my book. She's out of her depth and won't cause you trouble. Take the Beretta I gave Lachie…"

"He told me that Kelso took both that and the rifle!"

"Shit…of course!" He withdrew the Glock from his waistband. "Take this. Keep the woman quiet. I'll bring Cavendish over in a moment."

Bonnie disappeared through the heavy doors into the darkness of the stairwell and Bryson moved quickly to the side of Cavendish. He clutched roughly at his collar.

"You haven't a clue who I am have you?"

Cavendish started in surprise at the gruff question. "You're a Scotsman and you're violent. That much I know."

"Correct on both points, pal. You're about to find out how violent. Now, you spoke to Kelso yesterday," he lied. "You told him about the yacht that's approaching the harbour and that it was being crewed by someone called Murdo Monteith who might be bringing arms into the country from the USA. Now, you're going to tell me everything you know about Monteith and how you came by whatever information."

"I think it better if I remained silent."

"Kelso tried that and then told me everything. If I took your hood off you'd see that he isn't around here anymore. So I *don't* think it's better if you remained silent and I'm going to ask you again," insisted Bryson. "If you don't answer I'm going to shoot you in the left knee. Once you overcome the agony, I'll ask again. If you don't answer, I'll shoot you in the right knee. You'll never walk again. After that it gets gory. Ankles and elbows get involved."

Without a gun of any kind on his person, he took the *sgian dubh* from his boot and pressed the butt against Cavendish's knee. "Now, tell me about Monteith and how you know about the arms shipment!"

Cavendish's bowel was turning its contents to liquid and persuaded him that perhaps he'd better comply with his interrogator's request. He succumbed.

"Th...there's not much to tell. I was contacted and advised that this man was crewing on the racing yacht due to arrive today and that he was a member of the proscribed organisation, *Seed of the Gaels*. There was some mention of the fact that he might be carrying weapons for use by the organisation."

"Who told you this and what was your mission?"

Cavendish breathed deeply and didn't answer until Bryson pressed the knife butt into his knee.

"You were warned. Say goodbye to your left knee!"

"Wait...wait! He swallowed, his mouth suddenly dry. "I was asked by MI5 to monitor the situation. Kelso was going to let off a few harmless shots so there would be a news story implicating Scottish terrorists."

"And you work for the Home Office?"

The grain sack moved, suggesting a nodding head inside it.

Bryson dragged him to his feet and hauled him over to the stairwell. He pulled him inside and lowered him to the floor behind the large doors which he closed over allowing only a small amount of light to penetrate.

"Your eyes will become accustomed to the gloom, Bonnie. I need you, Lachie and Charlie to keep these two quiet. They won't cause you any trouble but if you're tested, shoot them in the shin. Maximum pain and complete disability without the trauma of immediate mortality. I'll be back shortly. Then I'm going after Kelso but God alone knows where he's headed and anyway, he'll be miles away by now."

Macdonald spoke from the darkness. "Dumfries!"

"Eh?"

"He'll be going to Dumfries. He's got a rifle and the First Minister is opening something. It was on the news in the minibus."

Bryson raised his eyes to a darkened ceiling. "Shit... you're right. That's *exactly* where he'll be headed."

Bonnie chipped in. "Well, he won't get far! You took his money and the tank was empty. We were driving on fumes when we got to Stranraer. I was just going to suggest we put something in the tank when you spotted this church."

Bryson shook his head. "That's my next problem. Right now I'm off to the harbour. Back shortly!"

Chapter Forty-three

Absence Makes the Heart Grow Fonder

Ogilvie levered his backside from the desk of Miss Evans and responded to Pennington's overheard intercom request to her to have him enter his office. Despite Evans' advanced years, matronly demeanour and humour by-pass, Ogilvie expended considerable efforts in attempting to charm her. As the boss's gatekeeper she was important and he reckoned that there may be benefits to be had merely by treating her as if she was one of the younger and more attractive members of staff upon whom he lavished much more licentious attention.

He entered Pennington's office and accepted his invitation to sit in the chair beside his imposing desk.

"This Scottish business, Jeremy. I'm getting a lot of flak. Tried to contact Kelso. Radio silence. Asked after Cavendish. Turns out he's gone to Scotland to '*assist*' Kelso". He pronounced the sibilants in the word as might someone mimicking a gas escape. "That can only end in tears. His secretary also said *he* was unobtainable!"

"Funny that," interrupted Ogilvie. "I tried to contact Treasure just ten minutes ago and there was no reply."

"So we've three operatives plus whoever Kelso's involved from his team of desperadoes and can't make contact with any of them?"

Ogilvie looked puzzled. "Signal problems? Stranraer isn't the dead centre of Silicon Valley."

Pennington sighed. "I suppose that's the most likely explanation." He changed the subject. "Just met with Admiral Eisenberg. The CIA is most anxious about our mission to silence the more assertive of our Scottish brethren. Leaned on us quite heavily. I was able to reassure him that we were on top of things."

"We are, boss although I've had to postpone our meeting with Police Scotland. They're pushing us for evidence that the SNP members are involved in the shooting in Glasgow and our evidence is threadbare. Kelso and his team didn't leave the evidence in the flat we needed to make the connection."

"Kelso's never let us down in the past. I'm counting on him to deliver." He pursed his lips evincing frustration. "Also, just had advance notice that the Historical Enquiries Team, a division of the Police Service of Northern Ireland are about to issue declassified papers and an official report which puts MI5 behind the eight-ball. They've uncovered evidence that British military intelligence was behind a plot to have the Ulster Volunteer Force attack the primary school at Belleeks in County Armagh in order to kill children and teachers. *Children* and fucking *teachers*! Back then our idiots thought that a civil war in Northern Ireland would clean out the IRA. When this hits the papers, the Scottish Nationalists will make the not unreasonable assumption that if we behaved like this in Ireland why on earth wouldn't we do the same in

Scotland - particularly given the much more substantial resources there as opposed to Ireland."

"Well, Ireland has Guinness!"

Pennington was in no mood for Ogilvie's banter.

"This operation just *can't* go belly up, Jeremy!"

"I'm sure it won't, boss." He hesitated. "Not sure about using Treasure on the front line, though!"

Pennington bit his lower lip thoughtfully. "Hmm, I'm a tad uncomfortable myself but she's been excellent in all that's been asked of her thus far, eh?"

"She has. But this time we're asking her to place an explosive device. She's not been trained for this. Has she the temperament?"

"She and Kelso have the ability to make contact with each other. They're both aware of the five code words that signify a legitimate signal sent without duress. She's not stupid. If she needs help she knows she has a more experienced agent in the field beside her."

"I suppose that's some reassurance, right enough." Ogilvie attempted encouragement. "I'll keep trying to contact her boss. I'll give you an update."

"Try Cavendish as well. He's as much use as an ashtray on a motorbike but we'd better try to support him."

Ogilvie rose to leave the office. Pennington shouted at his retreating figure.

"Kelso as well!"

Chapter Forty-four

Brothers in Arms

Bryson drove Maugham's car back to the harbour and parked. With as much insouciance as he could muster, he walked over to the throng of spectators and media people who had gathered at a space on the harbour wall set aside for *The Butcher's Apron*. Taller than most, he looked out at the approaching yacht. A small diesel-powered boat towed it the last few yards and it docked to much cheering. Champagne corks popped and music blared from a CD speaker set up to permit Cliff Richards to sing '*Congratulations*' to the crew.

Bryson moved to the edge of the crowd and spotted the younger brother who had been adopted along with him twenty-five years earlier and upon whom he'd not set eyes on for some twelve years. Unexpectedly, he felt tears sting his eyes. *Too long, too long!* He recovered his composure and watched as Monteith placed the cushioned fenders over the side as the craft edged slowly towards the pier. All of the crew moved towards the bow where they celebrated their arrival. Monteith smiled and appeared as caught up in the celebrations as the others but made himself busy towards aft. As everyone's attention was focussed upon the bow, Bryson watched as his young brother leaned over, opened a Swiss Army knife and surreptitiously punctured

two of the fenders before cutting the rope that held them
to the craft. Instantly each dropped into the depths.
Monteith then busied himself undoing the remaining rope
ends and again checking to ensure that no one was
watching, threw the ropes overboard. Slowly he made his
way forward and joined the rest of the crew, even accepting
a bottle of fizz handed him by a fellow crew member,
drinking it and returning the bottle. Bryson looked on,
puzzled from the rear of the crowd. *What the fuck is he
doing?*

After a while a few media people stepped aboard as
interviews were conducted. Some crew came ashore and
formalities eased. Still Monteith focussed upon tasks
around the yacht as did one or two other crew members.
He moved towards the rear of the yacht along with a
few *aficionados* on the wharf who pointed and
commented at various aspects of the craft. Exhibiting
an outward confidence that he'd learned over the years
normally persuaded people of his right to do whenever
he was doing, he stepped aboard the yacht and walked
up behind Monteith who was busily engaged in looping
a length of rope into a coil.

"How's my wee brother?"

Monteith didn't flinch but stopped his task
immediately and turned around.

"Jack!"

Both men embraced. Monteith fought for words but
floundered. Holding him tight, Bryson spoke directly
into his ear.

"Later, brother…later. Right now I've got to get you
off this boat and out of here. I don't know what you've
been up to but the security services have you marked

out as trouble. For all I know there are guns trained on you as we speak." Still he held him close.

"Wh…what?" Monteith attempted to release himself from Bryson's embrace but found himself held tight.

"Listen, Murdo. I'm not messing about here. The security services have you and me in their sights. I intercepted a message by accident that fingers you as a gun-runner for some Scottish mob."

At this, Bryson eased his grip and the brothers stepped back to view each other.

Monteith grinned widely. "Jeez, you're a sight for sore eyes, Jack. I don't see you for God knows how long and you arrive out of the blue and give me a tall tale about me being a gun smuggler without so much as a by-your-leave."

"I don't give a flying fuck whether you are or aren't! I just know that the might of MI5 and the fucking Home Office, for Christ's sake are up against you and me both and if we stand here much longer we could be looking at the inside of a jail or the inside of a morgue!" He looked around sniffing for danger but finding none. "Come with me!"

Monteith protested mildly. "Jack!"

Bryson held his adopted brother's elbow in a firm grip. Monteith didn't resist and in moments both were on the quayside and circumnavigating the crowd.

"This seems all a bit far-fetched, Jack!"

"You can tell me all about it in the car. We're going up to the church at the top of the town. I've three sweet students, a Home Office spymaster and a bomb-planter there and when we get there you're going to help me track down the guy who set me up and was meant to take you down today!"

"Eh?"

"All will be revealed. All I need you to do is go along with everything I ask right now. We can have a beer later and I'll explain everything...although I'm headed to Dubai to rescue my daughter and her man on the first available flight."

"Wee Rachael? She's married? And you need to rescue her?"

Bryson smiled. "It's a long story, brother!" He reached out and grasped Monteith's forearm which he squeezed affectionately.

He drove on.

* * *

The community centre in East Kilbride was thronged with local residents as Cabinet Secretary for Justice, Alan Lafferty drew the winning raffle ticket and announced that first prize; a spa day for two at up-market Stobo Castle, had been won by blue; twenty-two. As good-natured cheers and boos greeted the announcement, Lafferty's phone vibrated. Calculating that he'd completed his task and that his local constituents would forgive him taking the call, he noticed that the person calling was Scotland's Chief Constable, Andrew Miller. He put the phone to his ear and turned his back on the crowd, shouldering an exit door and pushing out into an empty corridor the better to hear the transmission.

"Minister! Andy Miller."

"Hi Andy. What's new?"

"Thought you might like to know that MI5 are pulling back from fingering SNP members as having been involved at the scene of that shooting."

"Jeez, I'm mighty relieved at that Andy. Is this news public?"

"Not yet but although I've nothing in writing, I took the call on conference so my deputy witnessed the change in their position."

"So I can release this to the media?"

"No reason why not, Minister."

"Thanks, Andy. I can sleep tonight!"

Chapter Forty-five

Chasing Kelso

Bryson pulled up just outside the car park he'd left some twenty minutes earlier.

"Sit still, Murdo. I'll fetch you in a second."

Monteith watched curiously as Bryson crossed the road to where a large articulated lorry was purring while the driver unloaded items on a trolley. He exited the store and pushed the trolley up a ramp and into the front of the wagon. While the driver was engaged with his inventory, with great effort, Bryson lifted upright the heavy platform the driver had used and closed the rear doors, locking them from the outside and confining the driver to the inside of the pantechnicon. Placing his thumb and forefinger together, he twisted his right hand as a signal to Monteith to switch off the ignition of the Ford Mondeo and beckoned him to join him.

"What the holy fuck are you doing, Jack?"

"Borrowing a lorry. I've a group of people to transport and the bastard I'm chasing stole my minibus."

"Oh, things are making a *lot* more sense!" chided Monteith sarcastically.

"They will in a minute."

Each brother climbed into the cab and Bryson set about attempting to establish sufficient of the controls to drive the massive vehicle uphill to the church.

Monteith delved into the glove compartment and pulled out a manual.

"Brother, you are driving a Renault T520 Maxispace Encamion." He looked at the images on the cover and turned around. "Jesus. H. Christ! This thing is the size of a small house. Look back there. It's like it's got its own kitchen and bedroom! He lifted the armrest that separated his seat from the driver. "Dear God! They've put a fridge down here!" He lifted a can. "Want a beer?"

Bryson was preoccupied by the complexity of driving the huge vehicle through the narrow roads towards the church.

"Why are you chasing this guy, Jack? Tell me that at least."

"He has threatened to have Rachael put in an Arab jail, he's up here in the pay of the British Government trying to create incidents that'll allow Westminster to put troops on the streets like they did in Northern Ireland and he might yet succeed. He's fucked off in the direction of Dumfries with a Beretta and a Lee-Enfield rifle."

"What's he trying to do?"

"He had me shoot at a BBC newsreader, he wanted me to shoot the man with the Lambeg drum in an Orange Walk, he was going to fire at you on the basis that the name of the yacht was a provocation and he'd heard you had arms aboard." He turned his head and looked at his brother. "That's what you cut adrift from the yacht!"

"Eh?"

"You cut two orange things and they sank. Were there weapons in them?"

"Jesus, Jack. You've a fertile imagination."

Bryson returned his attention to the task of manoeuvring the giant juggernaut to a halt outside the church.

"Later!"

They each stepped down from the articulated lorry.

"Keep your own counsel in here until I explain what's going on."

Gingerly he opened the door to the stairwell. Everyone was seated with Bonnie some four steps above everyone else. Beside her on the step were the contents of Maugham's pockets and purse.

"Everyone okay?" asked Bryson.

"Can't tell about your friend in the hood. He's been quiet and might be injured. Unless I open him up I can't see if he needs treatment."

Bryson kicked the sole of Cavendish's shoe. "You okay in there?"

"I'm fine," grumbled Cavendish.

Bonnie sought his attention. "This was in her purse. Thought you might like to look at it." She returned the Glock. Bryson stepped up the few stairs as Bonnie shone her phone torch on a piece of paper. Bryson squinted at it. It read;

- *Mix*
- *Civil*
- *Livid*
- *Mild*
- *Dill*

Bryson looked at Bonnie in recognition of the list of words before him and told her what she already knew. "These are the same words that Kelso had."

"More interesting is that there's more than just a passing connection between Mirren Maugham …that's the name she has on a staff pass for the Scottish Government by the way…and Kelso."

Bryson looked puzzled.

"Remember I'm studying English and Latin at University."

Bryson's look of puzzlement didn't alter. "These words are English, eh?"

"These words…they're not words…they're numbers!"

"Numbers?"

"Yes. Every letter in these words represents a number. 'So the letters in *Mix* is 1,000, 1 and 10. Civil is 100,1,5,1 and 50. Roman numerals. What you have here are two people with a list of common numbers. They could represent phone numbers, letters and pages in books. Anything!" She took a beat. "All UK mobile phone numbers are eleven numbers long but the first number is always zero. That leaves ten digits. I phoned the first ten digits of these words and her phone rang."

Bryson smiled his approval. "Jesus, Bonnie. You're top notch!"

Bonnie smiled at his appreciation. Macdonald and Singh caught each other's glance in the gloom. Each noted the other's admiration of Bonnie's sleuthing.

Bryson took control. "Right! Everybody up. We all stay together until I decide what happens next. Outside everyone. I've organised transport!"

As everyone made their way to the pantechnicon, Bonnie quizzed Bryson.

"Who's your new friend?"

"My wee brother. Introductions later."

Maugham and Cavendish remained silent and sombre as they climbed aboard. Macdonald and Singh despite earlier apprehensions were much impressed by the interior of the large cabin.

"There's a bed back here," gushed Singh.

"And a wee kitchen!" exclaimed Macdonald. Both joined Cavendish and Maugham seated on the bed. Bonnie sat on a stool she fished from a compartment under the sink. Monteith joined his brother in the driver's compartment and Bryson started the journey by reversing the leviathan some distance by using a television screen showing the rear of the vehicle. Achieving a small roundabout, he ignored the nicety of attempting to go around it and merely reversed over it. The elevated surface didn't trouble the lorry and the undulation wasn't even noticed by those in the cab.

Bryson headed off in the direction of Dumfries.

"So what makes it your business to catch this guy?"

"We served together in the SAS. We know each other. If I don't take him down, he'll take *me* down. Plus he has contacts with MI5. If he doesn't nail me, *they* certainly will. As a final supplementary point, Lachie in the back there reckons he's headed to Dumfries to take a shot at the First Minister of Scotland who's opening a health centre in Dumfries. That would certainly bring people on to the streets and give Westminster cause to quell the disruption that would certainly follow."

"So you're a Nationalist now?"

"Nope! No politics! But I can't stand back and allow an assassination; political or otherwise if I can stop it."

Ahead in a lay-by the minibus was parked with its bonnet raised.

"There's the fucker!" He guided the articulated lorry into the lay-by at the rear of the minibus. It seemed unoccupied.

He shouted over his shoulder. "You were right, Bonnie. He's out of gas! As the huge lorry hissed and settled as he turned off the power, he issued instructions. "Murdo. You stay here and make sure no one leaves. The three students are sound. The other two are not." He pulled the gun from his waistband.

"And what are you going to do?"

"I'm going after Kelso."

"With a Glock? You said he has a Lee-Enfield and a Beretta."

Bryson looked at his brother suspiciously. "Since when were you able to identify a handgun just by looking at it?"

Monteith ignored the question. "You'll be out-gunned. He could take you out from distance."

"I removed the sights. He'd have to get lucky. Look after these people. Remember there's a guy in the back. He might need the toilet or something."

A smirr of Scottish rain had begun to descend; barely detectable upon the skin but soaking victims as comprehensively as if falling in a river. As Bryson climbed down the considerable height from the driver's cab, a bullet whistled past him and settled in the turf near the hedgerow edging the lay-by.

Instinctively he dropped into a crouch and tried to establish the source of the shot. Scanning a nearby wooded area it became obvious that Kelso had attempted some cover there. A flash of colour moving left to right between trees gave away his position.

Arming the Glock, Bryson kept low and followed the contour of a hedge which led to the edge of the forest. Breathing heavily, he reached the protection of some large pines and listened for activity. Detecting none he reminded himself that Kelso was a trained warrior, skilled in all aspects of combat. He'd be skilled at camouflage and knew how to use available resources to make himself invisible should he wish to do so. *I'll make haste slowly,* he told himself. *All he needs to do is find a safe spot, make himself hard to spot, wait for me to arrive and take me out. It'd be easy.*

Inside the pine forest it was sunless and gloomy. Bryson picked his way between the trees, staying low. A bullet thwacked into a nearby tree forcing him to hold his position for some minutes. Some further distance into the forest he was hailed from ahead.

"Jack! Why are we at odds here? We've both earned a few bob. We're both ahead of the game. Let's not fuck things up. We both know there'd be no certainty about how this could finish." There was a silence. "Eh, Jack? What do you say? Can we make peace?"

Bryson remained silent, using Kelso's shouted offer in order to establish his position. Another bullet found a branch above his head.

He decided to respond.

"Can't trust you, Kelso. You would have seen me dead or jailed. You'd have seen my daughter jailed. We were comrades once. You betrayed a trust." He moved again, low and slow to a position beneath Kelso's estimated position.

"Don't be stupid, Bryson. Your daughter's safe. We should let bygones be bygones. I put a lot of money your way."

Now confident he'd established Kelso's position, Bryson moved sideways and climbed slowly up the hill maintaining his silence. Occasional gorse bushes, still bursting with yellow flowers helped cover his journey upwards. Some minutes passed. Carefully he studied the dark landscape within the forest and eventually noticed two legs protruding from a bush where Kelso was lying, a small log in front of him for some protection. Bryson moved silently further up the hill until he stood behind him.

I should just shoot the fucker in the back. Instead he pointed the Glock at Kelso and spoke evenly. "Game's up Kelso. I have you from the back. Lay the rifle down. Throw the Beretta away and stand up. Do not turn round!"

Through the foliage, he could see Kelso lower his head in defeat. After a moment the tone was still defiant.

"And how do I *know* you have me from the back?"

Bryson aimed his gun slightly to the right and pulled the trigger. A bullet smashed into the log against which Kelso had laid the rifle.

"Okay…okay….but…Jack this is crazy. We should both just go our separate ways. No hard feelings." He played his last card. "For old time's sake, Jack… old time's sake!"

Bryson repeated himself word for word.

"I have you from the back. Lay the rifle down. Throw the Beretta away and stand up. Do not turn round!"

After some moments, the Lee-Enfield was thrown to the left and Kelso stood upright.

"Now the Beretta!"

Immobilised in defeat for some seconds, Kelso sprang to life. Holding the handgun, he ducked and sprinted to the nearby cover of some birch trees and ran downhill, his momentum taking him ever faster.

"Fuck it!" growled Bryson to himself as he followed his quarry if not at quite the pace he set.

Tripping on a root, Kelso tumbled down a steep incline but rolled and continued his escape. Again he found his speed slightly out of control as he descended the hill, every so often crashing into undergrowth and leaping fallen trees. Bryson followed on by tracking the noise made by a now-panicked Kelso as he headed downhill, arms swinging to maintain his balance. Every so often he'd have Kelso in his sights but didn't shoot, preferring to follow on. Kelso careened downwards, leaping fallen logs and ducking low branches, moving left and right as if emulating the swerves and sidesteps of a young Welsh fly-half.

Thirty years earlier, local farmer Campbell Forbes had read an article on an economic analysis which showed that returns on investment when planting pines on unprofitable Scottish moors and hills would generate rates of return between ten and seventeen percent, he borrowed heavily and over five years worked to put in the ground thousands of sturdy *Pinus sylvestris*. As the largest and longest-lived tree in the Caledonian Forest, the Scots Pine is a keystone species in the ecosystem and over the years farmer Forbes had seen a decent return on investment as his trees reached maturity and were felled for lumber. His son Calum when younger had had other uses for the forest though and had preferred to make use of it as a private and mysterious place where he and his two friends could create dens and build small fires over which they'd cook link sausages impaled on green-sticks. To fashion each of these, the boys would use dead wood where possible but the need for green-sticks that wouldn't burn when held over the fire necessitated cutting live branches.

It was one of these branches, now five feet from the ground and somewhat more substantial but just as pointed as when young Calum had cut it some twenty years later that violently pierced the left eye of John Edward Kelso. So great was his downward momentum that the sharp branch punctured his eye socket, devastating his temporal lobe, destroying the brain stem and severing his spinal cord. He died immediately. The strong limb bent but nevertheless held the weight of Kelso giving Bryson pause for thought when he came upon the body, limp, semi-upright but still quietly showing signs of some slight residual movement.

Chapter Forty-six

Loose Ends

Bryson strode back to the pantechnicon where he lifted the rifle and both pistols into the cab and climbed in.

"Where's your pal?" asked Monteith.

"Believe it or not, the eegit killed himself by accident. I left him where he was. Took the guns."

Bonnie eased her way forward. "Can we have a quick chat outside...the three of us?"

Bryson looked at her, perplexed. "Outside?"

She nodded and Monteith exited the passenger's door as she and Bryson climbed down from the cabin.

Bonnie took the lead and said awkwardly, "My name *is* Bonnie Ogilvie." She paused... "My *full* name is Constable Bonnie Ogilvie."

"And mine is *Sergeant* Murdo Monteith."

"What the fu..."

Kelso's phone rang to mask Bryson's confusion. He glanced at it, taking a keener interest when the name 'Rachael' appeared on the screen. He held a hand up stilling further conversation as he gave attention to the call.

"Rachael?"

"Hi, dad."

"Peter talked some sense into me. We've passed through security and are now in a queue boarding a plane to Milan. Neither of us know quite what's going on but Peter reckoned you couldn't have known all you did about our holiday unless you had information…well anyway, we decided not to take any chances. We collected the money, booked the tickets and thought we could spend a few days in Italy before you visit us in England and explain just what the hell is going on!"

Bryson sensed the smile in her voice.

"Rachael, I'd be delighted. I've just collected my passport and was just preparing to fly out to Dubai and bring you both home by the scruff of the neck. Tell Peter I owe him a pint!" He placed his hand on the shoulder of Monteith. "And I might bring my wee brother Murdo with me"… He looked at him quizzically. "That is if he doesn't arrest me first."

"Uncle Murdo's with you?"

"Aye. And he's telling me he's a cop or a soldier or something. Can't wait to find out which."

Rachael's voice rose a tone. "Uncle Murdo! I haven't seen him since I was a baby! She responded to nudgings from her husband. "We're getting on the plane. Need to go. I'll phone you from Milan."

Bryson turned the phone off and replaced it in the pocket of his jeans. His grin suggested relief rather than humour.

"That was my daughter, Rachael. She's safe!" He remembered the earlier conversation. "You were saying how you were Constables and Sergeants?"

"Police Scotland," advanced Bonnie.

"On special detachment," clarified Monteith.

Bonnie took up the story. "There's a small team of us. The Scottish Government don't have devolved responsibilities for national security but they're aware that nevertheless the country faces threats not only from afar but also from within. It was put to us that while the security services, Special Branch, MI5, and MI6 might seek to do their utmost in protecting our interests, it might just be useful if Police Scotland formed a special unit to make sure that internal threats don't escape our attention."

Monteith took up the story. "And it looks like it was just as well. This has all the hallmarks of dirty dealing by someone! *Someone* paid Kelso to act as he did. We were both assigned to work undercover with *Seed of the Gaels*. I was over in the States for a while following up stories we'd been hearing of money being raised for weapons being brought into Scotland and Bonnie was at this end dealing with the organisation in Glasgow."

"I'm also a genuine student though. Women can multi-task."

"Well fuck me gently!" murmured Bryson.

Monteith took charge. "We've been talking. Here's what we need to do. We're going to drive this colossus back into Stranraer, let you and the boys off at a boozer to relax after your busy day, let the guy out of the back and take a statement from him about the bad man who stole his lorry but first…we thought you might want to interview the two we have trussed up in the back cabin. You have latitude in these matters that we don't. But we can film anything they say to you before we take a statement. We decide what's happening to them once you have a chat with them."

"So, am I in trouble?"

"Probably not. Once we film this pair and if they explain their involvement with the security services, this'll be hushed up quicker than ice melting on a hot stove although I've a nice man back in the States that might end up being of interest to the CIA."

Bonnie consulted a list. "We figure there have been several offences committed; attempted murder…"

"No way! countered Bryson. I was the best shot in the British Army. I was directed to scare the woman not wound her!"

"Attempted murder, five charges of kidnapping that I can count, theft of a vehicle…two, in fact…being in possession of a prohibited weapon, common assault, serious assault…"

"Serious assault? Christ, you kicked Kelso right in the goolies!"

A smile quickened upon her lips. "I'm an officer of the law," she grinned.

"Right in the haw-maws!" he repeated.

Monteith intervened. "These offences will be disappeared. Trust me, brother. You single-handedly stopped a car bomb being exploded in Stranraer. You're a hero! Now what's needed is for you to upset that pair in the back and then reassure Lachie and Charlie that all will be well and that they'll be tucked up tight in their own beds tonight. Bonnie and I will visit them together in Lachie's flat tomorrow evening to take their statements."

"So the sooner I get Sonny and Cher in there to talk, the sooner I get to go to the pub?"

"Got it in one."

"Do they know you're cops?"

Monteith shook his head. "Nope. Just don't do anything that could get you arrested."

* * *

Bryson went to a large metallic compartment attached to the lorry's undercarriage just aft of the driver's cabin and removed a heavy tool box. Holding it in one hand, he climbed back aboard and went through to the back where the four passengers were seated.

Wordlessly he opened the toolbox and took out a chisel and hammer, weighed the hammer in his hand and returned it choosing a heavier mallet instead. Still silent, he leaned over to the cooker and turned on a gas ring whereupon he laid the chisel in a position where its tip would heat quickly. He pulled the bag from Cavendish's head surprising him and gave him a cartoon grin as he again weighed the mallet in his left hand, manoeuvring the heated chisel as if to test its readiness.

Cavendish looked even more apprehensive than Maugham.

"Your friend Kelso is dead I'm afraid," volunteered Bryson distractedly. "As a dodo," he continued.

After a few moments, Maugham was first to speak. "What are you going to do with those tools?"

"Well, I'm not building a fucking chest of drawers!"

In the driver's cabin, Bonnie and Monteith suppressed a laugh.

"Look, I'm just a civil servant," offered Maugham her eyes not leaving the chisel.

"Aye, sure!" Bryson lifted the chisel and blew on the now red-hot tip.

Cavendish chimed in on descant. "I'm only a civil servant as well!"

"Fingers or toes?" murmured Bryson as if to himself. "Eh, you first, Misses. Would you step over to the sink please? It makes less of a mess. I'm more interested in what Cavendish here can tell me and he's more likely to talk if he sees you lose a few digits." He eyed Cavendish. "Eh, pal?"

Maugham decided to save herself, asking nervously. "What? Look what is it you want to know?"

Bryson leaned over and turned the gas off and placed both implements on the sink top out of camera shot.

In the forward cabin, both Monteith and Bonnie each surreptitiously turned their respective phone camera to record.

"What is your name and why were you sent to plant a bomb beneath a car at Stranraer Harbour?"

For the next twenty minutes Maugham slowly revealed her role as *Treasure*, her contact with Kelso, his mission, her work within MI5 and her placement within the senior levels of governance in Scotland, explaining tearfully that she saw herself more as a backroom analyst and how she wasn't suited to blood and guts. Following suit, Cavendish did the same, explaining his contact with Pennington, his role in supervising Kelso and the supply of a rifle for his use.

Satisfied, Bryson leaned backwards and hailed the twosome in the driver's cabin. "Get all that?"

Both emerged and Bonnie spoke for each. "My name is Constable Bonnie Gabriel, Police Scotland. This is Sergeant Murdo Monteith. I could arrest you under Section one of the Criminal Justice (Scotland) Act 2016 for more offences than you could fucking shake a sick at but I can't be arsed. Someone who gives a shit about due process can do that down at the station. Do you understand just how deep this shit is?"

Maugham nodded as Macdonald and Singh looked at one another aghast.

"Bonnie's a cop? whispered Macdonald.

"Her language is a bit ripe!" retorted Singh.

Monteith intervened. "Now, it'll be up to our bosses to determine whether any of this will be necessary given that this could blow up into the biggest political row since Guy Fawkes found somewhere dry to store his dynamite."

"Right now, we're heading back to Stranraer. Miss Maugham, you're driving Cavendish, Constable Gabriel and me back to Edinburgh for another chat about what you've been up to. Boys, you're going for a quick pint then Jack here will escort you home to your loved ones. We'll be round to your house tomorrow night Lachie to take statements if that's all right."

"Sure!" Both students could scarcely contain their relief.

Once we drop you off, we have to let the poor guy out of the back of this vehicle and take a statement."

"See you tomorrow!"

* * *

The following evening, Charlie and Lachie sat awaiting the arrival of Bonnie and Monteith, each of them two cans of lager down and opening a third.

Behind them as background to their excited conversation, the radio played music prior to the Scottish news being announced.

"The time is seven o'clock and these are the BBC news headlines in Scotland today."

The newsreader continued.

"The Chairman and Vice-Chairman of the Scottish National Party have been charged with several counts of sexual assault and will appear in court tomorrow. Both men vehemently deny the charges.

In breaking news, Mike Hudson, the SNP List MSP for Central Scotland has been suspended by the party's internal disciplinary committee as a consequence of a relationship he is alleged to have developed with an eighteen year old woman. Photographs have emerged in newspapers today and no comment has as yet been forthcoming from Mr. Hudson.

In a new Vox poll today the Nationalist Government has lost ground and has dropped three points, reducing their lead over the Conservative Party, putting in question their governance of Scotland at the next elections.

A jogger lost his life last night when out running in woods near Stranraer. The accident happened when the forty-four year male old lost his balance and collided with a tree.

Finally, Kilmarnock host Motherwell tonight at Rugby Park. In their last meeting Kilmarnock scored five goals without reply."

Macdonald and Singh had remained motionless as the news headlines were being read. Each had their drink paused before their lips. Macdonald spoke first.

"Turn that shite off, Charlie!"

About the Author

Ron Culley is the author of several books and a play, covering a range of topics. His entry in *Who's Who* describes his hobbies *inter alia* as 'reading biographies, Scottish, Irish and American politics, public speaking, Humanism, Robert Burns, laughing out loud, socialising, irreverence, song-writing, Glasgow memorabilia and in an attempt to encourage more people to make use of dictionaries, 'convivial temulence and contumacy.' Ron is the proud father of four strapping boys and lives with his wife Jean in the south side of Glasgow, Scotland, the city and country he loves.

CPSIA information can be obtained
at www.ICGtesting.com
Printed in the USA
BVHW080838130519
548116BV00001B/14/P

9 781786 235015